Simply Learning, Simply Best!

Simply Learning, Simply Best!

倍斯特出版事業有限公司
Best Publishing Ltd.

新托福100+

iBT
聽力

MP3

韋爾◎ 著

《三大聽力學習法》
同步強化其他項技能閱讀、寫作和口說實力
整合能力提升，四個單項分數狂飆升

1 **「記筆記能力」**：掌握關鍵重點，等同答對題目，考取高分。

2 **「填空測驗」**：提升聽「細節性」聽力訊息和拼字能力，聽力逆衝28+高分。

3 **「摘要能力」**：聽一段訊息後，能以口述和寫作方式即刻表達出關鍵考點，
　　　練聽力＋同步搞定寫作和口說整合題型。

Author's Preface
作者序

　　新托福聽力的測驗時間約為一小時，測驗中包含兩段校園場景的對話和四段學術場景的講座。書籍的規劃則包含了三個主要架構：❶漸進式的影子跟讀練習（包含校園場景和學術講座）、❷學術講座和❸校園場景的實戰練習。而其實在官方試題 TPO 中其實會找到出題的規律，包含常見的服務諮詢和 office hour 中會討論的問題。在第一部分的影子跟讀中收錄了「獎學金」和「研究中心動物遺失」，後者是改以更趣味式的長篇對話，讓學習者練習影子跟讀練習，在學習上更不枯燥。第二和第三部分的話，除了延續了新托福試題和提供解析外，加入了試題音檔的影子跟讀練習、記筆記練習、聽力填空練習和聽力摘要練習。

　　「試題音檔的影子跟讀練習」是很必要的練習，因為聽力「專注力」的提升能有效補足僅單靠題海策略和寫題目看答案與解析後分數仍停滯在某分數的問題。另外規劃了「記筆記」練習，主要是新托福聽力能記

筆記，實際練習這部分能提升讀者答較細節性的題目。（但考生須注意的是，聽力理解力遠比記筆記更重要，要拿捏這部分。）而「聽力填空練習」則是檢視自己拼字能力、提升聽細節性訊息和口譯能力，也能提升傳統聽力或口譯試題中 spot dictation 的答題能力。最後是「摘要練習」，是重新聽原音檔後，能寫出一段摘要或完整口述所聽到的訊息，這部分能大幅提升考生在答寫作和口說整合題型的問題、寫作和口譯能力，當中運用到「聽」與「寫」還有「聽」與「說」之間的關聯性。考生可以播放一段原音檔後，摘要給同學或友人聽，也可以播放原音檔後，在紙上寫出這段音檔的摘要。

　　書籍特色除了納入所提到的學習方法外，在內容上則考量到更生活化，以更貼近生活層面為主的內容。很多時候 office hour 不見得在詢問課業，反而是跟熟識的老師聊聊其他生活小事，課業問題反而自己去圖書館就搞定了。在校園場景中，包含了聊到兩性問題談論到《Why Men Want Sex and Women Need Love》中 four men who went fishing 的趣味小故事。另外有考量到大多數考生，在考完且唸完研究所後，其實還是要面臨就業跟未來規劃等的問題，也納入了可能去問老師們關於未來規劃和求職的問題，其中提到幾本書《Lean In》、《Business Model You》、《Getting There》、

《The Achievement Habit》、《Where You Go Is Not Who You Will Be》。在學習上，提到了《Peak》、《Outliers》、《Give and Take》、哈利波特和天龍八部。在協助學生找回自信中提到了《The School of Greatness》、股神巴菲特。

在校園場景中，除了學術話題（例如：共同演化等）外，也融入更生活化題材，包含了與生活息息相關的咖啡和《The Compound Effect》、《The Power of Habit》、年輕世代的面臨的 underachievement 問題、費爾普斯和《The Power of Moments》，讓讀者在備考外，也有較不一樣的感受。最後其實感謝的是協助審稿和校對的洪婉婷，像個良師益友般，對書籍提供了寶貴的建議，從她身上學習到很多。還要感謝倍斯特出版給予此次出書的機會。最後祝所有讀者都能考取理想成績。

韋爾 敬上

Editor's
編者序 Preface

　　新托福考試其實在制訂完整的學習規劃後，就能漸進的達到所需要的申請成績。有些考生則過於慌亂，而未能達到與自己本身相對應的成績或是缺乏更正確的引導，使得自己走了更多迂迴的路，才考到理想的成績。這本新托福聽力書納入了更具整合性、更全面的規劃，利用「聽」、「說」、「讀」和「寫」之間的關聯性，由聽力強化新托福中的「口說」和「寫作」整合題型的答題能力。這樣的規劃更能補足「單一」備考和狂寫 TPO 題目等備考方式所不足的部分，讓考生在最短時間內達到成效。

　　此外，準備考試僅是人生中一個短暫的過程。其實在求學結束後都會面臨求職和與未來規劃等相關的問題，在考取理想學校後，也可以趁這長段的求學時間思考下自己的未來，最後祝所有考生都能獲取理想成績。

倍斯特編輯部 敬上

Instructions
使用說明

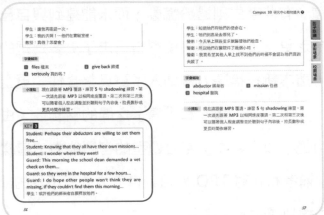

「短對話」影子跟讀

* 拆成數個關鍵句，漸進式引導，難度適中，且每個小練習均搭配字彙輔助，任何學習者都能輕易上手。
* 由「**短對話**」影子跟讀強化應對校園場景的題型，大幅提升應考實力。

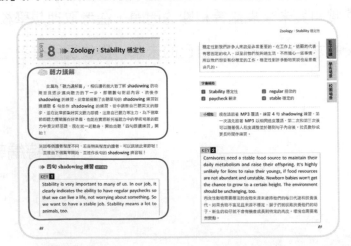

「學術場景」影子跟讀強化

* 詳盡使用說明，練習聽單句到數句的「**學術場景**」影子跟讀練習，漸進式銜接聽簡短句子到獨立完成寫 TPO 聽力試題，照書中的練習走，練習數次至數十次，聽力專注力和聽力成績都會莫名狂飆，重點是自己就能完成備考，考完還會驚嘆原來新托福聽力不難 XDD。
* 程度佳的考生可以視自己的英文程度，跳過「**影子跟讀講解篇**」這個篇章的練習，直接寫下兩個 part 練習。

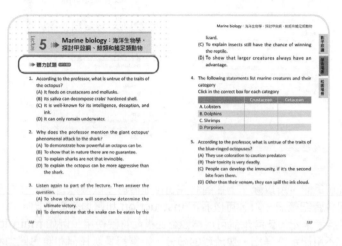

「短對話」影子跟讀

✻ 立即開始練習吧！書籍中學術場景收錄 7 篇實戰練習，校園場景 11 篇實戰練習。

✻ 寫完練習後，有疑惑的部分就對著解析看，務必要了解錯的部分在哪，才能提升應考答題能力。

✻ 每個單元於寫完試題後，均包含了「影子跟讀練習」的規劃，聽力音檔內容也以中英對照的方式呈現，便於讀者學習和練習影子跟讀。聽力學習中，很重要的一點，不是在於寫題目的量，而是寫試題後「聽力專注力」也有一定程度的提升，所以寫完試題、對完答案和觀看解析後，務必重新播放音檔至少做數次影子跟讀練習，才能強化學習成果。

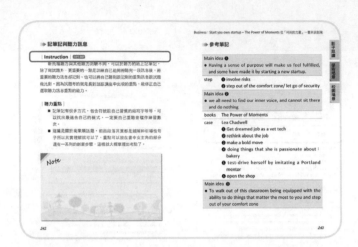

※ 新托福聽力能記筆記，所以除了上述的寫完題目並做影子跟讀練習外，要再重新聽過一次音檔後，自己練習記筆記一次，可以看下 instruction 和聽力重點說明，也可以自己記完筆記後，對照參考筆記，參考筆記可以再濃縮並搭配符號使用，例如 main idea 的部分，其實有聽懂就不用記那麼詳細，**像流程的部分**，通常都是新托福和雅思聽力和閱讀考點，掌握流程中所做的事很重要，而有些則是考聽到訊息後，能否具備「分類」和「歸納」主題的能力，其實都是考驗「**聽**」和「**讀**」的整合能力，多練習後就能強化「**click the right box**」這類的表格題。此外，強化這部分的能力，也能提升自己的簡報、口譯和口說能力喔！

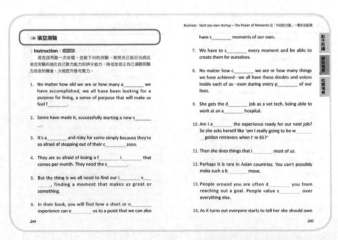

※ 完成寫試題、影子跟讀練習、記筆記後，還不能鬆口氣，要接續練習填空測驗的練習。這部分的練習可以修正是否漏聽訊息外，還可以提升拼字能力喔！

➠ 摘要能力

| Instruction | MP3 028

除了閱讀測驗外，其實培養能在聽完一大段訊息後，以口述講述剛才聽到的聽力訊息是學習語言和表達很重要的一件事，讓自己養成具備這樣的能力，除了能在聽力測驗中獲取高分外，也能在新托福寫作跟口說的整合題型上大有斬獲喔！所以快來練習，除了書中提供的參考答案外，自己可以試著重新聽過音檔一遍後，摘要出英文訊息並朗讀出來。

Note

➠ 參考答案

Three traits of the octopus package them with the ability to inhabit in different marine habitats, taking down preys such as crustaceans and mollusks. Despite these they have their natural enemies, too. They are vulnerable to the attack of cetaceans, sharks, pinnipeds, sea otters, or sea birds. However, another phenomenal attack of the giant octopus takes down a shark, which leads us to think that the size matters when it comes to the attack. We cannot really say about the outcome since things can change in a blink of the eye. Shrimps, crabs, and lobsters belong to the category of the crustaceans. Cetaceans, on the other hand, refer to whales, dolphins, and porpoises. The defense mechanisms have allowed animals to have a high successful survival rate. Octopuses, with the ability to spill ink, is one of the examples, although this will not always work. Aside from the ink cloud, the venom and coloration are also the defense mechanism. Blue-ringed octopuses are the representative, and their venom can kill you in a minute.

彭子顧讀　學術場景　校園場景

★ 最後則是超重要的「摘要」能力，練習這部分能大幅提升答新托福「口說」和「寫作」整合題型的能力，一舉數得，等同準備聽力這個項目，也同時準備了「口說」跟「寫作」。另外要注意的是，請務必先自己練習一次並寫下答案或口述，然後再看參考答案喔！（先看答案其實降低自己實際考試時的應對能力。）

CONTENTS 目次

Part 1 影子跟讀

校園話題

學術場景

Part 2　學術場景

Part 3　校園話題

Part 1

影子跟讀

篇章概述

影子跟讀篇規劃了各 10 個單元的校園場景和學術講座的練習，並包含的學習輔助說明，逐步練習能大幅提升聽說能力。另外，在校園場景中收錄了研究中心動物遺失小故事，邊練習聽力邊看看發生了什麼事吧！

Campus 1 ▶▶ 獎學金 ❶

 聽力講解

　　此篇為「聽力講解篇」，相信讀者能大致了解 shadowing 的功用並且逐步邁向聽力的下一步，即聽數句對話內容，然後作 shadowing 的練習，此章節規劃了由聽單句的 shadowing 練習到聽連續 5 句並作 shadowing 的練習，從中調整自己聽英文的腳步，並在此章節紮好英文聽力基礎，注意自己聽力專注力，為下個章節即聽力實戰篇作好準備，也能在實際新托福聽力中的學術場景的聽力中奠定好基礎，現在就一起動身，開始由聽「單句跟讀練習」開始！

※因每個讀者程度不同，若是稍具程度的讀者，可以跳過此章節喔！
　直接由下個篇章開始，直接作長句的 shadowing 練習喔！

▶▶ 單句 shadowing 練習 `MP3 001`

KEY 1

Student: I'm here to discuss my grades actually.
學生：我來這裡實際上是要討論我的分數。

字彙輔助

1. discuss 討論
2. grade 分數
3. actually 實際上

小提點 現在請跟著 MP3 覆誦，練習單句 shadowing 練習，第一次請先跟著 MP3 以相同速度覆誦，第二次和第三次後可以隨著個人程度調整並於聽到句子內容後，拉長數秒或更長時間作練習。

KEY 2

Professor: Oh! Is there a problem? Grading a bit too high or what?

教授：嗚。有什麼問題嗎？是評量的太高分了還是怎麼了嗎？

字彙輔助

1. is there a problem 有什麼問題嗎？
2. grading 評分
3. a bit 有點

小提點 現在請跟著 MP3 覆誦，練習單句 shadowing 練習，第一次請先跟著 MP3 以相同速度覆誦，第二次和第三次後可以隨著個人程度調整並於聽到句子內容後，拉長數秒或更長時間作練習。

KEY 3

Student: The thing is... I need the scholarship... You know...

學生：事情是…我需要獎學金…你知道的…。

1. thing 事情
2. need 需要
3. scholarship 獎學金

小提點 現在請跟著 MP3 覆誦,練習單句 shadowing 練習,第一次請先跟著 MP3 以相同速度覆誦,第二次和第三次後可以隨著個人程度調整並於聽到句子內容後,拉長數秒或更長時間作練習。

KEY 4

Student: I'm having a little financial constrain. So the scholarship is my only way out...

學生:我有些財務困境…所以獎學金是唯一解決的辦法…。

字彙輔助

1. financial 財務
2. constraint 限制
3. scholarship 獎學金

小提點 現在請跟著 MP3 覆誦,練習單句 shadowing 練習,第一次請先跟著 MP3 以相同速度覆誦,第二次和第三次後可以隨著個人程度調整並於聽到句子內容後,拉長數秒或更長時間作練習。

影子跟讀

學術場景

校園場景

KEY 5

Professor: it goes according to the grading policy...

教授：會根據評分規定走…。

字彙輔助

1 go …走、進行

2 according to 根據

3 grading policy 評分規定

小提點　現在請跟著 MP3 覆誦，練習單句 shadowing 練習，第一次請先跟著 MP3 以相同速度覆誦，第二次和第三次後可以隨著個人程度調整並於聽到句子內容後，拉長數秒或更長時間作練習。

KEY 6

Professor: I'm afraid there is nothing I can do.

教授：我想我無能為力。

字彙輔助

1 I'm afraid 我想（委婉的拒絕時使用）

2 nothing 沒有

小提點　現在請跟著 MP3 覆誦，練習單句 shadowing 練習，第一次請先跟著 MP3 以相同速度覆誦，第二次和第三次後可以隨著個人程度調整並於聽到句子內容後，拉長數秒或更長時間作練習。

 **聽力講解**

　　此篇為「聽力講解篇」，相信讀者能大致了解 shadowing 的功用並且逐步邁向聽力的下一步，即聽數句對話內容，然後作 shadowing 的練習，此章節規劃了由聽單句的 shadowing 練習到聽連續 5 句並作 shadowing 的練習，從中調整自己聽英文的腳步，並在此章節絮好英文聽力基礎，注意自己聽力專注力，為下個章節即聽力實戰篇作好準備，也能在實際新托福聽力中的學術場景的聽力中奠定好基礎，現在就一起動身，開始由聽「單句跟讀練習」開始！

※因每個讀者程度不同，若是稍具程度的讀者，可以跳過此章節喔！
　直接由下個篇章開始，直接作長句的 shadowing 練習喔！

▶▶ **單句 shadowing 練習** `MP3 002`

KEY 1

Professor: Altering academic records won't be fair to other students.
教授： 更改學業紀錄對其他學生來説不公平。

字彙輔助

1 altering 更改　　　　　**2** academic records 學業紀錄

小提點　現在請跟著 MP3 覆誦，練習單句 shadowing 練習，第一次請先跟著 MP3 以相同速度覆誦，第二次和第三次後可以隨著個人程度調整並於聽到句子內容後，拉長數秒或更長時間作練習。

KEY 2

Student: Is there any other ways or other things I can do to boost the grades?

學生：有任何其他方法或其他事情是我能做來提高分數嗎？

字彙輔助

1 other ways 其他方法　　　**2** boost 提高

小提點　現在請跟著 MP3 覆誦，練習單句 shadowing 練習，第一次請先跟著 MP3 以相同速度覆誦，第二次和第三次後可以隨著個人程度調整並於聽到句子內容後，拉長數秒或更長時間作練習。

KEY 3

Student: Like writing an extra report or something.

學生：像是寫額外的報告或什麼的。

字彙輔助

① writing 寫　　　② extra 額外的

小提點　現在請跟著 MP3 覆誦，練習單句 shadowing 練習，第一次請先跟著 MP3 以相同速度覆誦，第二次和第三次後可以隨著個人程度調整並於聽到句子內容後，拉長數秒或更長時間作練習。

KEY 4

Professor: Since the final report weighs 40%, why don't you work a little harder on that.

教授：既然期末報告佔比重的百分之四十，不如你在期末報告上更努力吧。

字彙輔助

① weighs 40% 佔比重百分之四十

小提點　現在請跟著 MP3 覆誦，練習單句 shadowing 練習，第一次請先跟著 MP3 以相同速度覆誦，第二次和第三次後可以隨著個人程度調整並於聽到句子內容後，拉長數秒或更長時間作練習。

KEY 5

Student: But how can I be sure I get to certain grades?

學生：但是如何確保我會得到確切的分數呢？

字彙輔助

1 be sure 確保

2 certain 確切的

小提點　現在請跟著 MP3 覆誦，練習單句 shadowing 練習，第一次請先跟著 MP3 以相同速度覆誦，第二次和第三次後可以隨著個人程度調整並於聽到句子內容後，拉長數秒或更長時間作練習。

KEY 6

Student: Grades... which meet the standard for scholarship.

學生：分數…達到獎學金的標準呢。

字彙輔助

1 grade 分數

2 standard 標準

小提點　現在請跟著 MP3 覆誦，練習單句 shadowing 練習，第一次請先跟著 MP3 以相同速度覆誦，第二次和第三次後可以隨著個人程度調整並於聽到句子內容後，拉長數秒或更長時間作練習。

聽力講解

　　此篇為「聽力講解篇」，相信讀者能大致了解 shadowing 的功用並且逐步邁向聽力的下一步，即聽數句對話內容，然後作 shadowing 的練習，此章節規劃了由聽單句的 shadowing 練習到聽連續 5 句並作 shadowing 的練習，從中調整自己聽英文的腳步，並在此章節紮好英文聽力基礎，注意自己聽力專注力，為下個章節即聽力實戰篇作好準備，也能在實際新托福聽力中的學術場景的聽力中奠定好基礎，現在就一起動身，開始由聽「單句跟讀練習」開始！

※因每個讀者程度不同，若是稍具程度的讀者，可以跳過此章節喔！
　直接由下個篇章開始，直接作長句的 shadowing 練習喔！

▶▶ 雙句 shadowing 練習 `MP3 003`

KEY 1

Professor: Why don't you discuss the details of the report every week with me.
Professor: That way you will know which part should be edited out.

教授：為什麼你不乾脆每週與我討論報告的細節。
教授：這樣的話，你就能知道哪些部分是需要被修改掉的了。

字彙輔助

1 discuss 討論 　　**2** details of the report 報告的細節

小提點　現在請跟著 MP3 覆誦，第二次和第三次後可以隨著個人程度調整並於聽到句子內容後，拉長數秒或更長時間作練習。

KEY **2**

Student: I think that's a fantastic idea!

Student: It means I won't digress from the main topic.

學生：我認為這是很棒的想法…。

學生：這意謂著我的報告將不會離題。

字彙輔助

1 digress 使…離題

小提點　現在請跟著 MP3 覆誦，第二次和第三次後可以隨著個人程度調整並於聽到句子內容後，拉長數秒或更長時間作練習。

KEY **3**

Student: The final report handed to you will be almost to an A+ level.

Professor: I can't be certain for that.

學生：遞交給你的期末報告會近乎到 A+ 的等級了。
教授：這我就不能保證。

字彙輔助

1 almost to an A+ level 近乎到 A+的等級了

小提點　現在請跟著 MP3 覆誦，第二次和第三次後可以隨著個人
程度調整並於聽到句子內容後，拉長數秒或更長時間作練
習。

KEY 4

Professor: I think it'll be a great start for you.
Student: I can't believe after two years in this university,
教授：我認為這對你來說會是很棒的開端。
學生：我不敢相信在大學唸兩年了。

字彙輔助

1 office hours 諮詢時段

小提點　現在請跟著 MP3 覆誦，第二次和第三次後可以隨著個人
程度調整並於聽到句子內容後，拉長數秒或更長時間作練
習。

KEY 5

Student: It's actually the first time I'm using office hours.

Professor: That's what office hours are all about…

學生：實際上這是我首次使用諮詢時段。

教授：這就是諮詢時段的目的…。

字彙輔助

1 the first time 首次　　　**2** office hours 諮詢時段

小提點　現在請跟著 MP3 覆誦，第二次和第三次後可以隨著個人程度調整並於聽到句子內容後，拉長數秒或更長時間作練習。

KEY 6

Professor: Answering questions and many other things...

Student: Thanks anyway...

教授：回答問題和許多事情…。

學生：無論如何，謝謝了。

字彙輔助

1 answering 回答　　　**2** questions 問題

小提點　現在請跟著 MP3 覆誦，第二次和第三次後可以隨著個人程度調整並於聽到句子內容後，拉長數秒或更長時間作練習。

29

聽力講解

　　此篇為「聽力講解篇」，相信讀者能大致了解 shadowing 的功用並且逐步邁向聽力的下一步，即聽數句對話內容，然後作 shadowing 的練習，此章節規劃了由聽單句的 shadowing 練習到聽連續 5 句並作 shadowing 的練習，從中調整自己聽英文的腳步，並在此章節紮好英文聽力基礎，注意自己聽力專注力，為下個章節即聽力實戰篇作好準備，也能在實際新托福聽力中的學術場景的聽力中奠定好基礎，現在就一起動身，開始由聽「單句跟讀練習」開始！

※因每個讀者程度不同，若是稍具程度的讀者，可以跳過此章節喔！
　直接由下個篇章開始，直接作長句的 shadowing 練習喔！

▶▶ **三句 shadowing 練習** MP3 004

KEY **1**

Student: I will make sure every component is what you have asked for⋯
Professor: I will be hard on you, too
Professor: Hopefully you will get the scholarship⋯
學生：我會確保每個部分都是你所要求的...。
教授：我也會嚴格對你。
教授：希望你能拿到獎學金。

30

字彙輔助

1. every component 每個部分
2. be hard on you 對你嚴格
3. get that scholarship 拿到獎學金

小提點　現在請跟著 MP3 覆誦，第一次請先跟著 MP3 以相同速度覆誦，第二次和第三次後可以隨著個人程度調整並於聽到句子內容後，拉長數秒或更長時間作練習。

KEY **2**

> Professor: I was just heading out…
>
> Professor: Anything I can help you with….?
>
> Student: I forgot to tell you that several animals are missing from the research center…
>
> 教授：我正要外出呢...。
>
> 教授：有什麼我可以幫你的嗎...？
>
> 學生：我忘了要跟你說研究中心的幾個動物失蹤了...。

字彙輔助

1. Anything I can help you with 什麼事情

小提點　現在請跟著 MP3 覆誦，第一次請先跟著 MP3 以相同速度覆誦，第二次和第三次後可以隨著個人程度調整並於聽到句子內容後，拉長數秒或更長時間作練習。

KEY 3

Professor: How did that happen?

Professor: It's impossible...

Professor: They are not agile...

教授：這是怎麼發生的呢？

教授：這怎麼可能...。

教授：他們沒那麼敏捷...。

字彙輔助

1. agile 敏捷的

小提點 現在請跟著 MP3 覆誦，第一次請先跟著 MP3 以相同速度覆誦，第二次和第三次後可以隨著個人程度調整並於聽到句子內容後，拉長數秒或更長時間作練習。

KEY 4

Student: That's what I thought...

Student: but it turns out... they are just as agile as monkeys...

Student: so what should I do?

學生：我也是這樣想的。

學生：但是結果是...他們就像是猴子一樣敏捷...。

學生：所以我該怎麼做呢？

字彙輔助

① monkeys 猴子

小提點　現在請跟著 MP3 覆誦，第一次請先跟著 MP3 以相同速度覆誦，第二次和第三次後可以隨著個人程度調整並於聽到句子內容後，拉長數秒或更長時間作練習。

KEY 5

Student: Should I call the police...

Professor: I just don't think the police should be involved in this...

Student: Perhaps someone stole them...

學生：我該報警嗎？

教授：我不認為應該讓警方介入...。

學生：或許有人偷走他們...。

字彙輔助

① call the police 報警　　② be involved in 牽涉其中

③ stole 偷走

小提點　現在請跟著 MP3 覆誦，第一次請先跟著 MP3 以相同速度覆誦，第二次和第三次後可以隨著個人程度調整並於聽到句子內容後，拉長數秒或更長時間作練習。

Campus **5**　　研究中心動物遺失 ❷

🌥 聽力講解

　　此篇為「聽力講解篇」，相信讀者能大致了解 shadowing 的功用並且逐步邁向聽力的下一步，即聽數句對話內容，然後作 shadowing 的練習，此章節規劃了由聽單句的 shadowing 練習到聽連續 5 句並作 shadowing 的練習，從中調整自己聽英文的腳步，並在此章節紮好英文聽力基礎，注意自己聽力專注力，為下個章節即聽力實戰篇作好準備，也能在實際新托福聽力中的學術場景的聽力中奠定好基礎，現在就一起動身，開始由聽「單句跟讀練習」開始！

※因每個讀者程度不同，若是稍具程度的讀者，可以跳過此章節喔！
　直接由下個篇章開始，直接作長句的 shadowing 練習喔！

▶▶ 三句 shadowing 練習 MP3 005

KEY 1

Professor: For what?
Student: Cooking? Perhaps?
Student: you know... with Thanksgiving coming up

教授：偷走他們幹嘛？
學生：煮來吃？或是？

學生：你知道的…隨著感恩節的到來…。

字彙輔助

1　cooking 烹煮
2　Perhaps 或是
3　Thanksgiving 感恩節

小提點　現在請跟著 MP3 覆誦，練習 3 句 shadowing 練習，第一次請先跟著 MP3 以相同速度覆誦，第二次和第三次後可以隨著個人程度調整並於聽到句子內容後，拉長數秒或更長時間作練習。

KEY 2

Student: People might misinterpret those rosters as turkeys...
Professor: stop joking around...
Professor: I do need you to give me the precise numbers

學生：人們可能誤把公雞當成火雞了…。
教授：別再開玩笑了…。
教授：我需要你給我一個精確的數字。

字彙輔助

1　misinterpret 誤解成
2　rosters 公雞
3　turkeys 火雞

小提點 現在請跟著 MP3 覆誦，練習 3 句 shadowing 練習，第一次請先跟著 MP3 以相同速度覆誦，第二次和第三次後可以隨著個人程度調整並於聽到句子內容後，拉長數秒或更長時間作練習。

KEY 3

Professor: and of course, which animals...

Student: I will check with the guard at the research center

Student: I do have another question

教授：還有…當然…是哪些動物失蹤。

學生：我會跟研究中心的警衛確認。

學生：我還有另一個問題。

字彙輔助

1 check 確認　　　　**2** guard 警衛

3 question 問題

小提點 現在請跟著 MP3 覆誦，練習 3 句 shadowing 練習，第一次請先跟著 MP3 以相同速度覆誦，第二次和第三次後可以隨著個人程度調整並於聽到句子內容後，拉長數秒或更長時間作練習。

KEY 4

Professor: Shoot...

Student: Since they are missing...

Student: There is no way that we can work on our mid-term papers.

教授：快説…。

學生：既然他們失蹤了…。

學生：我們就不可能繼續研究完成期中報告了。

字彙輔助

1 **shoot** 快説

2 **missing** 失蹤

3 **mid-term papers** 期中報告

小提點　現在請跟著 **MP3** 覆誦，練習 **3** 句 shadowing 練習，第一次請先跟著 **MP3** 以相同速度覆誦，第二次和第三次後可以隨著個人程度調整並於聽到句子內容後，拉長數秒或更長時間作練習。

聽力講解

　　此篇為「聽力講解篇」，相信讀者能大致了解 shadowing 的功用並且逐步邁向聽力的下一步，即聽數句對話內容，然後作 shadowing 的練習，此章節規劃了由聽單句的 shadowing 練習到聽連續 5 句並作 shadowing 的練習，從中調整自己聽英文的腳步，並在此章節紮好英文聽力基礎，注意自己聽力專注力，為下個章節即聽力實戰篇作好準備，也能在實際新托福聽力中的學術場景的聽力中奠定好基礎，現在就一起動身，開始由聽「單句跟讀練習」開始！

※因每個讀者程度不同，若是稍具程度的讀者，可以跳過此章節喔！
　直接由下個篇章開始，直接作長句的 shadowing 練習喔！

▶▶ 三句 shadowing 練習　MP3 006

KEY 1

Student: I don't want to restart examining those animals all over...
Professor: Good point...
Student: Is it possible for us to just hand in what we've documented..so far...?

學生：我不想要重新開始檢查那些動物…。

教授：說到重點了。

學生：我們有可能只交我們目前所記載的部分嗎？

字彙輔助

1. restart 重新開始
2. examining 檢查
3. document 記載

小提點　現在請跟著 MP3 覆誦，練習 3 句 shadowing 練習，第一次請先跟著 MP3 以相同速度覆誦，第二次和第三次後可以隨著個人程度調整並於聽到句子內容後，拉長數秒或更長時間作練習。

KEY **2**

Professor: That would be too easy for you guys... .

Professor: Certainly unfair to others...

Student: Others?

學生：那會對你們來說太簡單了…。

教授：對其他人來說很不公平…。

學生：其他人？

字彙輔助

1. too easy 太簡單
2. unfair 不公平

3 others 其他人

小提點 現在請跟著 MP3 覆誦，練習 3 句 shadowing 練習，第一次請先跟著 MP3 以相同速度覆誦，第二次和第三次後可以隨著個人程度調整並於聽到句子內容後，拉長數秒或更長時間作練習。

KEY **3**

Professor: Other students…who keep a good eye on their animals...?
Student: I don't want to blame on luck...
Student: but it's an accident...

教授：那些有留神關注他們動物的其他學生？
教授：我不想要歸咎在運氣上…。
學生：但這是意外…。

字彙輔助

1 keep a good eye 留神關注　　**2** blame 責怪
3 accident 意外

小提點 現在請跟著 MP3 覆誦，練習 3 句 shadowing 練習，第一次請先跟著 MP3 以相同速度覆誦，第二次和第三次後可以隨著個人程度調整並於聽到句子內容後，拉長數秒或

更長時間作練習。

KEY 4

Student: It's true that we are out of luck...
Professor: I have another idea...
Student: What?

學生：真的是我們運氣不好啊！
教授：我有另一個想法。
學生：什麼。

字彙輔助

1 out of luck 運氣不好　　**2** another idea 另一個想法
3 what 什麼

小提點　　現在請跟著 MP3 覆誦，練習 3 句 shadowing 練習，第一次請先跟著 MP3 以相同速度覆誦，第二次和第三次後可以隨著個人程度調整並於聽到句子內容後，拉長數秒或更長時間作練習。

聽力講解

　　此篇為「聽力講解篇」，相信讀者能大致了解 shadowing 的功用並且逐步邁向聽力的下一步，即聽數句對話內容，然後作 shadowing 的練習，此章節規劃了由聽單句的 shadowing 練習到聽連續 5 句並作 shadowing 的練習，從中調整自己聽英文的腳步，並在此章節紮好英文聽力基礎，注意自己聽力專注力，為下個章節即聽力實戰篇作好準備，也能在實際新托福聽力中的學術場景的聽力中奠定好基礎，現在就一起動身，開始由聽「單句跟讀練習」開始！

※因每個讀者程度不同，若是稍具程度的讀者，可以跳過此章節喔！
　直接由下個篇章開始，直接作長句的 shadowing 練習喔！

▶▶ 三句 shadowing 練習 　MP3 007

KEY 1

Professor: I'm gonna divide you guys into other groups...
Professor: it's week 3... now
Professor: So from week 4-8, you will join the other groups.

教授：我會將你們幾個分到其他組裡。
教授：現在是第三週…。

教授：所以從第四週到第八週，你們將加入其他組。

字彙輔助

1 divide 分成　　　　　　2 group 組
3 week 週

小提點　現在請跟著 MP3 覆誦，練習 3 句 shadowing 練習，第一次請先跟著 MP3 以相同速度覆誦，第二次和第三次後可以隨著個人程度調整並於聽到句子內容後，拉長數秒或更長時間作練習。

KEY 2

Professor: You can write down what you've observed from other groups...
Professor: For the mid-term paper…hand in two reports to me...
Professor: Problem solved...

教授：你可以寫下由其他組中觀察到的動物…。
教授：至於期中報告…遞交兩份報告給我…。
教授：問題解決了…。

字彙輔助

1 write down 寫下　　　　2 observe 觀察
3 problem solved 問題解決

影子跟讀

學術場景

校園場景

現在請跟著 MP3 覆誦，練習 3 句 shadowing 練習，第一次請先跟著 MP3 以相同速度覆誦，第二次和第三次後可以隨著個人程度調整並於聽到句子內容後，拉長數秒或更長時間作練習。

KEY 3

Student: Ok...
Student: but what about those missing animals...
Student: Aren't we responsible for them being missing...

學生：好的⋯。
學生：但是關於那些失蹤的動物呢⋯？
學生：牠們的失蹤，我們難道沒有責任嗎？

字彙輔助

1. missing 失蹤
2. animals 動物
3. responsible 責任的

小提點 現在請跟著 MP3 覆誦，練習 3 句 shadowing 練習，第一次請先跟著 MP3 以相同速度覆誦，第二次和第三次後可以隨著個人程度調整並於聽到句子內容後，拉長數秒或更長時間作練習。

KEY 4

Professor: I don't want to be too hard on you guys...
Professor: but clearly it's a result of your negligence
Student: I feel bad about what happened....

教授：我不想要對你們太嚴格⋯。
教授：但是顯然這是你們疏忽的結果⋯。
學生：對此我也感到很難過

字彙輔助

1 too hard 太嚴格　　　2 result 結果
3 negligence 疏忽

小提點　現在請跟著 MP3 覆誦，練習 3 句 shadowing 練習，第一次請先跟著 MP3 以相同速度覆誦，第二次和第三次後可以隨著個人程度調整並於聽到句子內容後，拉長數秒或更長時間作練習。

聽力講解

　　此篇為「聽力講解篇」，相信讀者能大致了解 shadowing 的功用並且逐步邁向聽力的下一步，即聽數句對話內容，然後作 shadowing 的練習，此章節規劃了由聽單句的 shadowing 練習到聽連續 5 句並作 shadowing 的練習，從中調整自己聽英文的腳步，並在此章節紮好英文聽力基礎，注意自己聽力專注力，為下個章節即聽力實戰篇作好準備，也能在實際新托福聽力中的學術場景的聽力中奠定好基礎，現在就一起動身，開始由聽「單句跟讀練習」開始！

※因每個讀者程度不同，若是稍具程度的讀者，可以跳過此章節喔！
　　直接由下個篇章開始，直接作長句的 shadowing 練習喔！

▶▶ 四句 shadowing 練習 〔MP3 008〕

KEY 1

Student: Should I put some posters on the bulletin boards

Student: Like what they have done for missing dogs...

Professor: Great idea...

Professor: I guess I will leave that to you..

學生：我該把一些海報放到佈告欄嗎？

學生：像是他們會替失蹤的狗狗做的那樣…。

教授：很棒的想法。

教授：我想我就把這部分交給你了。

字彙輔助

1　posters 海報　　　　　　2　bulletin boards 佈告欄

3　missing dogs 失蹤的狗狗

小提點　現在請跟著 MP3 覆誦，練習 4 句 shadowing 練習，第一次請先跟著 MP3 以相同速度覆誦，第二次和第三次後可以隨著個人程度調整並於聽到句子內容後，拉長數秒或更長時間作練習。

KEY 2

Student: Me?

Student: No... Absolutely not...

Student: I mean I would love to find them..., but

Student: I'm not the artistic type...

學生：我嗎？

學生：不…絕對不能…。

學生：我指的是我也樂意能找到他們…，但是。

學生：我不是藝術類型的。

1 absolutely not 絕對不能   2 love 喜愛

3 artistic 藝術類型的

小提點　現在請跟著 MP3 覆誦，練習 4 句 shadowing 練習，第
　　　　一次請先跟著 MP3 以相同速度覆誦，第二次和第三次後
　　　　可以隨著個人程度調整並於聽到句子內容後，拉長數秒或
　　　　更長時間作練習。

KEY 3

Student: I'm the athletic type... .

Student: me, writing on those posters... .

Student: will ruin their chances of getting found...

Professor: Ok.. Then find someone who is good at writing
those characters...

學生：我是運動型的…。

學生：我，寫那些海報…。

學生：會破壞找到他們的機會…。

教授：好的…那麼找位擅長寫那些字體的…。

字彙輔助

1 athletic 運動型的   2 ruin 破壞

3 chances 機會

| 小提點 | 現在請跟著 MP3 覆誦，練習 4 句 shadowing 練習，第一次請先跟著 MP3 以相同速度覆誦，第二次和第三次後可以隨著個人程度調整並於聽到句子內容後，拉長數秒或更長時間作練習。 |

影子跟讀　學術場景　校園場景

聽力講解

　　此篇為「聽力講解篇」，相信讀者能大致了解 shadowing 的功用並且逐步邁向聽力的下一步，即聽數句對話內容，然後作 shadowing 的練習，此章節規劃了由聽單句的 shadowing 練習到聽連續 5 句並作 shadowing 的練習，從中調整自己聽英文的腳步，並在此章節紮好英文聽力基礎，注意自己聽力專注力，為下個章節即聽力實戰篇作好準備，也能在實際新托福聽力中的學術場景的聽力中奠定好基礎，現在就一起動身，開始由聽「單句跟讀練習」開始！

※因每個讀者程度不同，若是稍具程度的讀者，可以跳過此章節喔！
　直接由下個篇章開始，直接作長句的 shadowing 練習喔！

▶▶ 五句 shadowing 練習 MP3 009

KEY 1

Professor: I'll announce my decision in class...
Student: Ok...
Professor: What are you looking at...?
Student: The sky... .
Student: It's as blue as I am now...

教授：我會在課堂中宣布我的決定…。

影子跟讀

學術場景

校園場景

學生：好的…。

教授：你在看什麼呢？

學生：天空…。

學生：就像我現在這樣憂鬱…。

字彙輔助

1 announce 宣布　　　2 the sky 天空

3 blue 憂鬱

小提點　現在請跟著 MP3 覆誦，練習 5 句 shadowing 練習，第一次請先跟著 MP3 以相同速度覆誦，第二次和第三次後可以隨著個人程度調整並於聽到句子內容後，拉長數秒或更長時間作練習。

KEY 2

Professor: what happened at the center was not your fault.

Student: Almost 3 weeks... now gone...

Student: I now know why

Student: stealing hurts...

Student: I would never do something like that

教授：在研究中心發生的事不是你的錯…。

學生：幾乎照顧了三週…現在全沒了

學生：我現在懂為什麼了。

學生：偷竊傷人…。

學生：我絕不會做像這樣的事情。

字彙輔助

1 fault 錯　　　　　　　　　　　**2** stealing 偷竊

3 never do something like that 絕不會做像這樣的事情

小提點 現在請跟著 MP3 覆誦，練習 5 句 shadowing 練習，第一次請先跟著 MP3 以相同速度覆誦，第二次和第三次後可以隨著個人程度調整並於聽到句子內容後，拉長數秒或更長時間作練習。

KEY **3**

Student: My lab partner actually named the goat "clouds"

Student: since her fur is just like clouds...

Professor: Cute...

Professor: not so bad for a nickname... I guess

Student: I wonder how my lab partner would handle this

學生：我的實驗夥伴還真的命名山羊為「雲朵」。

學生：因為牠的毛就像是雲朵般…。

教授：可愛…。

教授：我想愛…以綽號來說還蠻不錯的…。

學生：我真的不知道我的實驗夥伴會怎麼應對這件事。

字彙輔助

1 lab partner 實驗夥伴　　　2 cute 可愛

3 not so bad for a nickname 以綽號來說還蠻不錯的

小提點　現在請跟著 MP3 覆誦，練習 5 句 shadowing 練習，第一次請先跟著 MP3 以相同速度覆誦，第二次和第三次後可以隨著個人程度調整並於聽到句子內容後，拉長數秒或更長時間作練習。

聽力講解

　　此篇為「聽力講解篇」，相信讀者能大致了解 shadowing 的功用並且逐步邁向聽力的下一步，即聽數句對話內容，然後作 shadowing 的練習，此章節規劃了由聽單句的 shadowing 練習到聽連續 5 句並作 shadowing 的練習，從中調整自己聽英文的腳步，並在此章節紮好英文聽力基礎，注意自己聽力專注力，為下個章節即聽力實戰篇作好準備，也能在實際新托福聽力中的學術場景的聽力中奠定好基礎，現在就一起動身，開始由聽「單句跟讀練習」開始！

※因每個讀者程度不同，若是稍具程度的讀者，可以跳過此章節喔！
　直接由下個篇章開始，直接作長句的 shadowing 練習喔！

▶▶ 五句 shadowing 練習 MP3 010

KEY 1

Student: I just don't want to hurt her feelings...
Student: She sure can't take this... .
Professor: She will know eventually...
Professor: So just tell her... the truth
Professor: Why don't we walk back to the lab

學生：我只是不想要傷到她的感受…。

學生：她肯定無法承受的…。

教授：她最終會知道的…。

教授：所以就告訴她吧…。

教授：我們為何不走回實驗室呢？

字彙輔助

1. hurt her feelings 傷到她的感受
2. she sure can't take this 她肯定無法承受的
3. lab 實驗室

小提點　現在請跟著 MP3 覆誦，練習 **5** 句 shadowing 練習，第一次請先跟著 MP3 以相同速度覆誦，第二次和第三次後可以隨著個人程度調整並於聽到句子內容後，拉長數秒或更長時間作練習。

KEY **2**

Professor: I happen to have some files I need to give back

Student: Sure...

(10 minutes later)

Student: I'm gonna check again

Student: Oh my goodness! ... They are in the lab

Professor: seriously? How?

教授：我碰巧有幾個檔案需要歸還。

學生：好的…。

（十分鐘後）

學生：讓我再確認一次。

學生：我的天啊！…他們在實驗室裡。

教授：真假？怎麼會？

字彙輔助

1 files 檔案　　　　　**2** give back 歸還

3 seriously 真的嗎？

小提點　現在請跟著 MP3 覆誦，練習 5 句 shadowing 練習，第一次請先跟著 MP3 以相同速度覆誦，第二次和第三次後可以隨著個人程度調整並於聽到句子內容後，拉長數秒或更長時間作練習。

KEY **3**

Student: Perhaps their abductors were willing to set them free...

Student: Knowing that they all have their own missions...

Student: I wonder where they went!

Guard: This morning the school dean demanded a vet check on them... so they were in the hospital for a few hours...

Guard: I do hope other people won't think they were missing, if they couldn't find them this morning...

學生：或許他們的綁架者自願釋放牠們。

學生：知道牠們有牠們的使命在。

學生：牠們到底是去哪兒了。

警衛：今天早上院長要求獸醫替牠們檢查。所以牠們在醫院待了幾個小時 。

警衛：我真希望其他人早上找不到牠們的時候不會認為牠們真的失蹤了 。

字彙輔助

1 abductor 綁架者   2 mission 任務

3 hospital 醫院

小提點 　現在請跟著 MP3 覆誦，練習 5 句 shadowing 練習，第一次請先跟著 MP3 以相同速度覆誦，第二次和第三次後可以隨著個人程度調整並於聽到句子內容後，拉長數秒或更長時間作練習。

Lecture 1 ►► Ecology：水的重要性
The Importance of Water

 聽力講解

　　此篇為「聽力講解篇」，相信讀者能大致了解 shadowing 的功用並且逐步邁向聽力的下一步，即聽數句對話內容，然後作 shadowing 的練習，此章節規劃了由聽單句的 shadowing 練習到連續聽 4 句並作 shadowing 的練習，從中調整自己聽英文的腳步，並在此章節奠好英文聽力基礎，注意自己聽力專注力，為下個章節即聽力實戰篇作好準備，也能在實際新托福聽力中的學術場景的聽力中奠定好基礎，現在就一起動身，開始由聽「單句跟讀練習」開始！

※因每個讀者程度不同，若是稍具程度的讀者，可以跳過此章節喔！
　　直接由下個篇章開始，直接作長句的 shadowing 練習喔！

►► 單句 shadowing 練習 MP3 011

KEY 1

Water is so essential in our lives that we cannot live without it.
水在我們生活中是如此重要以至於我們生活不可缺少它。

字彙輔助

1 water 水　　　　　2 essential 重要的

小提點　現在請跟著 MP3 覆誦，第一次請先跟著 MP3 以相同速度覆誦，第二次和第三次後可以隨著個人程度調整並於聽到句子內容後，拉長數秒或更長時間作練習。

KEY 2

We need to drink a certain amount of water to keep our body stable.

我們需要飲用到定量的水來維持我們身體的恆定。

字彙輔助

1 stable 穩定的

小提點　現在請跟著 MP3 覆誦，第一次請先跟著 MP3 以相同速度覆誦，第二次和第三次後可以隨著個人程度調整並於聽到句子內容後，拉長數秒或更長時間作練習。

KEY 3

The imbalance can cause dehydration and severe organ failures.

失衡會引起脫水和嚴重的器官衰竭。

1 imbalance 失衡　　2 dehydration 脫水
3 severe 嚴重的　　4 organ 器官

小提點 現在請跟著 MP3 覆誦，第一次請先跟著 MP3 以相同速度覆誦，第二次和第三次後可以隨著個人程度調整並於聽到句子內容後，拉長數秒或更長時間作練習。

KEY 4

Nowadays, we seem to take the water we use for granted.

現今，我們似乎將使用水當成理所當然。

字彙輔助

1 use 使用

小提點 現在請跟著 MP3 覆誦，第一次請先跟著 MP3 以相同速度覆誦，第二次和第三次後可以隨著個人程度調整並於聽到句子內容後，拉長數秒或更長時間作練習。

KEY 5

In some countries, sanitary water may need certain efforts to get.

在有些國家，衛生的飲用水需要相當程度的努力才能取得。

字彙輔助

1 sanitary 衛生的

2 certain 確切的

小提點　現在請跟著 MP3 覆誦，第一次請先跟著 MP3 以相同速度覆誦，第二次和第三次後可以隨著個人程度調整並於聽到句子內容後，拉長數秒或更長時間作練習。

KEY 6

Not living in those kinds of situations makes it unlikely for us to think about the importance of water... even a drop of it.

沒有實際生活在那樣的情況下，使我們忽略了去思考水的重要性…既使是一滴水也沒有。

字彙輔助

1 situation 情況

2 unlikely 不可能地

3 importance 重要性

4 drop 滴

小提點　現在請跟著 MP3 覆誦，第一次請先跟著 MP3 以相同速度覆誦，第二次和第三次後可以隨著個人程度調整並於聽到句子內容後，拉長數秒或更長時間作練習。

Lecture 2 ▶▶ American history：
美國歷史，亂世佳人看南北戰爭

🌥 聽力講解

　　此篇為「聽力講解篇」，相信讀者能大致了解 shadowing 的功用並且逐步邁向聽力的下一步，即聽數句對話內容，然後作 shadowing 的練習，此章節規劃了由聽單句的 shadowing 練習到連續聽 4 句並作 shadowing 的練習，從中調整自己聽英文的腳步，並在此章節紮好英文聽力基礎，注意自己聽力專注力，為下個章節即聽力實戰篇作好準備，也能在實際新托福聽力中的學術場景的聽力中奠定好基礎，現在就一起動身，開始由聽「單句跟讀練習」開始！

※因每個讀者程度不同，若是稍具程度的讀者，可以跳過此章節喔！
　直接由下個篇章開始，直接作長句的 shadowing 練習喔！

▶▶ 單句 shadowing 練習 MP3 012

KEY 1

I suppose you remember all the facts and exact dates of historical events from high school...
我相信你們高中的時候都記過所有歷史事件的史實和確切的日期。

字彙輔助

■ 1 exact 確切的　　　　　　　■ 2 historical 歷史的

小提點　現在請跟著 MP3 覆誦，第一次請先跟著 MP3 以相同速度覆誦，第二次和第三次後可以隨著個人程度調整並於聽到句子內容後，拉長數秒或更長時間作練習。

KEY 2

Therefore, I want you to take a look at the historical events through a different lens.
所以我想要你們透過不同面相來看歷史事件。

字彙輔助

■ 1 take a look at 看待　　　　■ 2 different 不同的
■ 3 len 視角

小提點　現在請跟著 MP3 覆誦，第一次請先跟著 MP3 以相同速度覆誦，第二次和第三次後可以隨著個人程度調整並於聽到句子內容後，拉長數秒或更長時間作練習。

KEY 3

Watching a film is a good way to start. At least, it won't be that boring, right?

觀看電影也是個開始的好方法。至少不會那麼無聊，對吧？

字彙輔助

1 film 電影　　　　　　　　2 start 開始

小提點　現在請跟著 MP3 覆誦，第一次請先跟著 MP3 以相同速度覆誦，第二次和第三次後可以隨著個人程度調整並於聽到句子內容後，拉長數秒或更長時間作練習。

KEY 4

Slavery has been a big issue throughout the history of the United States.

縱觀美國史，奴隸制度一直是一個重大的議題。

字彙輔助

1 Slavery 奴隸制度　　　　　2 issue 議題

小提點　現在請跟著 MP3 覆誦，第一次請先跟著 MP3 以相同速度覆誦，第二次和第三次後可以隨著個人程度調整並於聽到句子內容後，拉長數秒或更長時間作練習。

KEY 5

The root cause of the American Civil War was slavery.
美國南北戰爭的主要原因是奴隸制度。

字彙輔助

1. American Civil War 美國南北戰爭

小提點　現在請跟著 MP3 覆誦，第一次請先跟著 MP3 以相同速度覆誦，第二次和第三次後可以隨著個人程度調整並於聽到句子內容後，拉長數秒或更長時間作練習。

KEY 6

This caused the secession of seven southern states and many other things.
這些都導致了七個南方美國聯邦國家的分離和許多其他事情。

字彙輔助

1. cause 導致
2. secession 分離
3. southern 南方的

小提點　現在請跟著 MP3 覆誦，練習單句 shadowing 練習，第一次請先跟著 MP3 以相同速度覆誦，第二次和第三次後可以隨著個人程度調整並於聽到句子內容後，拉長數秒或更長時間作練習。

3 ▶▶ American History：
美國歷史，亂世佳人看南北戰爭

🌧 聽力講解

　　此篇為「聽力講解篇」，相信讀者能大致了解 shadowing 的功用並且逐步邁向聽力的下一步，即聽數句對話內容，然後作 shadowing 的練習，此章節規劃了由聽單句的 shadowing 練習到連續聽 4 句並作 shadowing 的練習，從中調整自己聽英文的腳步，並在此章節紮好英文聽力基礎，注意自己聽力專注力，為下個章節即聽力實戰篇作好準備，也能在實際新托福聽力中的學術場景的聽力中奠定好基礎，現在就一起動身，開始由聽「單句跟讀練習」開始！

※因每個讀者程度不同，若是稍具程度的讀者，可以跳過此章節喔！
　直接由下個篇章開始，直接作長句的 shadowing 練習喔！

▶▶ 單句 shadowing 練習 `MP3 013`

KEY 1

Disunion has also led people to rethink about slavery, but in places where cotton yields a huge profit, slavery expanded.
分裂已經導致人們重新思考奴隸制度，但是在棉花能產生高利潤的地區，奴隸制度的問題卻加劇。

字彙輔助

1 disunion 分裂   2 yield 產生

3 expand 擴張

小提點   現在請跟著 MP3 覆誦，第一次請先跟著 MP3 以相同速度覆誦，第二次和第三次後可以隨著個人程度調整並於聽到句子內容後，拉長數秒或更長時間作練習。

KEY 2

The fear that the emancipation of slavery would lead to the collapse of the economy was also the reason.

對於解放奴隸的恐懼導致了經濟的崩塌也是主因。

字彙輔助

1 emancipation 解放   2 collapse 崩解

3 economy 經濟

小提點   現在請跟著 MP3 覆誦，第一次請先跟著 MP3 以相同速度覆誦，第二次和第三次後可以隨著個人程度調整並於聽到句子內容後，拉長數秒或更長時間作練習。

KEY 3

Gone with the Wind is a well-structured movie that links its theme with the history of the United States.

電影中亂世佳人就是結構完整的電影，電影連結了美國歷史和其主題。

字彙輔助

1. well-structured 結構完整的　　2. link 連結
3. theme 主題

小提點　現在請跟著 MP3 覆誦，第一次請先跟著 MP3 以相同速度覆誦，第二次和第三次後可以隨著個人程度調整並於聽到句子內容後，拉長數秒或更長時間作練習。

KEY 4

Back then, cotton was a major crop.

在當時，棉花是主要經濟作物。

字彙輔助

1. cotton 棉花　　　　　　　2. major 主要的
3. crop 作物

小提點　現在請跟著 MP3 覆誦，第一次請先跟著 MP3 以相同速度覆誦，第二次和第三次後可以隨著個人程度調整並於聽到句子內容後，拉長數秒或更長時間作練習。

KEY 5

One of the heroines, Scarlett O'Hara lives at Tara in Georgia where her family owns cotton plantations

其中一位女主角，思嘉莉歐哈拉住在喬治亞的塔拉，在哪裡她的家裡擁有著棉花種植所。

字彙輔助

1 heroine 女主角

2 own 擁有

3 plantation 種植所

小提點 現在請跟著 MP3 覆誦，第一次請先跟著 MP3 以相同速度覆誦，第二次和第三次後可以隨著個人程度調整並於聽到句子內容後，拉長數秒或更長時間作練習。

KEY 6

She is about to attend Ashley's wedding at Twelve Oaks.

而且她正要參加艾許麗在十二橡樹園的婚禮。

字彙輔助

1 wedding 婚禮

小提點 現在請跟著 MP3 覆誦，第一次請先跟著 MP3 以相同速度覆誦，第二次和第三次後可以隨著個人程度調整並於聽到句子內容後，拉長數秒或更長時間作練習。

4 ▶▶ Nutrition：營養學，食物攝取

☁ 聽力講解

　　此篇為「聽力講解篇」，相信讀者能大致了解 shadowing 的功用並且逐步邁向聽力的下一步，即聽數句對話內容，然後作 shadowing 的練習，此章節規劃了由聽單句的 shadowing 練習到聽連續 4 句並作 shadowing 的練習，從中調整自己聽英文的腳步，並在此章節紮好英文聽力基礎，注意自己聽力專注力，為下個章節即聽力實戰篇作好準備，也能在實際新托福聽力中的學術場景的聽力中奠定好基礎，現在就一起動身，開始由聽「雙句跟讀練習」開始！

※因每個讀者程度不同，若是稍具程度的讀者，可以跳過此章節喔！
　直接由下個篇章開始，直接作長句的 shadowing 練習喔！

▶▶ 雙句 shadowing 練習 MP3 014

KEY 1

Nowadays, foods have labels with calories. It's actually a good thing.

現今，食物都附有卡路里的標籤。這樣其實是件好事。

字彙輔助

1. Nowadays 現今
2. label 標籤
3. calories 卡路里

小提點　現在請跟著 MP3 覆誦，練習單句 shadowing 練習，第一次請先跟著 MP3 以相同速度覆誦，第二次和第三次後可以隨著個人程度調整並於聽到句子內容後，拉長數秒或更長時間作練習。

KEY 2

You get to know the amount of the calories you consume. No one wants to wake up in the morning and be told by a dear friend or a colleague how much weight you have gained.

你能知道你所需要攝取的卡路里量。沒有人想要在早上起床後，被親愛的友人或同事告知你怎麼體重增加了這麼多。

字彙輔助

1. consume 攝取
2. wake up 起床
3. weight 體重

小提點　現在請跟著 MP3 覆誦，練習單句 shadowing 練習，第一次請先跟著 MP3 以相同速度覆誦，第二次和第三次後

影子跟讀

學術場景

校園場景

可以隨著個人程度調整並於聽到句子內容後，拉長數秒或更長時間作練習。

KEY 3

Not to mention it's not good for your health. We are responsible for what we eat.
更別提這樣對你的健康有害。我們都需要對我們攝取的食物負起責任。

字彙輔助

1. Not to mention 更別提
2. health 健康
3. are responsible for 對……負起責任

小提點 現在請跟著 MP3 覆誦，練習單句 shadowing 練習，第一次請先跟著 MP3 以相同速度覆誦，第二次和第三次後可以隨著個人程度調整並於聽到句子內容後，拉長數秒或更長時間作練習。

KEY 4

Whatever goes in our mouth can have a huge impact on our future health. A person might be diagnosed with intestinal cancer if one regularly consumes unhealthy foods.
任何放進我們嘴裡的食物都對我們未來的健康有著重大的影響。一個人可能即刻被診斷出有大腸癌，如果定期攝取不健康的食物。

字彙輔助

1 condition 情況　　　2 diagnose 診斷

3 intestine 腸道

小提點　現在請跟著 MP3 覆誦，練習單句 shadowing 練習，第一次請先跟著 MP3 以相同速度覆誦，第二次和第三次後可以隨著個人程度調整並於聽到句子內容後，拉長數秒或更長時間作練習。

KEY 5

So before the next time you put anything into your mouth, take a look at the food labels. There is no harm in that.

所以下次當你將任何食物放進口中時，看下食物標籤吧。有益無害。

字彙輔助

1 mouth 嘴巴　　　2 label 標籤

3 harm 損害

小提點　現在請跟著 MP3 覆誦，練習單句 shadowing 練習，第一次請先跟著 MP3 以相同速度覆誦，第二次和第三次後可以隨著個人程度調整並於聽到句子內容後，拉長數秒或更長時間作練習。

5 ▶▶ Sociology：社會學，第一印象與外貌

 聽力講解

　　此篇為「聽力講解篇」，相信讀者能大致了解 shadowing 的功用並且逐步邁向聽力的下一步，即聽數句對話內容，然後作 shadowing 的練習，此章節規劃了由聽單句的 shadowing 練習到聽連續 4 句並作 shadowing 的練習，從中調整自己聽英文的腳步，並在此章節紮好英文聽力基礎，注意自己聽力專注力，為下個章節即聽力實戰篇作好準備，也能在實際新托福聽力中的學術場景的聽力中奠定好基礎，現在就一起動身，開始由聽「雙句跟讀練習」開始！

※因每個讀者程度不同，若是稍具程度的讀者，可以跳過此章節喔！
　直接由下個篇章開始，直接作長句的 shadowing 練習喔！

▶▶ 雙句 shadowing 練習 MP3 015

KEY 1

It's often said that first impressions are lasting. It's true that the first impression will last for a significant portion of time.

據説通常第一印象是持久的。第一印象其實真的佔了很大的部分。

字彙輔助

1 impression 印象　　　2 lasting 持久的

3 significant 重要的

小提點　現在請跟著 MP3 覆誦，練習 2 句 shadowing 練習，第
一次請先跟著 MP3 以相同速度覆誦，第二次和第三次後
可以隨著個人程度調整並於聽到句子內容後，拉長數秒或
更長時間作練習。

KEY 2

The major factor on top of the list that influences a
person's impression is one's appearance. We are judged
by how well we look.

在影響一個人第一印象的清單裡，首要的主因就是一個人的外
表。我們會因為我們看起來的樣子受到評論。

字彙輔助

1 influence 影響　　　2 appearance 外表

3 judge 評定

小提點　現在請跟著 MP3 覆誦，練習 2 句 shadowing 練習，第
一次請先跟著 MP3 以相同速度覆誦，第二次和第三次後
可以隨著個人程度調整並於聽到句子內容後，拉長數秒或
更長時間作練習。

KEY 3

It's not that people are shallow or something. But we tend to value others by looking from how that person looks.

不是說人們很膚淺或什麼的。但是我們傾向藉由一個人看起來如何而評價對方。

字彙輔助

1. shallow 膚淺的
2. tend to 傾向
3. value 評價

小提點　現在請跟著 MP3 覆誦，練習 2 句 shadowing 練習，第一次請先跟著 MP3 以相同速度覆誦，第二次和第三次後可以隨著個人程度調整並於聽到句子內容後，拉長數秒或更長時間作練習。

KEY 4

Is that person clean-cut? That's also why people try so hard to make best of themselves when they go to the interview.

這個人看起來乾淨整潔嗎？這也是為什麼人們去面試時很盡其所能展現自己。

字彙輔助

1. clean-cut 乾淨整潔的
2. make best of 充分利用
3. interview 面試

小提點　現在請跟著 MP3 覆誦，練習 2 句 shadowing 練習，第一次請先跟著 MP3 以相同速度覆誦，第二次和第三次後可以隨著個人程度調整並於聽到句子內容後，拉長數秒或更長時間作練習。

KEY 5

Guys are wearing some make-up to cover some flaws. It's not female's preference anymore.

男人敷上一些化妝品來遮蓋一些瑕疵。這不再是女性的偏好了。

字彙輔助

1 make-up 化妝品　　　　2 flaw 瑕疵

3 preference 偏好

小提點　現在請跟著 MP3 覆誦，練習 2 句 shadowing 練習，第一次請先跟著 MP3 以相同速度覆誦，第二次和第三次後可以隨著個人程度調整並於聽到句子內容後，拉長數秒或更長時間作練習。

6 ▶▶ Sociology：社會學，整形

🌥 聽力講解

　　此篇為「聽力講解篇」，相信讀者能大致了解 shadowing 的功用並且逐步邁向聽力的下一步，即聽數句對話內容，然後作 shadowing 的練習，此章節規劃了由聽單句的 shadowing 練習到連續聽 4 句並作 shadowing 的練習，從中調整自己聽英文的腳步，並在此章節紮好英文聽力基礎，注意自己聽力專注力，為下個章節即聽力實戰篇作好準備，也能在實際新托福聽力中的學術場景的聽力中奠定好基礎，現在就一起動身，開始由聽「三句跟讀練習」開始！

※因每個讀者程度不同，若是稍具程度的讀者，可以跳過此章節喔！
　　直接由下個篇章開始，直接作長句的 shadowing 練習喔！

▶▶ 三句 shadowing 練習 `MP3 016`

KEY 1

People desire to be around handsome guys or beautiful ladies. But how good a person looks has a lot to do with the hereditary traits he or she inherits. In the past, it was unchangeable.

人們渴望環繞在英俊的男子或漂亮的女士週圍。但是一個人看起來多好與他或她所遺傳的遺傳特質息息相關。在過去，這是無法改變的。

字彙輔助

1 unchangeable 無法改變的

小提點 現在請跟著 MP3 覆誦，第一次請先跟著 MP3 以相同速度覆誦，第二次和第三次後可以隨著個人程度調整並於聽到句子內容後，拉長數秒或更長時間作練習。

KEY **2**

You cannot possibly change your genes, but nowadays people can have plastic surgery to alter their fate. Catalogues of the list of people are provided for clients to choose from.

你不可能改變你的基因，但是現今人們可以由整型手術來改變他們的命運。目錄清單上的人選會提供給客戶挑選。

字彙輔助

1 catalogue 目錄

小提點 現在請跟著 MP3 覆誦，第一次請先跟著 MP3 以相同速度覆誦，第二次和第三次後可以隨著個人程度調整並於聽

到句子內容後，拉長數秒或更長時間作練習。

KEY 3

Since people value so much how good they look, doctors want to exploit this opportunity to make a fortune out of it. It's now become a somewhat popular phenomenon.

既然人們極重視他們看起來多好。醫生想要利用機會去大賺一筆。這已經或多或少是個流行的現象了。

字彙輔助

1 exploit 利用

2 opportunity 機會

小提點　現在請跟著 MP3 覆誦，第一次請先跟著 MP3 以相同速度覆誦，第二次和第三次後可以隨著個人程度調整並於聽到句子內容後，拉長數秒或更長時間作練習。

KEY 4

The trend has swept many countries even among men. Sometimes good-looking people make a comparison with others and then make an appointment with doctors. They want to be incredibly good-looking.

這個趨勢已橫掃許多國家，甚至是對男人都造成影響。有時候好看的人與他人比較而又與醫生約定排程。他們想要超好看。

字彙輔助

1　trend 趨勢

2　comparison 比較

小提點　現在請跟著 MP3 覆誦，第一次請先跟著 MP3 以相同速度覆誦，第二次和第三次後可以隨著個人程度調整並於聽到句子內容後，拉長數秒或更長時間作練習。

KEY 5

It distorts some values that we had in the past. Sometimes it's not even the money that we are talking about. It does cost people's lives from time to time.

這扭曲了一些我們過去有的價值。有時候我們所談論的甚至不是金錢。有時候犧牲的是人的性命。

字彙輔助

1　distort 扭曲

2　money 金錢

小提點　現在請跟著 MP3 覆誦，第一次請先跟著 MP3 以相同速度覆誦，第二次和第三次後可以隨著個人程度調整並於聽到句子內容後，拉長數秒或更長時間作練習。

7 ▶▶ Business：Advertisement
廣告充斥在生活週遭

🌸 聽力講解

　　此篇為「聽力講解篇」，相信讀者能大致了解 shadowing 的功用並且逐步邁向聽力的下一步，即聽數句對話內容，然後作 shadowing 的練習，此章節規劃了由聽單句的 shadowing 練習到連續聽 4 句並作 shadowing 的練習，從中調整自己聽英文的腳步，並在此章節紮好英文聽力基礎，注意自己聽力專注力，為下個章節即聽力實戰篇作好準備，也能在實際新托福聽力中的學術場景的聽力中奠定好基礎，現在就一起動身，開始由聽「四句跟讀練習」開始！

※因每個讀者程度不同，若是稍具程度的讀者，可以跳過此章節喔！
　直接由下個篇章開始，直接作長句的 shadowing 練習喔！

▶▶ 四句 shadowing 練習 `MP3 017`

KEY 1

Everyday when we wake up, bombarded messages pop up. They have become a constant annoying nuisance. Sometimes we cannot help but feel we don't need a constant reminder of something. Those messages are just so rampant that stopping using the smartphone seems the only way out.

每天當我們起床，轟炸式的訊息出現。他們已經成了不斷令人感到討厭的麻煩事。有時候我們不得不覺得我們不需要這樣子的連續提醒…那些訊息是如此的猖獗以至於似乎停止使用手機是唯一的解決辦法。

字彙輔助

1　bombarded 轟炸式的　　　2　constant 不斷的、連續的

3　annoying 擾人的　　　　　4　nuisance 麻煩事

5　reminder 提醒　　　　　　6　rampant 蔓延的

小提點　現在請跟著 MP3 覆誦，練習 4 句 shadowing 練習，第一次請先跟著 MP3 以相同速度覆誦，第二次和第三次後可以隨著個人程度調整並於聽到句子內容後，拉長數秒或更長時間作練習。

KEY 2

But walking along the streets, you still get to see the billboards and many other things. Advertisements are everywhere. All of a sudden, it's like you need a weekend getaway or something.

但是沿著街道走去，你仍可以看到那些廣告刊版和許多其他事。廣告無所不在。突然間，就像是你需要周末大逃亡或什麼的。

字彙輔助

1 billboards 廣告刊版　　2 Advertisement 廣告
3 everywhere 到處　　　　4 getaway 逃亡

小提點 現在請跟著 MP3 覆誦，練習 4 句 shadowing 練習，第一次請先跟著 MP3 以相同速度覆誦，第二次和第三次後可以隨著個人程度調整並於聽到句子內容後，拉長數秒或更長時間作練習。

KEY 3

Just like to some places somewhat remote from the cities, preferably rainforests... kidding. But sometimes being in a place like that can actually make your mind serene... It's like you can finally have some time alone and can contemplate or meditate or something.

就像是逃到一些地方，有點遠離都市，更可能是雨林…開玩笑的。但是有時候在一個像那樣子的地方確實能讓你的心靈感到寧靜…像是你最終能有些獨處的時間和可以思考或沉思著一些事。

字彙輔助

1 remote 偏遠的　　　　2 preferably 偏好
3 serene 寧靜的　　　　4 contemplate 沉思、深入思考
5 meditate 沉思、冥想

小提點 現在請跟著 MP3 覆誦，練習 4 句 shadowing 練習，第一次請先跟著 MP3 以相同速度覆誦，第二次和第三次後可以隨著個人程度調整並於聽到句子內容後，拉長數秒或更長時間作練習。

8 ▶▶ Zoology：Stability 穩定性

🌫️ 聽力講解

　　此篇為「聽力講解篇」，相信讀者能大致了解 shadowing 的功用並且逐步邁向聽力的下一步，即聽數句對話內容，然後作 shadowing 的練習，此章節規劃了由聽單句的 shadowing 練習到連續聽 4 句並作 shadowing 的練習，從中調整自己聽英文的腳步，並在此章節紮好英文聽力基礎，注意自己聽力專注力，為下個章節即聽力實戰篇作好準備，也能在實際新托福聽力中的學術場景的聽力中奠定好基礎，現在就一起動身，開始由聽「四句跟讀練習」開始！

※因每個讀者程度不同，若是稍具程度的讀者，可以跳過此章節喔！
　直接由下個篇章開始，直接作長句的 shadowing 練習喔！

▶▶ 四句 shadowing 練習 MP3 018

KEY 1

Stability is very important to many of us. In our job, it clearly indicates the ability to have regular paychecks so that we can live a life, not worrying about something. So we want to have a stable job. Stability means a lot to animals, too.

穩定性對我們許多人來說是非常重要的。在工作上，這顯然代表有著固定的收入，以至於我們能夠過生活，不用擔心一些事情。所以我們想要有份穩定的工作。穩定性對許多動物來說也是意義非凡的。

字彙輔助

1 Stability 穩定性   2 regular 規律的

3 paycheck 薪津   4 stable 穩定的

小提點 現在請跟著 MP3 覆誦，練習 4 句 shadowing 練習，第一次請先跟著 MP3 以相同速度覆誦，第二次和第二次後可以隨著個人程度調整並於聽到句子內容後，拉長數秒或更長時間作練習。

KEY 2

Carnivores need a stable food source to maintain their daily metabolism and raise their offspring. It's highly unlikely for lions to raise their young, if food resources are not abundant and stable. Newborn babies won't get the chance to grow to a certain height. The environment should be unchanging, too.

肉食性動物需要穩定的食物來源來維持他們的每日代謝和扶養後代。如果食物不富足且來源不穩定，獅子們就很難扶養他們的幼子。新生的幼仔就不會有機會成長到特定的高度。環境也需要毫無變動。

小提點　現在請跟著 MP3 覆誦，練習 4 句 shadowing 練習，第一次請先跟著 MP3 以相同速度覆誦，第二次和第三次後可以隨著個人程度調整並於聽到句子內容後，拉長數秒或更長時間作練習。

KEY 3

A drastic change to the surroundings can be lethal to the newborns since they are susceptible to subtle changes in the environment. Drought, for example, can be a huge factor in determining the survival of the population. It's also an indication as a result of a lack of rain, and most animals in Africa are expecting the rainy season to arrive so that there will be enough of food for the species, not just for carnivores, but also herbivores.

環境的急遽改變也會對於幼仔造成致命影響，因為他們很容易受到環境中細微變化的影響。例如，乾旱就可能是決定族群生存的重大影響因素。這也可能是顯示著缺乏降雨的結果，而且大部分在非洲的動物都期待著雨季的降臨，如此物種才能夠有足夠的食物，不只是對肉食動物而言，對草食動物也是相同的。

字彙輔助

1 drastic 急遽的

2 lethal 致命的

3 susceptible 易受攻擊的

4 subtle 微妙的、難捉摸的

5 survival 生存

6 population 族群

7 indication 指標

8 herbivore 草食性動物

小提點 現在請跟著 MP3 覆誦，練習 4 句 shadowing 練習，第一次請先跟著 MP3 以相同速度覆誦，第二次和第三次後可以隨著個人程度調整並於聽到句子內容後，拉長數秒或更長時間作練習。

9 ▶▶ Business：Marketing Through Social Platforms 透過社交平台行銷

☁ 聽力講解

　　此篇為「聽力講解篇」，相信讀者能大致了解 shadowing 的功用並且逐步邁向聽力的下一步，即聽數句對話內容，然後作 shadowing 的練習，此章節規劃了由聽單句的 shadowing 練習到連續聽 4 句並作 shadowing 的練習，從中調整自己聽英文的腳步，並在此章節紮好英文聽力基礎，注意自己聽力專注力，為下個章節即聽力實戰篇作好準備，也能在實際新托福聽力中的學術場景的聽力中奠定好基礎，現在就一起動身，開始由聽「單句跟讀練習」開始！

※因每個讀者程度不同，若是稍具程度的讀者，可以跳過此章節喔！直接由下個篇章開始，直接作長句的 shadowing 練習喔！

▶▶ 四句 shadowing 練習 　MP3 019

KEY 1

It has been known that prolonged viewing on the screens of smartphones and computers has caused a widespread concern among educators and parents since it has a detrimental effect on our health. Blue light from these digital devices does cause eye strain, but warnings from the news headlines or health-conscious parents and educators have a very insignificant influence on users of digital devices. What prevents them from doing so has a lot to do with intriguing commercials, appealing footage, and user habits.

眾所皆知，長期觀看智慧型手機和電腦已引起教育者和家長廣泛的關心，因為這對我們的健康會造成有害影響。這些數位裝置的藍光的確會導致眼睛疲勞，但來自新聞頭條或關注健康的家長及教育者的警告對數位裝置的使用者沒有顯著影響，原因跟有趣的廣告，吸引人的影片及使用者習慣有關。

字彙輔助

1. prolonged 冗長的
2. widespread 廣佈的
3. detrimental 有害的
4. digital 數位的
5. insignificant 微不足道的
6. commercials 廣告
7. footages 連續鏡頭

小提點　現在請跟著 MP3 覆誦，練習 4 句 shadowing 練習，第一次請先跟著 MP3 以相同速度覆誦，第二次和第三次後可以隨著個人程度調整並於聽到句子內容後，拉長數秒或更長時間作練習。

KEY 2

As competition among companies has become more and more competitive, it is not uncommon for those companies to lure consumers by using innovative technologies or eye-catching videos. A video footage of a blue lobster moving in the aquarium will soon capture the eyes of viewers. The surge of viewers will sooner or later generate more profits for the company. The number of viewers and people who click the like button will be the measurement for ad companies to decide whether this video will bring profits and generate orders.

隨著公司間的競爭越來越激烈，那些公司用創新科技或引人注目的影片吸引消費者是很普遍的。在水族館裡移動的藍色龍蝦影片很快地就能捕捉觀眾的目光。觀眾數量的暴增遲早會替公司帶來更多利潤。觀眾數量和按讚的人數將是廣告公司用來決定這段影片是否能帶來利潤並帶來訂單的衡量方式。

字彙輔助

1 competitive 競爭的
2 uncommon 不普遍的
3 lobster 龍蝦
4 aquarium 水族館
5 profit 利潤
6 measurement 測量、尺寸
7 generate 產生

小提點　現在請跟著 MP3 覆誦，練習 4 句 shadowing 練習，第一次請先跟著 MP3 以相同速度覆誦，第二次和第三次後可以隨著個人程度調整並於聽到句子內容後，拉長數秒或更長時間作練習。

KEY 3

In addition, novelty also has a say in the viewing population. Among all video footage, animals are by far one of the most interesting ones to viewers. It is said that animals with a novelty not only add color to the entire video, but soon generate hit after hit, which is what clients want. They want significant hits within an hour or less. The less time taken, the better.

此外，新奇的內容也能決定觀賞者的人數。目前在所有影片中，動物對觀賞者來說是最有趣的。據說帶有新奇動物元素，不但增加整部影片的趣味，也能很快地產生點閱率，而這正是顧客想要的。他們想要在一小時或更短時間內有大量點閱率。花的時間越少越好。

字彙輔助

1 interesting 令人感到有趣的　　**2** novelty 新奇

3 entire 完整的　　**4** significant 有意義的

小提點　現在請跟著 MP3 覆誦，練習 4 句 shadowing 練習，第一次請先跟著 MP3 以相同速度覆誦，第二次和第三次後可以隨著個人程度調整並於聽到句子內容後，拉長數秒或更長時間作練習。

10 ▶▶▶ Literature：Sea Wolf 海狼

🌧 聽力講解

　　此篇為「聽力講解篇」，相信讀者能大致了解 shadowing 的功用並且逐步邁向聽力的下一步，即聽數句對話內容，然後作 shadowing 的練習，此章節規劃了由聽單句的 shadowing 練習到聽連續 4 句並作 shadowing 的練習，從中調整自己聽英文的腳步，並在此章節紮好英文聽力基礎，注意自己聽力專注力，為下個章節即聽力實戰篇作好準備，也能在實際新托福聽力中的學術場景的聽力中奠定好基礎，現在就一起動身，開始由聽「單句跟讀練習」開始！

※因每個讀者程度不同，若是稍具程度的讀者，可以跳過此章節喔！
　直接由下個篇章開始，直接作長句的 shadowing 練習喔！

▶▶ 四句 shadowing 練習 MP3 020

KEY 1

As the story progresses, we can't help but feel bad for crew members and several major characters on the Ghost. The incredible strength of Wolf Larsen makes him somewhat invincible from the attack of the crew members. Several themes make us feel there should be something happening to reverse the trend, and yes things are starting

to change. As the saying goes, no one holds all the cards.
隨著故事的進展，我們不得不對於在幽靈號上的船員和幾個主要角色感到同情。拉森船長的驚人力量使得他在受到船員攻擊後有點無可匹敵。幾個主題都使我們感到應該要有些事情出現來扭轉情勢，而是的，事情開始有了改變。有俗諺說：沒有人是總是佔盡優勢的。

字彙輔助

1. progress 進展
2. incredible 難以置信的、驚人的
3. strength 力量
4. invincible 無堅不摧的
5. reverse 顛倒、徹底改變
6. trend 趨勢

小提點　現在請跟著 MP3 覆誦，練習 4 句 shadowing 練習，第一次請先跟著 MP3 以相同速度覆誦，第二次和第三次後可以隨著個人程度調整並於聽到句子內容後，拉長數秒或更長時間作練習。

KEY 2

Wolf Larsen cannot always have the upper hand. Readers expect to see some changes, and everyone has his or her own weaknesses. It's just a matter of time. The story reaches the climax by revealing Wolf Larsen's weakness to the reader: the headache…The headache is probably a sign that shows he will not remain the king of the Ghost.

拉森船長不可能總是都占上風。讀者也期待要看到一些改變，而且每個人都有自己的弱點。只是時間早晚而已。故事藉由向讀者揭露了拉森船長來的弱點來到了高潮：頭痛..頭痛可能是個跡象，顯示出他不會維持幽靈號的王者。

字彙輔助

1. in the upper hand 佔上風
2. weakness 弱點
3. climax 高潮
4. reveal 揭露

小提點 現在請跟著 MP3 覆誦，練習 4 句 shadowing 練習，第一次請先跟著 MP3 以相同速度覆誦，第二次和第三次後可以隨著個人程度調整並於聽到句子內容後，拉長數秒或更長時間作練習。

KEY 3

With his physical condition deteriorating, it influences several aspects of Wolf Larsen, including his ability to move and his vision. The blindness of Wolf Larsen marks the end of his journey and takes us to the end of the whole story. The ruling of the sea is short-lived. The one-time powerful Larsen eventually meets his doom.

隨著他的身體情況惡化，也影響了拉森船長幾個部分，包含了他的移動能力和視力。拉森船長的失明標誌著他旅程的結束和帶領我們到了整個故事的尾端。統治大海是短暫的。曾經如此強大的拉森船長最終走向了滅亡。

字彙輔助

1 physical 身體的、肉體的

2 deteriorate 惡化

3 blindness 盲目、失明

4 journey 旅程

5 short-lived 短暫的

6 doom 厄運、毀滅、死亡

小提點 現在請跟著 MP3 覆誦，練習 **4** 句 shadowing 練習，第一次請先跟著 MP3 以相同速度覆誦，第二次和第三次後可以隨著個人程度調整並於聽到句子內容後，拉長數秒或更長時間作練習。

Part 2

學術場景

篇章概述

學術場景中收錄了 **7** 篇的新托福聽力實戰練習，除了寫試題對解析外，請務必要確實做跟讀練習、記筆記練習、填空練習和摘要練習。

其中摘要練習紮實提升新托福寫作和口説整合題的答題能力。運用聽、寫和説的關聯性，最短時間內獲取理想成績。

Lecture 1 ▶▶ Zoology：生物間的關係，很多時候視頻並未揭露全貌

▶▶ 聽力試題 (MP3 021)

1. According to the professor, what is untrue about the videos?
   (A) The intention of some videos on social platforms is to create hits.
   (B) People are able to view fine moments of animals through watching videos.
   (C) They somehow present a biased and incomplete part of the whole story.
   (D) They can only be uploaded by a photographer.

2. Listen again to part of the lecture. Then answer the question.
   (A) To show animals on the top of the food chain can be exempted from being the victim.
   (B) To show predators are powerful than prey.
   (C) To explain in nature top predators serve as a very important function.
   (D) To demonstrate top predators are carnivores.

3. The following statements list mantis' prey and mantis' natural enemies

Click the correct box for each one

	Mantis' prey	Mantis' natural enemy
A. hornets		
B. amphibians		
C. humming birds		
D. grasshoppers		

4. According to the professor, what is untrue about the honey badgers?

(A) They can withstand the sting of bees.

(B) They can withstand the bite of some snakes.

(C) To lions, they are not palatable.

(D) They can always take down pythons.

5. The following statements list mantises, snakes and their traits

Click the correct box for each trait

	Mantises	Snakes
A. are the prey of chameleons		
B. have secret armors		
C. sensitive to temperature changes		
D. susceptible to some amphibians		

▶▶ 新托福聽力解析

1. 這題詢問的是細節部分，關於聽力考點中敘述錯誤的部分。ABC 均為正確選項，而 D 的 They can **only** be uploaded by a photographer.，加上 only 後過於絕對，加上聽力敘述中沒有提到僅能由攝影師上傳，故答案為選項 D。

2. 這題是考聽力段落中的某句話意思為何。教授説：After all, only top predators can be immune from being someone else's prey. 的原因是 To show animals on the top of the food chain can be exempted from being the victim. 由此可得知答案為選項 A。

3. 這題是較整合且細節性的題目。讀者要從聽力敘述中區分螳螂的天敵跟獵物分別為何，而且敘述其實平均分散在每個段落，記筆記時要注意這部分。了解生物間的關係就能輕易答對這題。答案為 CD 和 AB。

4. 這題詢問的是細節部分，關於聽力考點中敘述錯誤的部分。這部分要定位在聽力後段 honey badger 的地方，C 選項中的 palatable 是 delicious 的同義詞要注意。D 選項的 always 也是過於絕對的詞，與聽力敘述不符，故答案為選項 D。

5. 這題是考生物與其特性的敘述。蛇的部分在聽力最尾段，專心聽且將螳螂和蛇的特性記下的話，蠻容易答對的。答案分別為 ABD 和 C。

....

答案： 1. D 2. A 3. CD/AB 4. D 5. ABD/C

影子跟讀練習 MP3 021

做完題目後，除了對答案知道錯的部分在哪外，更重要的是要修正自己聽力根本的問題，即聽力理解力和聽力專注力，聽力專注力的修正能逐步強化本身的聽力實力，所以現在請根據聽力內容「逐個段落」、「數個段落」或「整篇」進行跟讀練習，提升在實際考場時專注聽完每個訊息、定位出關鍵考點和搭配筆記回答完所有題目。Go!

| Professor |

Often we can see videos from all sources, whether it's uploading by a photographer who captures a really fine moment of some animals, insects, and plants, or it's from marketers or editors of social platforms, intending to increase hits. Sometimes people do it out of pleasure. Looking for more "likes" from Facebook pages through a computer screen gives people euphoria. Some are getting affirmation from virtual worlds.

通常我們透過所有能找到的來源觀看視頻，不論是攝影師所上傳，捕捉到有些動物、昆蟲和植物相當細微一刻的視頻，或者是由行銷人員或編輯們從社交平台意圖增加點擊率的視頻。有時候人們上傳視頻純粹是以此為樂。透過電腦螢幕看到臉書頁面有著更多的「讚」給予人們愉悅的感覺。

字彙輔助

1 sources 來源
2 upload 上傳
3 capture 捕捉
4 fine 細微的
5 intend 意圖
6 pleasure 樂趣
7 euphoria 幸福感
8 affirmation 肯定

Whatever the motive behind the scene, videos somehow present a biased and incomplete part of the whole story. For example, a video of a mantis killing several insects, such as grasshoppers or crickets, shows how skillful the mantis is. People start to label "the mantis" a certain name, misconstruing most people that all animals or insects have their natural enemy.

有些人可以因此從虛擬世界中獲得更多認同感。不論背後的動機為何，視頻在某種程度上表現出了整個故事背後偏見和不全面的部份。例如，視頻中螳螂殺死幾隻螳螂或蟋蟀的昆蟲，就顯示出螳螂捕食行為是多麼厲害。人們開始將給「螳螂」冠上特定的名字，使大多數的人誤解了所有動物或昆蟲都有著牠們的天敵。

字彙輔助

1 motive 動機
2 present 呈現
3 biased 偏見的
4 incomplete 不完整的
5 whole 整個的
6 grasshoppers 蚱蜢

7	crickets 蟋蟀	8	skillful 有技術的、熟練的
9	label 標籤	10	misconstrue 誤解

It's not that people don't have a basic idea of the biology. It's how uploaders edit the video in a certain way. What they fail to do is present viewers with a complete part of the story. For example, mantises seem so talented at hunting cockroaches and crickets beneath the grass, but can instantly get eaten by cranes and some chameleons the next moment. Presenting the whole thing will give viewers a more balanced idea of how nature works. After all, only top predators can be immune from being someone else's prey.

這不是表示人們沒有生物學的基本概念。這只是上傳者將視頻剪輯成某個方式。他們失敗的是未呈現出故事的全貌給觀看者。例如：螳螂在捕食草叢下的蟑螂和蟋蟀看似很有天賦，卻能在下一刻瞬間被鶴和有些變色龍吃掉。呈現全貌將給予觀看者對於自然界如何運作有著更平衡的概念。畢竟，僅有少數的頂端捕食者能夠免於成為其他生物的獵物。

字彙輔助

1	biology 生物學	2	uploaders 上傳者
3	talented 有才能的	4	cockroach 蟑螂
5	viewer 觀看者	6	balanced 平衡的
7	predator 掠食者	8	immune 免疫於

Here I want to show you a video clip about a mantis feeding on small insects, but its short-lived victory soon ends when a chameleon spots him under the bush. The tongue of the chameleon is so sticky and as you can see how fast it captures the mantis in a second. Other than chameleons, mantises are also the prey of vertebrates and invertebrates. They are not that powerful, right?

在此我想要展示一段關於螳螂捕食小型昆蟲的視頻，但是這短暫的勝利卻在變色龍於草叢下方即刻發現他的行蹤而告終。變色龍的舌頭是如此黏稠，所以你能看到它如何能轉眼間快速捕捉到螳螂。除了變色龍外，螳螂也是脊椎動物和無脊椎動物的獵物。它們沒那麼厲害了，對吧？

字彙輔助

1. insect 昆蟲
2. victory 勝利
3. chameleon 變色龍
4. tongue 舌頭
5. vertebrates 脊椎動物
6. invertebrate 無脊椎動物

| Student A |

Yes, they are not as powerful as they seem. Of course, they have secret armors and many other things, and they do attack small insects and humming birds when prey are within striking distance. They're still vulnerable to some amphibians, such as frogs.

是的，它們沒有表面上看起來那樣厲害。當然它們有著祕密的裝甲和許多其他部分，它們確實在攻擊範圍內的距離時會攻擊小型昆蟲和將蜂鳥當成獵物。他們也相當容易受到一些兩棲類的攻擊，例如青蛙等。

字彙輔助

1 powerful 強有力的   **2** secret 祕密的

3 armor 裝甲   **4** striking distance 攻擊範圍

5 amphibian 兩棲類動物

| Student B |

Yes, one time I saw a video from a friend of mine. It's a mantis getting taken down by a hornet. Perhaps I should have uploaded the video. I was like "You go hornet!" I'm not a big fan of mantises. They're weird to me. Some videos make them so invincible or something.

是的，有次我觀看一位朋友傳來的視頻。是螳螂不敵大黃蜂的視頻。或許我該上傳該視頻。我的反應是：大黃蜂，快進攻啊！我不是很喜歡螳螂。他們對我來說很奇怪。有些視頻使它們太無堅不摧了或什麼的。

字彙輔助

1 hornet 大黃蜂   **2** invincible 無堅不摧的

I think you guys have made some pretty good points. Back to what I said before, it's a partial part of the story. A honey badger can be named the king of the jungle or something simply because it can stand the attack of bees, withstand the bite of some snakes, and scare away some lions, but what videos fail to tell us is that the meat of honey badgers is not delicious. They are no match when it comes to getting into a fight with a lion. They have zero chances of winning. Just because lions do not like eating them does not make them more powerful than lions or even lions are afraid of them. The statement "lions are afraid of the honey badgers" comes from lacking a thorough understanding of the biology as well as biased videos.

我認為你們已經表達出了有些相當不錯的論點。回到我剛才提到的，這是故事的一部分。一隻蜜獾可以被命名為叢林之王或什麼的僅因為它能抵禦蜜蜂們的攻擊，忍受一些蛇咬和嚇走有些獅子。但是視頻沒有告訴我們的是，蜜獾的肉並不美味。他們在戰鬥時根本不是獅子的對手。他們毫無勝算。僅是因為獅子不喜歡吃它們的肉並不代表蜜獾比獅子厲害或甚至獅子怕它們。「獅子懼怕蜜獾」的陳述來自於缺乏對於生物學的透徹了解以及以偏概全的視頻。

字彙輔助

1. partial 部分的
2. badger 蜜獾
3. withstand 抵擋、禁得起
4. delicious 美味的
5. chance 機會
6. statement 聲明

7 understanding 了解　　8 biased 偏見的

They can easily get hunted down by lions. It's just not included in those videos. Another statement about honey badgers is also untrue. Of course, they do have the ability to take down snakes, but they do get eaten by pythons. Showing a photo or a video about the honey badger eating a python at night does not give a full story. Snakes are sensitive to temperature changes since they are reptiles. Temperature fluctuations influence their mobility at night. During the daytime, the situation can totally change. They're not that powerful.

蜜獾能輕易被獅子追殺。只是這些不包含在那些視頻裡。另一個關於蜜獾的陳述也不是真實的。它們有著打倒蛇的能力，但是蟒蛇也以它們為食。所以關於蜜獾在夜間捕食蟒蛇的照片或視頻並未給予故事較完整的一面。蛇因為是爬蟲類，對於溫度變化敏感。溫度變化影響他們在夜間的行動力。在白天，情況可能截然不同。蜜獾沒有那麼厲害。

字彙輔助

1 untrue 不真實的　　2 python 蟒蛇
3 sensitive 敏感的　　4 temperature 溫度
5 fluctuation 變化、波動　　6 mobility 移動性
7 situation 情況

| Student A |

I do think sometimes it's about the size. A couple weeks ago, I saw a video about a honey badger entwined by a python.

| 學生 A |

我認為有時候是體型。幾週前，我看到一個關於蜜獾被蟒蛇纏繞的視頻。

| Student B |

I don't think they trump lions and pythons because it's just so untrue. Plus, some videos are setup by photographers. Pretending they are rescuing an animal, but they're not. It's they who put the snare that traps those animals. From my viewpoint, uploading those videos does not make them an American hero or something. It doesn't change my perception of how nature works. It just doesn't work that way.

| 學生 B |

我不認為蜜獾勝過獅子和蟒蛇因為這是不真實的。再者，有些視頻是受到攝影師的鋪陳。假裝他們在拯救某個動物，然而卻不是。攝影師是放置陷阱捕抓那些動物者。從我的觀點，上傳那些視頻並不能使他們成為美國英雄或什麼的。也不會改變我對於自然界是如何運作的觀點。就是不會以那樣的方式運作。

字彙輔助

1 entwine 纏繞　　　　**2** trump 勝過

3 pretend 假裝　　　　**4** snare 陷阱

5 perception 觀點

| Professor |

Excellent points. The key point of what I'm telling you today is not about which species trumps or outshines which species. The point is to beware of every message you receive. Being able to tell right from wrong and having a critical thinking ability are essential to all of us so that bombarded messages won't influence us.

出色的論點。我今天所要告訴你們的關鍵點不在於哪個物種勝過或光芒蓋過某個物種。重點是小心每個你所接收到的資訊。能夠分辨對錯和有著批判性思考的能力，對我們所有人來說是很重要的。如此，我們才能不受到轟炸性訊息的影響。

字彙輔助

1 excellent 卓越的　　　**2** outshine 勝過、使失色、比…更優秀

3 beware of 小心　　　　**4** essential 重要的

5 bombarded 轟炸的　　　**6** message 訊息

1. According to the professor, what is untrue about the videos?

2. Listen again to part of the lecture. Then answer the question.
   Professor: presenting the whole thing will give viewers a more balanced idea of how nature works. After all, only top predators can be immune from being someone else's prey.

   Why does the professor say "After all, only top predators can be immune from being someone else's prey"?

3. The following statements list mantis' prey and mantis' natural enemies
   Click the correct box for each one

4. According to the professor, what is untrue of the honey badgers?

5. The following statements list mantises, snakes and their traits
   Click the correct box for each trait

▶▶ 記筆記與聽力訊息

| Instruction | MP3 **021**

　　新托福聽力與其他聽力測驗不同，可以於聽力的紙上記筆記，除了寫試題外，更重要的一點是訓練自己能夠將聽完一段訊息後，將重要的聽力訊息都記到。也可以將自己聽到跟記到的重點訊息跟試題做比對，因為試題考的就是長對話跟講座中出現的重點，能修正自己篩選聽力訊息重點的能力。

| 聽力重點 |

■ 記筆記有很多方式，包含符號跟自己習慣的縮寫字等等，可以找出最適合自己的模式，一定要自己重聽音檔作練習數次。

■ 這篇是關於動物學，**前面段落其實都是鋪陳所以其實理解就可以了，理解力遠比記筆記和答題技巧重要多了，重點可以放在所提到的動物間的關係，掌握提到的生物間的關係和特性就能答對整合題型，可以參考下列的表格中所記到的重點，有些地方可以再簡化些。**

Note

▶▶ 參考筆記

Main idea ❶ Videos：biased an incomplete	
details	❶ pleasure ❷ euphoria ❸ affirmation
Predatory—prey	mantis—grasshoppers, crickets
Main idea ❷ all animals：(have) natural enemies	
Predatory—prey	mantis—cockroaches, crickets
Prey—Predatory	mantis—cranes, chameleons
Main idea ❸ top predators：immunity	
Prey—Predatory	mantis—vertebrates, invertebrates
Main idea ❹ Victory： **short-lived，animals not as powerful as they seem**	
Predatory—prey	mantis—small insects, humming birds
Prey—Predatory	mantis—amphibians (e.g. frogs), a hornet
Main idea ❺	Statements about honey badgers：untrue ❶ lions are not afraid of the honey badgers ❷ they do get eaten/ entwined by pythons
details	Honey badgers ❶ stand the attack of bees ❷ withstand the bite of some snakes ❸ scare away some lions
details	Snakes ❶ sensitive to temperature fluctuations
Main idea ❻ **Beware of bombarded messages/critical thinking**	

Note

| Instruction | MP3 021

現在請再聽一次音檔,並做下列的測驗,檢視自己能否完成此填空測驗和強化自己聽力能力和拼字能力,降低並修正自己漏聽到聽力訊息的機會,大幅提升應考實力。

1. Videos u_____ by a photographer capture a really f _____ moment of some animals, insects, and plants.

2. Whether they are doing it for the p_____, getting more likes from others does give people e_____.

3. Whatever the motive behind the scene, videos somehow present a b_____ and i_____ part of the whole story.

4. Mantises do have the ability to take down insects, such as g_____ or c_____.

5. People do have a f_____ idea of the b_____. It's just that uploaders edit the video in a certain way.

6. For example, a mantis, which seems so t_____ at hunting c_____ and c_____ beneath the grass, can instantly get eaten by c_____ and some c_____ _____ the next moment.

7. Presenting the whole thing will give viewers a more b__ _____ idea of how n_____ works.

8. After all, only top p_____ can be i_____ from being someone else's prey.

9. Sometimes the victory is s_____ and will soon end when a c_____ spots the mantis right under the bush.

10. Other than chameleons, mantises are also the prey by v _____ and i_____.

11. Mantises are not as p_____ as they seem, even though they are equipped with secret a_____.

12. They do attack small insects and h_____ b_____ when prey are within s_____ d_____.

13. They are susceptible to that attack of some a_____, and they do get taken down by a h_____.

14. A honey b_____ can stand the attack of b_____, w_____ the bite of some snakes, and scare away some l_____.

15. What videos fail to tell us is that the m_____ of them

is not d_____.

16. They do have the ability to take down snakes, but they do get eaten by p_____.

17. Snakes are s_____ to t_____ changes since they are r_____.

18. Their m_____ during night time will be influenced by those f_____.

19. It doesn't change the student's p_____ of how nature works.

20. B_____ messages are everywhere, so it's important for us to have c_____ thinking ability.

| 答案 |

1. uploaded, fine
2. pleasure, euphoria
3. biased, incomplete
4. grasshoppers, crickets
5. fundamental, biology
6. talented, cockroaches, crickets, cranes, chameleons
7. balanced, nature
8. predators, immune
9. short-lived, chameleon

10. vertebrates, invertebrates
11. powerful, armors
12. humming, birds, striking, distance
13. amphibians, hornet
14. badger, bees, withstand, lions
15. meat, delicious
16. pythons
17. sensitive, temperature, reptiles
18. mobility, fluctuations
19. perception
20. Bombarded, critical

▶▶ 摘要能力

| Instruction | MP3 021

　　除了閱讀測驗外，其實培養能在聽完一大段訊息後，以口述講述剛才聽到的聽力訊息是學習語言和表達很重要的一件事，讓自己養成具備這樣的能力，除了能在聽力測驗中獲取高分外，也能在新托福寫作跟口說的整合題型上大有斬獲喔！所以快來練習，除了書中提供的參考答案外，自己可以試著重新聽過音檔一遍後，摘要出英文訊息並朗讀出來。

Note

▶▶ 參考答案

Videos can be used for several purposes. Whatever the motives behind, they send messages to us through a different lens. Often the video presented to us reveals an incomplete part of the story, so it is important for us to look at what's behind. Species can be so powerful in edited videos, but the point is that they all have their natural enemies. The victory for some insects or animals can be short-lived. Only the top predators can be immune from being someone else's food.

Viewers sometimes get misconstrued by the idea uploaders or editors are trying to convey. The statement about the honey badger is the best example. Honey badgers are shaped into some forms that most people deem them as powerful creatures, but we should keep in mind that they have their limits and natural enemies, too. In our life, bombarded messages are everywhere, and we need to be aware of every message that we have received.

2 ▶▶ Psychology：Coffee and the Compound Effect 心理學，咖啡和累加效應

▶▶ **聽力試題** `MP3 022`

1. What aspect of coffee does the professor mainly discuss?
   (A) Its history and development
   (B) It can be used as an example to elucidate the theory of the Compound Effect.
   (C) The importance of decorations and comfort in a coffee shop.
   (D) The main reasons why buying coffee of other brands is better than buying coffee of huge brands.

2. How does the professor present the idea to the class?
   (A) She invites experts to warn student how costly a cup of coffee can be.
   (B) She shows students the result of buying coffee of huge brands and coffee of other brands in a given time.
   (C) She talks mainly about coffee of huge brands.
   (D) She talks at length about other coffee brands.

3. Why does the professor mention "the 22k salary"?
   (A) Because she values student's response.

(B) Because it's the modern-day phenomenon

(C) Because it's an indicator and it's relatively costly to people earning that amount of salary

(D) Because it's a comment given by well-known experts

4. Listen again to part of the lecture. Then answer the question.

(A) To show how amnesia can do to people, and people forget things.

(B) To warn consumers the importance of taking notes on what you have purchased.

(C) To let consumers know they should do a basic calculus before buying expensive appliances.

(D) To show small amount of money beguiles us into thinking it's harmless.

5. Listen again to part of the lecture. Then answer the question.

(A) She wants students to stay slim and fit.

(B) She wants students to know drinking water improves health.

(C) To solidify what she has said so far.

(D) To let students know the theory can be applied to the calorie, too.

▶▶ 新托福聽力解析

1. 這題詢問的是段落主旨的部分，這題主要是說咖啡能夠用於解釋 Compound Effect 這個理論，所以答案要選 B，It can be used as an example to elucidate the theory of the Compound Effect。

2. 這題是詢問教授是如何將想法呈現在課堂中，教授其實是用一定時間內買別品牌咖啡和星巴克咖啡做比較讓學生了解，所以最符合的是選項 B，She shows students the result of buying coffee of huge brands and coffee of other brands in a given time。

3. 這題是詢問為什麼教授提到 22k，其實主要原因不是因為這是社會現象等，最主要是因為這是指標等，故可以得知答案為選項 C，Because it's an indicator and it's relatively costly to people earning that amount of salary。

4. 這題詢問學生為什麼會講該段話，They have no idea where they have spent the money, and they don't seem to recall what they have spent it on. It's a small thing that we can easily ignore. 其實指的就是 To show small amount of money beguiles us into thinking it's harmless. 故答案為選項 D。

5. 這題是考教授怎麼以自己為例子，可以從敘述中推測出，教授最主要是想要強化自己之前提到論點，所以以自己為例子，故答案為選項 C。

....

答案：1. B 2. B 3. C 4. D 5. C

影子跟讀練習 MP3 022

做完題目後，除了對答案知道錯的部分在哪外，更重要的是要修正自己聽力根本的問題，即聽力理解力和聽力專注力，聽力專注力的修正能逐步強化本身的聽力實力，所以現在請根據聽力內容「逐個段落」、「數個段落」或「整篇」進行跟讀練習，提升在實際考場時專注聽完每個訊息、定位出關鍵考點和搭配筆記回答完所有題目。Go!

A cup of coffee from big brands? Hmm… so tempting. Sorry for setting a bad example myself, but it actually is a good start for today's topic "the compound effect". What does a cup of coffee have to do with this? Everyday whether you are on your way to the office, or whether you are feeling exhausted after a long day at school, it's so tempting to have a cup of coffee, sitting in a comfy chair and a room with a perfect lighting. All of a sudden, fatigue and other things are overridden…like it's just a cup of coffee or it's just NT150 dollars.

一杯來自咖啡大廠的咖啡…嗯..如此吸引人…抱歉自己做了很不好的示範，但是實際上卻是今天主題「累加效應」很好的開端。一杯咖啡與這個有甚麼關聯性呢？每天不論你是前往上班途中或是你在學校漫長的一天後身感疲憊，有杯咖啡是如此吸引人，坐在舒適的椅子和有著恰如其分的燈光下。突然間，疲累和其他事情都被蓋過了…像是只是一杯咖啡或者是僅花費 150 元新台幣。

1. tempting 吸引人的
2. compound 增加、加重
3. exhausted 疲憊的
4. fatigue 疲倦
5. override 撤銷、推翻、使無效

Although we have been warned or urged not to spend money buying a coffee, we just cannot help buying it whenever we feel there is a need for us to lighten up our mood or something. We have put behind what many experts have said or mentioned in those articles. But little things do matter. Doing a basic calculation yourself, you can surely find how significant that is. Accumulated fees can somehow astound most of us.

　　雖然我們已受到警告或規勸不要將金錢花費在購買咖啡，但是每當我們覺得有需要能讓我們打起精神或什麼的，我們又無法克制地買了它。我們將許多專家所說的話或在那些文章中提到的部分都拋諸到腦後。但是這一丁點的小事卻至關重要。自己做一個基本計算，你可以確定發現影響會是多麼重大。累積的費用令我們大多數的人感到吃驚。

1. warn 警告
2. urge 催促、激勵
3. lighten up 愉快起來
4. accumulated 累積的

5 astound 使震驚

Let me do a basic calculation for you. A white-collar office lady who buys another brand's coffee, whose price is significantly lower than that of the big brand's. Say 55 NT dollars for a latte. She buys a cup of coffee per day. There are 52 weeks in a year. She buys 5 cups of coffee per week. We multiply that by 52, and the result is NT14300 dollars per year.

讓我做簡單的計算給你們看。一個白領上班族女性買了其他品牌的咖啡，價格遠比大廠牌的咖啡便宜。假定是每杯拿鐵 55 元新台幣的價格。她每天都買一杯咖啡。一年裡頭共有 52 週。她每週賞 5 杯咖啡。我們將每杯價格乘以 52，結果是每年將花費新台幣 14300 元。

| Student A |

Wow…that certainly is significant to today's salary. No wonder, an expert once said, if you're earning a 22k salary right after you graduate, then you probably shouldn't be drinking coffee of huge brands, and it's the accumulated fee of other brands… Coffee of other brands is almost one thirds of huge brand's coffee, and I'm not drinking it even if I'm earning more than a 22 salary.

| 學生 A |

哇…這對於現今的薪水真的很可觀。難怪有專家曾說，如果你是畢業後賺取 2 萬 2 千元月薪的人，那麼你可能真的不該喝大廠牌咖啡。這是其他品牌的累加費用…其它廠牌的咖啡花費幾乎是大廠牌咖啡的三分之一，即使我的薪水高於 22K 我也不喝它。

| Professor |

That's pretty smart.

| 教授 |

相當聰明。

| Student B |

Sometimes people just don't think it's a big deal or something. That's why people have a hard time looking at what's in their pocket at the end of the month. They have no idea where they've spent the money and they don't seem to recall what they have spent it on. It's a small thing that we can easily ignore. According to the fee calculation, you can buy an iPhone, if you quit drinking coffee for two years.

| 學生 B |

有時候人們不認為這是什麼大事或什麼的。這也是為什麼人們在每個月月底的期間，看著他們的荷包面有難色。他們不知道自己將金錢花費到哪裡了和他們回憶不起他們將錢花費在什麼上面了。這是很些微的小事，而我們卻輕易地忽略。根據累加的費用，你可以購買一隻 iPhone 了，如果你停止飲用咖啡兩年。

| **Professor** |

Excellent observations. Now I want to show you a basic calculation. NT 150 dollars per cup, 5 cups per week, 52 weeks per year. We are looking at NT39000 dollars which is close to two months' income for a new grad. It's scary. We are responsible for every choice we make. Every day we tend to ignore little things. Some of my students even have loans, but they are not making smart choices. They live paycheck to paycheck, not realizing it is the little things they have to pay attention to. So, I want you all to start your day by being acutely aware of the decisions you make.

卓越的觀察。現在我想要藉基本的計算。每杯咖啡、、是新台幣 150 元，一週五杯，一年 52 周。我們在看 台幣 39000 元。幾乎是一個畢業生近兩個月的月薪。這相當驚人。我們必須對於我們每個選擇負起責任。每天我們頃向忽略相當微不足道的小事情。我的學生中有些人甚至有學生貸款，他們每天卻沒有做出每個聰明的選擇。他們是月光族，沒有意識到是這些小事情才是他們需要注意的部分。所以我想要你們在每一天都很清楚自己所做的決定 。

字彙輔助

1. it's not a big deal 沒什麼大不了的　2. pocket 荷包
3. recall 回憶　4. ignore 忽略
5. calculated 計算的　6. observation 觀察
7. income 收入　8. paycheck 薪資
9. acutely 敏銳地

Being willing to change is always a great start in life. For example, before starting a family of my own, I used to buy unnecessary things, thinking that money is easily earned. Now I don't want to drink coffee any more. Instead I drink water. A lot of water per day. Imagine how much money I have saved for the past two decades. The saved money can be used for other purposes, too. Another thing which also relates to today's topic "the compound effect" is the calorie. You're not only saving money, but calories.

願意改變總是生活中很棒的開始。例如，在我自己成家前，我過去曾購買許多不必要的東西，認為金錢是很容易賺取的。現在我不在喝咖啡了。取而代之的是我喝水，每天大量的水。想像在過去這 20 年中，我省了多少錢。節省的金錢也能夠用於其他用途上。另一件關於今天主題「累加效應」的是卡路里。你能節省不僅是金錢，還有卡路里。

字彙輔助

1. unnecessary 不必要的　2. imagine 想像

3 purpose 目的

4 calorie 卡路里

....

You can do a basic calculation youself⋯I'm not doing it for you. You can check the beverage you frequently drink, and do a basic calculation. You'll also be astonished by the calories you have consumed over the year. You get to utilize the theory in so many ways and your life will improve significantly⋯Look at me⋯a slim figure at my age. I'm saying NO to desserts that go well with coffee, but I do enjoy watching my colleagues doing so. Just kidding! Now please open to page 52..it's a theory that is related to what we've discussed so far⋯⋯

你可以自己替自己計算一下⋯我沒有要替你們計算。你可以檢查每個你常喝的飲料，做下基本的計算。你會發現過去一年裡你攝取了多少卡路里且感到吃驚。你能夠在很多地方使用這個理論，而且你的生活會有顯著的改變⋯看我⋯以我的年紀來說，我是苗條的。我也拒絕品嚐與咖啡極搭的甜點，但是我很享受看著我的同事去做這件事⋯沒有啦⋯只是開玩笑！現在請翻開到第 52 頁⋯是關於一個我們目前為止所討論過的理論⋯。

字彙輔助

1 beverage 飲料

2 frequently 頻繁地

3 astonish 驚訝

4 consume 消耗、花費

5 utilize 利用

6 colleague 同事

▶▶ 試題聽力原文

1. What aspect of coffee does the professor mainly discuss?
2. How does the professor present the idea to the class?
3. Why does the professor mention "a 22k salary"?
4. Listen again to part of the lecture. Then answer the question.

   Students: Sometimes people just don't think it's a big deal or something. That's why people have a hard time looking at what's in their pocket at the end of the month. They have no idea where they've spent the money and they don't seem to recall what they have spent it on. It's a small thing that we easily ignore. According to the fee calculation, you can buy an iPhone, if you quit drinking coffee for two years.

   Why does the student say "They have no idea where they've spent the money and they don't seem to recall what they have spent it on. It's a small thing that we easily ignore."?

5. Listen again to part of the lecture. Then answer the question.

   Professor: Being willing to change is always a great start in life. For example, before starting a family of my own, I used to buy unnecessary things, thinking that money is easily earned. Now I don't drink coffee any more. Instead I drink water. A lot of water per day. Imagine how much money I have saved for the past two decades. The saved money can be used for other purposes, too. Another thing which also relates to today's topic "the compound effect" is the calorie. You're not only saving money, but calories.

Why does the professor mention herself as an example?

Note

▶▶ 記筆記與聽力訊息

　　新托福聽力與其他聽力測驗不同，可以於聽力的紙上記筆記，除了寫試題外，更重要的一點是訓練自己能夠將聽完一段訊息後，將重要的聽力訊息都記到。也可以將自己聽到跟記到的重點訊息跟試題做比對，因為試題考的就是長對話跟講座中出現的重點，能修正自己篩選聽力訊息重點的能力。

| 聽力重點 |

- 記筆記有很多方式，包含符號跟自己習慣的縮寫字等等，可以找出最適合自己的模式，一定要自己重聽音檔作練習數次。
- 這篇是關於商業概念和心理學，**段落中很多其實都是鋪陳，其實跟著聽力訊息走很容易理解，有理解的部分就不用記，而且這篇跟生活很相關，重點可以放在所提到別的廠牌咖啡和大廠牌的咖啡的關係和差異，以及文中提到的概念和應用，這樣就可以不管題目怎麼換都不影響答題。**

▶▶ **參考筆記**

Main idea ❶

- the compound effect/concept
- little things do matter./can't recall money spent it on
- accumulated fees can somehow astound most of us.

example	❶ feelings get overridden by other factors
result	❶ normal brand：the result is NT14300 dollars per year/ 5 cups of coffee per week ❷ coffee of huge brands：NT 39000 dollars

Main idea ❷

They live paycheck to paycheck, not realizing it is the little thing they have to pay attention to. Start your next day by being acutely aware of every choice you make.

application	❶ can be used in other things, such as **calories**

Note

▶▶ 填空測驗

| Instruction | MP3 022

現在請再聽一次音檔，並做下列的測驗，檢視自己能否完成此填空測驗和強化自己聽力能力和拼字能力，降低並修正自己漏聽到聽力訊息的機會，大幅提升英考實力。

1. It's t_____ to have a cup of coffee from big brands to start the day.

2. Today's topic is "the C_____ effect".

3. Sometimes we are feeling e_____ after a long day at school.

4. It's nice to have a cup of coffee, sitting in a c_____ chair and a room with a p_____ lighting.

5. But all of a sudden, f_____ and other factors overwhelm the feelings of not buying.

6. We have been w_____ or u_____ not to spend money on buying coffee.

7. Coffee does make us feel that there is a need for us to drink it so that our mood can be l_____.

8. You can do a basic c_____ by counting a_____ f_____.

9. We m_____ that by 52, and the result is NT14300 dollars per year.

10. No wonder, an e_____ once said, if you're earning a 22k salary right after you g_____, then you probably shouldn't be drinking coffee of huge brands.

11. That's why people have a hard time looking at their p__ at the end of every month.

12. They don't seem to recall anything major or that c_____ they spent it on.

13. We tend to i_____ the small thing.

14. The amount is NT 39000 dollars…almost twice of a graduate's m_____ i_____.

15. We are responsible for every choice we make, but sometimes people are not making every s_____ c__ _____ every day.

16. They live p_____ to p_____, not realizing it is the little things they have to pay attention to.

17. The professor used to buy u_____ things, thinking that money is easily earned.

18. Another thing which also relates to today's topic "the compound effect" is c_____.

19. You can check the b_____ you frequently purchase, and do a basic calculation. You'll also be a_____ by the calorie you have c_____ over the year.

20. Just by look at me... a s_____ f_____ at my age. I'm saying no to a desert that goes well with coffee, but I'm enjoying watching my colleague doing that... just kidding.

| 答案 |

1. tempting
2. Compound
3. exhausted
4. comfy, perfect
5. fatigue
6. warned, urged
7. lightened
8. calculation, accumulated, fees
9. multiple
10. expert, graduate
11. pocket

12. costly
13. ignore
14. monthly, income
15. smart, choice
16. paycheck, paycheck
17. unnecessary
18. calories
19. beverage, astonished, consumed
20. slim figure, desert

影子跟讀

學術場景

校園場景

Note

▶▶ 摘要能力

　　除了閱讀測驗外，其實培養能在聽完一大段訊息後，以口述講述剛才聽到的聽力訊息是學習語言和表達很重要的一件事，讓自己養成具備這樣的能力，除了能在聽力測驗中獲取高分外，也能在新托福寫作跟口說的整合題型上大有斬獲喔！所以快來練習，除了書中提供的參考答案外，自己可以試著重新聽過音檔一遍後，摘要出英文訊息並朗讀出來。

Note

▶▶ 參考答案

It's tempting to start our day with a cup of coffee from big brands. Although we have been warned that little things do matter, we are making that kind of decision. The feeling of having it outweighs the feeling of not buying it. Doing a basic calculation can reveal how astonishing the accumulated fees can be. Multiple that by 52 weeks, and the end result is almost close to today's monthly salary for a new grad. We often ignore the small things that spend money on, and it's important for us to learn how to make smart choices every day. The professor suggests to start the day by being acutely aware of every choice you make and gives us examples of how she uses this on her own life. Other than the money we spend, the compound effect can be used in other aspects, too, such as calories.

Note

3 ▶▶ Psychology：Preparedness 卓越
成功者的準備超乎你想像，費爾普斯

▶▶ **聽力試題** (MP3 023)

1. How does the professor present the idea to the class?
   (A) By talking at length about jogging so that student can understand.
   (B) By describing the relationship between great athletes and ones who have an affair with fans.
   (C) By giving general ideas for students to relate and then give examples.
   (D) By researching different aspects of athletes.

2. What are the major differences between Phelps and other candidates?
   (A) The number of gold medals one has earned.
   (B) The environment where they are trained.
   (C) The environment where they grew up.
   (D) How experienced their coaches are.

3. Listen again to part of the lecture. Then answer the question.
   (A) To show preparing a competition often requires sacrifices.

(B) To show athletes only worry about daily consumption before the contest.

(C) To refute the popular idea that athletes do not need to have a rigorous diet plan.

(D) To show the life of athletes is not as great as we deem it is.

4. Listen again to part of the lecture. Then answer the question.

(A) To show following a strict guideline is a sure way to the top.

(B) To show we should prevent any distraction from happening.

(C) To show even if everything goes according to planned, we still cannot be sure who will win at the end.

(D) To show deviation is a guaranteed for winning.

5. Listen again to part of the lecture. Then answer the question.

(A) To show there are variables in life.

(B) To show foliage can be a hinderance to swimmer.

(C) To let students know swim suits can fall off.

(D) To show eyesight is important to swimmers.

▶▶ 新托福聽力解析

1. 這題詢問的是教授如何將想法呈現出，最主要的是 C 選項所提到的 By giving general ideas for students to relate and then give examples，主要是提的主要概念讓讀者能共鳴後再舉例讓學生了解。

2. 這題是詢問費爾普斯和其他候選人的主要差異在哪？答案為選項 B The environment where they are trained，在文末可以發現其實選手都受到良好訓練，但在泳池跟密西根湖的差異就可以看出，費爾普斯是在未知且不熟悉的環境下訓練，因此奠定他更好的應對水平。

3. 這題是詢問教授為什麼說 Athletes have a pretty strict daily consumption…… Preparing for a competition is often lonely and arduous.，從聽力敘述中可以推測出其實指的是選項 D，To show the life of athletes is not as great as we deem it is。

4. 這題是詢問教授為什麼說 even if there is nothing that deviates you from doing a rigorous training, there is no guarantee for winning，教授指的是 To show even if everything goes according to planned, we still cannot be sure who will win at the end 故答案為選項 C。

5. 這題是詢問教授為什麼說 anything can happen that day…… or your eyesight being impaired by foliage or something…其實最主要指的是 To show there are variables in life，所以可以得知答案為選項 A。

答案：1. C 2. B 3. D 4. C 5. A

影子跟讀練習 MP3 023

做完題目後，除了對答案知道錯的部分在哪外，更重要的是要修正自己聽力根本的問題，即聽力理解力和聽力專注力，聽力專注力的修正能逐步強化本身的聽力實力，所以現在請根據聽力內容「逐個段落」、「數個段落」或「整篇」進行跟讀練習，提升在實際考場時專注聽完每個訊息、定位出關鍵考點和搭配筆記回答完所有題目。Go!

| Professor |

Often we hear "chances favor the ready one"? What do we mean by the ready one? What do they mean when it comes to preparedness? Preparedness is such a broad concept that we feel we know it, but sometimes we don't. it is related to several levels of doing or planning things in advance to sound like you are doing something or achieving toward a certain result.

通常我們聽到「機會偏好準備好的人」？我們所謂的準備好的人指的是什麼呢？當提到準備，他們所指的是什麼？準備是如此廣的概念到我們覺得我們懂，但有時候我們不懂。這與我們要做或提前計劃的事情的幾個層級有關聯，使我們看起來像是你正在做什麼或朝著某個特定的結果邁進。

1 prepare 準備   2 preparedness 準備

3 achieve 達成   4 result 結果

Assume people exercise everyday. They wake up early in the morning, doing a little jogging. Often, they encounter their neighbors or nosy landlords, but they keep doing jogging after all. It's pretty relaxing and you get to burn down some calories. There is absolutely no pressure or low pressure. You can even pick up your jogging partners, preferably the one who is not going to outperform you. After the whole jogging thing is done, you get to eat your favorite meal of the day with your family members··· just assuming they all wake up that early. It's just a normal person's day, but if it is about the person who is doing this for a living, it is a totally different matter.

假設人們每天運動。他們早晨早起，從事小慢跑。通常他們遇到了他們的鄰居或煩人的房東們，但是他們畢竟還是在慢跑。這相當輕鬆而且能燃燒一些卡路里。全然沒有壓力或者是無壓力。你能夠挑選你的慢跑夥伴，最好是不會超越你跑步能力的對象。在完成一些慢跑後，你可以與你的家庭成員享用你今日最喜歡的餐點，假設他們也都起的很早。這只是一個普通人的一天，但是如果是對於一個以此為生的人來說，這全然是另一回事。

字彙輔助

1 assume 假定
2 encounter 面對
3 nosy 厭煩的
4 landlord 房東
5 burn down 耗掉
6 pressure 壓力
7 preferably 偏好
8 outperform 比⋯勝過

Athletes have a pretty strict daily consumption of every calorie they consume⋯not that charming, glamorous or fun, right. Preparing for a competition is often lonely and arduous. Everything matters. Chances are not going to favor those who seem lazy or lack of discipline, or who do not set a strict routine for themselves, right?

運動員對於他們每日所攝取的每項卡路里有相當嚴格的的限制⋯沒那麼吸引人、光鮮或有趣了對吧！準備　個比賽通常是寂寞且艱辛的。每件事情都很重要。機會不會給予那些看起來似乎很懶散且缺乏紀律的人或是不對自己有著嚴格行程要求的人，對吧？

字彙輔助

1 Athlete 運動員
2 strict 嚴格的
3 consumption 消耗
4 glamorous 有魅力的
5 arduous 艱辛的
8 favor 偏愛
7 discipline 紀律
8 routine 行程

| Student A |

That's right. That's why business owners are so pissed off when they find out athletes are not doing what they are supposed to do. Some were having affairs with their fans, and that damaged the reputation of their team. I saw that on the news.

| 學生 A |

對的…這也是為什麼商業經營者對於發現運動員沒有做好自己本分時會感到如此生氣。有些甚至與他們的粉絲有婚外情，這也損及他們團隊的名聲。我是從新聞看到的。

| Student B |

Perhaps that will distract them. Other teams who work so hard will have an excellent chance to win if the team from the news keeps doing things that deviate them from achieving their goals.

| 學生 B |

或許這會使他們分心。其他那麼努力的團隊會有極佳的勝算，如果新聞中的這個團隊持續做讓與他們完成目標所背道而馳的事。

字彙輔助

1. pissed of 生氣
2. damage 損害
3. reputation 名聲
4. distract 分心
5. excellent 卓越的

| **Professor** |

Glad that you're aware of that. It's taking them away from focusing on what they are doing, which is winning the competitions. Any small thing can be a great hindrance to achieving their team goals.

| 教授 |

很高興你察覺到這個。這全然使他們背馳他們正專注的事情上，也就是贏得比賽。任何小事情都會是達成團體目標的障礙。

So being well-prepared is harder than it sounds. You have to focus on different little things, and even if there is nothing that deviates you from doing a rigorous training, there is no guarantee for winning. All candidates are trained in a certain way. They all have an amazing body figure and they all know what they are doing. They all have experts that guide them throughout the whole preparation. So what is the key to success? What do they have to do to win? Do they need something extra? Like preparing something else or things people don't do.

所以準備充分是比想像中難的。你必須專注在不同的小事上，即使沒有遇到任何使你做嚴格訓練時會分心的事，也不能保證能夠獲取勝利。所有候選人都以特定的方式進行訓練。他們有驚人的體格而且他們總是知道自己在做什麼。他們都有著專家在整場比賽中引導著他們。所以是什麼成功的關鍵呢？他們要做什麼才能獲取成功呢？他們會需要額外的準備嗎？像是準備其他事情或者人們不會做的事。

字彙輔助

1. hindrance 妨礙、障礙
2. achieve 達到
3. deviate 偏離
4. rigorous 嚴格的
5. guarantee 保證
6. candidate 候選人
7. amazing 驚人的
8. guide 引導
9. preparation 準備

A friend of mine is a pretty good swimmer himself…he gets up at a certain time, he follows the strict training by his coach…and so on…but that does not mean he is going to win an Olympic championship. What seems lacking from his preparation towards greater success?

我的一位友人就是位相當良好的游泳選手…他會在固定的時間起床，然後遵循他教練嚴格的訓練…等等的…但是這不意謂著他具備能夠贏得奧林匹亞競賽的實力。在他準備朝向成功的過程中似乎少了什麼呢？

Since we're talking about swimmers, I want to show you how other champions are doing so that you will have a clear idea between prepared and well-prepared. First, I want to show you the person you are all familiar with, Michael Phelps.

　　既然我們談到游泳選手，我想要讓你們知道其他冠軍是如何準備的。如此你們就能夠對於準備和充分準備有著清楚的想法。首選我想要展示的是你們都很熟悉的人物，費爾普斯。

字彙輔助

1 follow 遵循　　　　2 Olympic 奧林匹亞

3 champion 冠軍　　　4 mention 提到

5 familiar 熟悉的

I want you to look at the slide…the statement of "Bowman had once made Phelps swim in a Michigan pool in the dark, believing that he needed to be ready for any surprise." Do you see the difference? He has been trained in that kind of a situation, a situation he is so unfamiliar, but somehow gives him an edge over other candidates, who have been trained in a swimming pool or something.

　　我想要你們都看著簡報頁面…「教練飽文曾要費爾普斯在黑暗的密西根湖中游泳，相信他需要對任何意外做好準備」。你看出當中的差異了嗎？他是在如此不熟悉的環境下接受訓練，使得他比在泳池或在其他地方受訓的候選人有優勢。

字彙輔助

1 statement 聲明　　　2 Michigan 密西根

3 difference 差異　　　4 situation 情況

5 edge 優勢

There is a stark difference between swimming in a regular pool and swimming in a Michigan pool in the dark. In order to win, you need to be well-prepared. Here well-prepared is not limited to doing what your experts have told you⋯ like say swimming in a regular pool⋯anything can happen that day⋯whether it's your swim suit falling off or your eyesight being impaired by foliage or something⋯the thing is are you comfortable enough to swim naked if your swimming suit actually falls off⋯ here I'm not asking you to actually swim naked right after the class⋯I could be sued⋯ just pinpoint something⋯if you know what I mean⋯

在普通泳池或在夜晚密西根湖中游泳是有著顯著差異的。為了獲取勝利，你需要充分準備。這裡的充分準備不限定於做你的專家告知你的事項⋯像是例如在普通泳池游泳⋯任何事情能在那天發生⋯不論是你的泳裝掉落或者是你的視力受到樹葉或其他東西影響了⋯你能坦然的裸泳如果你的泳裝真的掉落嗎⋯這裡我不是要你們在課後都實際跑去裸泳⋯我可能會被告⋯只是指出一些⋯如果你知道我要講什麼的事⋯。

字彙輔助

1 stark 顯著的

2 regular 規律的

3 eyesight 視力

4 foliage 葉子

▶▶ 試題聽力原文

1. How does the professor present the idea to the class?

2. What are the major differences between Phelps and other candidates?

3. Listen again to part of the lecture. Then answer the question.

   Professor: Athletes have a pretty strict daily consumption of every calorie they consume…not that charming, glamorous or funny right. Preparing for a competition is often lonely and arduous. Everything matters. Chances are not going to favor those who seem lazy or lack of discipline, or who do not set a strict routine for themselves, right?

   Why does the professor say "Athletes have a pretty strict daily consumption of every calorie they consume…not that charming, glamorous or funny right. Preparing for a competition is often lonely and arduous.."?

4. Listen again to part of the lecture. Then answer the question.

   Professor: So being well-prepared is harder than it sounds. You have to focus on different little things, and even if there is nothing that deviates you from doing a rigorous training, there is no guarantee for winning. All candidates are trained in a certain way.

Why does the professor say "even if there is nothing that deviates you from doing a rigorous training, there is no guarantee for winning."?

5. Listen again to part of the lecture. Then answer the question.
Professor: Anything can happen that day⋯whether it's your swim suit falling off or your eyesight being impaired by foliage or something⋯the thing is are you comfortable enough to swim naked if your swimming suit actually falls off⋯ here I'm not asking you to actually swim naked right after the class.

Why does the professor say "anything can happen that day⋯whether it's your swim suit falling off or your eyesight being impaired by foliage or something⋯"?

▶▶ 記筆記與聽力訊息

| Instruction | MP3 023

　　新托福聽力與其他聽力測驗不同，可以於聽力的紙上記筆記，除了寫試題外，更重要的一點是訓練自己能夠將聽完一段訊息後，將重要的聽力訊息都記到。也可以將自己聽到跟記到的重點訊息跟試題做比對，因為試題考的就是長對話跟講座中出現的重點，能修正自己篩選聽力訊息重點的能力。

| 聽力重點 |

- 記筆記有很多方式，包含符號跟自己習慣的縮寫字等等，可以找出最適合自己的模式，一定要自己重聽音檔作練習數次。

- 這篇是關於心理學，**前面段落其實都是鋪陳不難理解，重點可以放在所提到的主要概念和提到的例子，可以參考下列表格的筆記，有掌握這些概念就可以答對主要考點，也可以在簡化記筆記的部分。**

Note

▶▶ 參考筆記

Main idea ❶

- Preparedness, be the ready one.
- Jogging may seem like a normal exercise people do every day, but for some people (athletes) who are doing this for a living, it's a totally different matter.

Main idea ❷

- The things athletes do can deviate them from achieving their goals or jeopardize their reputation.
- Any small thing can be a great hindrance to achieving their team goals.

Main idea ❸

- Should focus on other factors that lead to greater success

example   **Phelps**

❶ be ready for any surprise/unfamiliar

❷ a stark difference between swimming in a regular pool and swimming in a Michigan pool is the dark

Main idea ❹ be well-prepared to any situation

example   ❶ your swim suit falling off

❷ your eyesight being impaired by foliage or something

Note

....

....

....

....

....

....

....

....

....

....

....

....

▶▶ 填空測驗

| Instruction | MP3 **023**

　　現在請再聽一次音檔，並做下列的測驗，檢視自己能否完成此填空測驗和強化自己聽力能力和拼字能力，降低並修正自己漏聽到聽力訊息的機會，大幅提升英考實力。

1. P_____ is such a broad concept that we feel we know it, but sometimes we don't.

2. Often they e_____ their neighbors or nosy landlords, but they are doing jogging after all. It's pretty relaxing and you get to burn down several c_____.

3. You can even pick up your jogging p_____, preferably the one who is not going to o_____ you.

4. After the whole jogging thing is done, you get to eat your f_____ meal of the day with your family m_____.

5. Athletes have a pretty s_____ daily c_____ of every calorie they c_____.

6. Preparing for a competition is often l_____ and a_____.

7. C_____ are not going to favor those who seem lazy or lack of d_____, or who do not set a strict routine for themselves, right?

8. Some are having an affair with their fans, which d_____ the r_____ of their team.

9. Other teams who work so hard will have an e_____ chance to win if the team from the news keeps doing things that d_____ them from achieving their goals.

10. Any small thing can be a great h_____ to achieving their team goals.

11. Even if there is nothing that d_____ you from doing a r_____ training, there is no g_____ for winning.

12. All c_____ are t_____ in a certain way.

13. They all have an a_____ body f_____ and they all know what they are doing.

14. I want to show you how other c_____ are doing so that you will have a clear idea between prepared and well-prepared.

15. The s_____ of "Bowman had once made Phelps swim in a Michigan pool in the dark, believing that he needed to be ready for any s_____."

16. He has been trained in that kind of a situation, a situation he is so u_____, but somehow gives him an e_____ over other candidates, who have been trained in a swimming pool or something.

17. There is a s_____ difference between swimming in a r_____ pool and swimming in a Michigan pool is the dark.

18. Here well-prepared is not l_____ to doing what your e_____ have told you.

19. Anything can happen that day…whether it's is your swim suit falling off or your e_____ being i_____ by f_____ or something.

20. The thing is are you c_____ enough to swim n_____ if your swimming suit actually falls off.

| 答案 |

1. Preparedness
2. encounter, calories
3. partners, outperform

4. favorite, members
5. strict, consumption, consume
6. lonely, arduous
7. Chances, discipline
8. damage, reputation
9. excellent, deviate
10. hindrance
11. deviates, rigorous, guarantee
12. candidates, trained
13. amazing, figure
14. champions
15. statement, surprise
16. unfamiliar, edge
17. stark, regular
18. limited, experts
19. eyesight, impaired, foliage
20. comfortable, naked

▶▶ 摘要能力

| **Instruction** | MP3 023

　　除了閱讀測驗外，其實培養能在聽完一大段訊息後，以口述講述剛才聽到的聽力訊息是學習語言和表達很重要的一件事，讓自己養成具備這樣的能力，除了能在聽力測驗中獲取高分外，也能在新托福寫作跟口說的整合題型上大有斬獲喔！所以快來練習，除了書中提供的參考答案外，自己可以試著重新聽過音檔一遍後，摘要出英文訊息並朗讀出來。

Note

▶▶ 參考答案

Preparedness is such a broad concept that it affects us in many ways. Jogging may seem like a normal exercise people do every day, but for some people who are doing this for a living, it's totally a different matter. Athletes are not as glamorous as they seem since they have to follow a strict guideline. The things they do can deviate them from achieving their goals or can jeopardize their reputation. Any small thing can be a great hindrance for them to achieving their team goals. Even if they are following a rigorous training, there is no guarantee for winning. Well-trained athletes still need to know those factors that influence them to get closer to greater success. Being well-prepared also means pushing your limits to a certain point so that you are really well-prepared. Phelps, for example, is trained in an unfamiliar environment that makes him stand out from the rest.

4 ▶▶ Biology：Co-evolution 共同演化，蠑螈和束帶蛇

▶▶ **聽力試題** (MP3 024)

1. According to the professor, what is untrue about the camouflage?

   (A) Chameleons use camouflage to protect themselves.

   (B) It can be used as a way to deceive predators.

   (C) It will not reduce the chance of getting caught.

   (D) Sometimes it will not work out.

2. Listen again to part of the lecture. Then answer the question.

   (A) Because big bullfrogs do not secrete neurotoxins.

   (B) Because bullfrogs will send salamanders free, but not golden dart frogs.

   (C) Because salamanders' cryptic colors can't scare them away.

   (D) To show neurotoxins can be used as a way for protection.

3. Listen again to part of the lecture. Then answer the question.

   (A) To show peacocks are in desperate of finding their mates

(B) To show peacocks can't use colors as a way to camouflage.

(C) To explain chances of survival will decrease if peacocks use coloration.

(D) To demonstrate the purpose of peacocks' coloration is different from that of other creatures.

4. The following statements list salamanders, garter snakes and their traits
    Click the correct box for each trait

	Salamanders	Garter snakes
A. use coloration to advertise their toxicity		
B. Use neurotoxin on the skin to protect themselves		
C. Secrete neurotoxins		
D. Develop resistance to the neurotoxin		

5. According to the professor, what is untrue about the coevolution?

(A) Salamanders and garter snakes belong to the type of prey-and-predatory.

(B) It only include two types.

(C) co-evolution means species evolving together.

(D) coevolution occurs when two or more species reciprocally affect each other's evolution.

▶▶ 新托福聽力解析

1. 這題詢問的是聽力細節的部份，C 選項的敘述多了 not，表示降低被捕獲的機會與聽力敘述相反，故答案為 C 選項。

2. 這題是詢問教授為什麼提到 A big bullfrog accidentally eating a salamander can eventually open its mouth and set the salamander free，其實主要是想要表達出 neurotoxins can be used as a way for protection，故答案為選項 D。

3. 這題是詢問為什麼教授說 Other times, you can spot species exhibit all forms of colors, but they are doing this not because they want to allure the mate, like peacocks showing their feathers，其實主要是表明 the purpose of peacocks' coloration is different from that of other creatures.，兩者的目的和功能均不同，故答案為選項 D。

4. 這題是需要具備整合聽力訊息和特點的能力，且要特別注意的是除了注意兩種生物的不同處外，生物間也有共同點，在這題中即是，兩種生物均能分泌神經毒素，要特別注意。

5. 這題詢問的是聽力細節的部份，B 選項中有 only 過於絕對，且在聽力開頭的共同演化舉例中就有三個舉例，所以可以推測不可能僅有兩種，故答案為選項 B。

⋯⋯⋯⋯⋯⋯⋯⋯⋯⋯⋯⋯⋯⋯⋯⋯⋯⋯⋯⋯⋯⋯⋯⋯⋯

答案：1. C 2. D 3. D 4. ABC/CD 5. B

影子跟讀練習 MP3 024

做完題目後，除了對答案知道錯的部分在哪外，更重要的是要修正自己聽力根本的問題，即聽力理解力和聽力專注力，聽力專注力的修正能逐步強化本身的聽力實力，所以現在請根據聽力內容「逐個段落」、「數個段落」或「整篇」進行跟讀練習，提升在實際考場時專注聽完每個訊息、定位出關鍵考點和搭配筆記回答完所有題目。Go!

| Professor |

I promise I won't bore you with The Origin of XXX… (chuckling)…actually it's not that boring…I'm beginning today's session by telling you today's topic…it's not that remote as it seems…It's very close to us actually. Today's topic is co-evolution. Co is a prefix which means together. Co-evolution means species evolving together…

| 教授 |

我保證我不會用「XXX 的起源」這本書來讓你們感到無聊透頂...（笑）...實際上它沒那麼無聊...我會告訴你們今天的課程來作為開頭...它不會像看起來那麼遙不可及... 它與我們實際上息息相關.今天的主題是共同演化。CO 字首意謂著「一起」的意思。共同演化意謂著物種一起的演化。

Let's take a look at the definition. "In biology,

coevolution occurs when two or more species reciprocally affect each other's evolution", and it includes different forms, such as mutual relationships, host-parasite, and predator-prey. This somehow fascinates me…Like how can they benefit or influence other organism? Growing up in a farm, I can almost taste the nature of all forms, capturing moments that snakes chasing their preys, witnessing their fangs injecting venom in the prey.

我們來看一下定義。「在生物學裡，共同演化發生於兩個或多個物種相互影響著彼此的演化」。共同演化包括不同的形式，像是相互關係、宿主和寄生關係和捕食者和獵物間的關係。這也或多或少令我感到沉迷。像是他們如何受益於或影響其他的生物有機體。於農場中長大，我可以幾乎嚐到大自然的各種形式，捕捉到蛇追捕他們獵物的時刻，目睹他們毒牙注射毒液到獵物裡。

字彙輔助

1. remote 偏遠的
2. co-evolution 共同演化
3. evolve 演化
4. definition 定義
5. reciprocally 互惠地
6. host-parasite 寄主寄生的
7. fascinate 吸引
8. witness 目睹
9. inject 注射
10. venom 毒液

But biology seems to have a way of its own. There are all kinds of mechanisms out there. Sometimes prey have developed a certain defense mechanism to protect themselves from danger. For example, chameleons camouflage themselves. A great deception to natural's predator. Even if the camouflage doesn't work out sometimes, this reduces their chances of getting captured by predators. The successful survival rate is increasing for the species. Other times, you can spot species exhibiting all forms of colors, but they are doing this not because they want to allure the mate, like peacocks showing their feathers. They are doing this because colorful colors tell predators that probably they have venom or they are not as pleasant as they seem.

但是生物學似乎有著自己的機制。有許多種的機制。有時候獵物發展出特定的防禦機制來保護自己免於危險。例如，變色龍偽裝自己。對自然界中的捕食者是最大的欺騙。即使偽裝有時候沒有發揮作用，這降低了他們被捕食者捕抓的機會。對物種來說生存成功率增加了。其他時候，你可以察覺到物種展示出所有形式的顏色，但是他們這麼做並不是他們想要吸引伴侶，像是孔雀展示自己的羽毛那樣。他們這麼做是因為多彩的顏色能夠告訴捕食者，可能他們有毒或是他們沒有看起來那樣美味。

字彙輔助

1 mechanism 機制
2 defense 防護
3 camouflage 偽裝
4 deception 欺騙
5 reduce 減低
6 successful 成功的
7 survival 生存
8 allure 吸引

| Student A |

Yep…I once saw golden dart frogs with different kinds of colors. They're pleasing to the eye. I like the blue one. Their venom is incredibly poisonous. Snakes that accidentally eat them can die in a second. It's pretty scary. They have colors that say "don't touch me". Some chameleons use color changes to scare away their predators, too. Although sometimes they still get eaten by some snakes.

| 學生 A |

是的…有次我看到有著各種不同顏色的箭毒蛙。很滿足視覺觀感。我喜歡藍色的。他們的毒性非常強。蛇不經意吃到箭毒蛙會一下子就死亡。這相當驚人。他們有顯示著「別碰我」的顏色。有些變色龍也使用顏色變化嚇走捕食者，儘管有時候變色龍仍被有些蛇類捕食。

| Student B |

It's pretty awesome to see golden dart frogs. They are like decorations in the rainforest. Their venom is used for different purposes. For example, the toxin is used on arrows for hunting. But what does this have to do with co-evolution?

學生 B

能目睹箭毒蛙相當棒。它們像是雨林裡的裝飾品。它們的毒性已經被利用於不同的地方，例如，毒性置於箭上頭用來捕獵。但是這與共同演化有什麼關聯性呢？

字彙輔助

1 golden dart frogs 箭毒蛙
2 incredibly 驚人地
3 poisonous 有毒的
4 accidentally 意外地
5 decoration 裝飾

......

Professor

I'm about to tell you. Don't be so hasty. There're other animals that use coloration to advertise their toxicity, too. For example, salamanders have vivid colors to ward off predators. They secrete neurotoxins, too. Neurotoxins on their skin can be a powerful weapon to protect them. A big bullfrog accidentally eating a salamander can eventually open its mouth and set the salamander free. Predators like snakes will eventually avoid animals with cryptic colors, such as salamanders and golden dart frogs, but the fact is they all have their natural enemies, too.

教授

我正要告訴你們…別這麼急嘛…有其他動物也會使用顏色宣傳著它們的毒性。例如，蝾螈有著鮮豔的顏色抵禦捕食者。它們也分泌神經毒素。它們皮膚上的神經毒素是保護它們的強大武器。大型的牛蛙不經意吃到蠑螈最終會將嘴巴張開並釋放蠑螈。捕食者像是蛇最終會避開捕食具神秘顏色的動物，像是蠑螈和箭毒蛙，但是事實是它們也都有自己的天敵。

Garter snakes, also known as ribbon snakes, are the predator of salamanders simply because they are not afraid of the toxin contained in the salamander's bodies. When you see a snake, which does not hesitate to attack salamanders, you're probably seeing a garter snake. They're just having their own snack time.

襪帶蛇也以束帶蛇而為人所知是蠑螈的捕食者，僅因為它們不懼怕蠑螈身體內所含的毒素。當你看到蛇毫不猶豫地攻擊蠑螈⋯你可能看到襪帶蛇。那是它們的零食時間。

They have developed a mechanism to resist the neurotoxins of the salamanders. This is a pretty remarkable improvement for biology. Ribbon snakes are undergoing a series of mutations to evolve a mechanism so that they are unafraid of the neurotoxins. Salamanders, on the other hand, are gradually evolving to a more powerful toxin to counter ribbon snakes' development. Surprisingly, garter snakes are continually evolving a stronger mechanism. This is what we call coevolution. This is the perfect example of the prey-and-predatory coevolution. It's like a race. Amazing, right? Salamanders and ribbon snakes are constantly seeking for ways to improve their way in order to survive. I just don't want you to feel bad for those salamanders. It's just part of the process of the natural selection.

它們已經發展出抵抗蠑螈的神經毒素。這是生物學中相當驚人的進步。束帶蛇正經歷一系列的突變演化出機制，如此它們就不懼怕神經毒素。蠑螈，另一方面，也逐漸演化出更強大的毒素來反制束帶蛇的進展。驚人地是，襪帶蛇正持續演化出更強的機制。這就是我們所稱的共同演化。這是獵物和捕食者共同演化的絕佳例子。這像是場比賽。令人吃驚，對吧？蠑螈和束帶蛇不斷地尋找方式來改進自我才得以生存。我不會希望你們對於那些被捕食的蠑螈感到難過。這只是天擇的一部分過程。

字彙輔助

1 resist 抵抗　　　2 remarkable 值得注意的、顯著的
3 mutation 突變　　4 process 過程

| Student A |

That's pretty amazing. Are we going to see the videos or will we be introduced to another form of coevolution today?

| 學生 A |

這相當驚人，我們會觀看視頻或我們今天會介紹另一個形式的共同演化嘛？

| Professor |

I guess we'll do that in the next session. Now, I want to tell you more about ribbon snakes. They are venomous, and like salamanders, they secrete neurotoxins, too. The venom they produce is pretty mild compared with that of snakes, such as rattle snakes and cobras.

| 教授 |

我想我們會在下堂課討論。現在我想要告訴你們更多關於束帶蛇的部分。它們實際上有毒，就如同蠑螈那樣，它們也分泌神經毒素。只是相較於響尾蛇與眼鏡蛇等其他蛇類，它們所分泌的神經毒素溫和許多。

字彙輔助

1 venomous 有毒的　　　2 produce 產生

3 mild 輕微的　　　　4 cobra 眼鏡蛇

▶▶ 試題聽力原文

1. According to the professor, what is untrue about camouflage?

2. Listen again to part of the lecture. Then answer the question.

   Professor: Neurotoxins on their skin can be a powerful weapon to protect them. A big bullfrog accidentally eating a salamander can eventually open its mouth and set the salamander free. Predators like snakes will eventually avoid animals with cryptic colors, such as salamanders and golden dart frogs, but the fact is they all have their natural enemies, too.

   Why does the professor mention "A big bullfrog accidentally eating a salamander can eventually open its mouth and set the salamander free."?

3. Listen again to part of the lecture. Then answer the question.

   Professor: Even if the camouflage doesn't work out sometimes, this reduces their chances of getting captured by predators. The successful survival rate is increasing for the species. Other times, you can spot species exhibiting all forms of colors, but they are doing this not because they want to allure the mate, like peacocks showing their feathers.

Why does the professor say, "Other times, you can spot species exhibiting all forms of colors, but they are doing this not because they want to allure the mate, like peacocks showing their feathers."?

4. The following statements list salamanders, garter snakes and their traits
   Click the correct box for each trait

5. According to the professor, what is untrue about coevolution?

▶▶ 記筆記與聽力訊息

| Instruction | MP3 024

　　新托福聽力與其他聽力測驗不同，可以於聽力的紙上記筆記，除了寫試題外，更重要的一點是訓練自己能夠將聽完一段訊息後，將重要的聽力訊息都記到。也可以將自己聽到跟記到的重點訊息跟試題做比對，因為試題考的就是長對話跟講座中出現的重點，能修正自己篩選聽力訊息重點的能力。

| 聽力重點 |

- 記筆記有很多方式，包含符號跟自己習慣的縮寫字等等，可以找出最適合自己的模式，一定要自己重聽音檔作練習數次。

- 這篇是關於生物學，**前面段落有對共同演化的定義，這部分有出現在考題最後一題，很容易被忽略，也要注意共同演化的應用部分，了解 ribbon snakes 和 salamanders 間的關係其實就差不多了，還有就是生物間的其他形式 camouflage, coloration 等**。

Note

Main idea ❶ co-evolution： **definition** (mutual, host-parasite, and predator-prey)
Main idea ❷ defense mechanism：camouflage, coloration
Main idea ❸ animals use **coloration to advertise their toxicity**
example　　salamanders
Main idea ❹ prey-and-predatory coevolution： **Salamanders and Garter snakes/ribbon snakes**
Ribbons snakes：mutation/mechanism to neurotoxins **Salamanders**：a more powerful toxin to counter ribbon snakes' development.

Note
....

....

....

▶▶ 填空測驗

| **Instruction** | MP3 024

　　現在請再聽一次音檔，並做下列的測驗，檢視自己能否完成此填空測驗和強化自己聽力能力和拼字能力，降低並修正自己漏聽到聽力訊息的機會，大幅提升應考實力。

1. Let's take a look at the d_____ here "In biology, c____ _____ occurs when two or more species r_____ affect each other's evolution".

2. it includes different forms, such as m_____ relationships, h_____, and predator-prey.

3. Growing in a farm, I can almost t_____ a nature of all forms, capturing m_____ that snakes chasing their prey, witnessing their f_____ injecting venom in the prey.

4. But biology seems to have a way of its own. Sometimes prey have developed a d_____ m_____ to protect themselves from dangers.

5. For example, chameleons' c_____ is a great d_____ ____ to natural's predator.

6. The s_____ s_____ rate is increasing for the

species. Other times, you can spot species e_____ all forms of colors, but they are doing this not because they want to a_____ the mate, like p_____ showing their feathers.

7. They are doing this because c_____ colors tell predators that probably they have venoms or they are not as p_____ as they seem.

8. The venoms of golden dart frogs are i_____ p_____ ____.

9. There're other animals that use c_____ to a_____ __ their t_____, too.

10. They s_____ neurotoxins, too. Neurotoxins on their skin can be a powerful w_____ to protect them.

11. A big b_____ accidentally eating a salamander can eventually open its m_____ and set the salamander free.

12. P_____ like snakes will eventually avoid animals with c_____ colors, such as salamanders and golden dart frogs, but the fact is they all have their natural enemies, too.

13. Garter snakes, also known as r_____ snakes, are the predator of the salamander simply because they are not afraid of the toxin c_____ in the salamander's body.

14. They have developed a mechanism to resist the n_____ of the salamander. This is a pretty r_____ i_____ for biology.

15. Ribbons snakes are undergoing a series of m_____ to e_____ a mechanism so that they are unafraid of the neurotoxins.

16. Surprisingly, garter snakes are c_____ evolving a s_____ mechanism. This is what we call coevolution.

17. This is the p_____ example of the prey-and-predatory coevolution.

18. Salamanders and ribbon snakes are c_____ seeking for ways to improving their way in order to s_____.

19. They are actually v_____, and like salamanders, they secrete neurotoxins, too.

20. The venom they produce is pretty m_____ compared with other snakes, such as rattle snakes and c_____.

1. definition, coevolution, reciprocally
2. mutual, host-parasite
3. taste, moments, fangs
4. defense, mechanism
5. camouflage, deception
6. successful, survival, exhibiting, allure, peacocks
7. colorful, pleasant
8. incredibly, poisonous
9. coloration, advertise, toxicity
10. secrete, weapon
11. bullfrog, mouth
12. Predators, cryptic
13. ribbon, contained
14. neurotoxins, remarkable, improvement
15. mutations, evolve
16. continually, stronger
17. perfect
18. constantly, survive
19. venomous
20. mild, cobras

▶▶ 摘要能力

| Instruction | MP3 024

　　除了閱讀測驗外，其實培養能在聽完一大段訊息後，以口述講述剛才聽到的聽力訊息是學習語言和表達很重要的一件事，讓自己養成具備這樣的能力，除了能在聽力測驗中獲取高分外，也能在新托福寫作跟口說的整合題型上大有斬獲喔！所以快來練習，除了書中提供的參考答案外，自己可以試著重新聽過音檔一遍後，摘要出英文訊息並朗讀出來。

Note

....

....

....

....

....

Co-evolution means species evolving together. "In biology, coevolution occurs when two or more species reciprocally affect each other's evolution", and it includes different forms, such as mutual relationships, host-parasite, and predator-prey.

The biology seems to have a way of its own for all kinds of species to develop mechanisms. Sometimes prey have developed a certain defense mechanism by camouflaging themselves or exhibiting all forms of colors.

Salamanders and golden dart frogs use coloration to advertise their toxicity, too. Vivid colors on the skin can do the trick to ward off predators.

Snakes and bullfrogs will let go of the meal of the salamander because its skin contains neurotoxins, but garter snakes are unafraid of the salamanders. They have developed a mechanism to resist the neurotoxins of the salamander.

Salamanders, on the other hand, are gradually evolving to a more powerful toxin to counter ribbon snakes' development. Surprisingly, garter snakes are continually evolving a stronger mechanism. This is the perfect example of the prey-and-predatory coevolution.

Note

▶▶ 聽力試題 (MP3 025)

1. According to the professor, what is untrue about the traits of the octopus?
   (A) It feeds on crustaceans and mollusks.
   (B) Its saliva can decompose crabs' hard shell.
   (C) It is well-known for its intelligence, deception, and ink.
   (D) It can only remain underwater.

2. Why does the professor mention the giant octopus' phenomenal attack to the shark?
   (A) To demonstrate how powerful an octopus can be.
   (B) To show that in nature there are no guarantee.
   (C) To explain sharks are not that invincible.
   (D) To explain the octopus can be more aggressive than the shark.

3. Listen again to part of the lecture. Then answer the question.
   (A) To show that size will somehow determine the ultimate victory.
   (B) To demonstrate that the snake can be eaten by the

lizard.

(C) To explain insects still have the chance of winning the reptile.

(D) To show that larger creatures always have an advantage.

4. The following statements list marine creatures and their category

Click the correct box for each category

	Crustacean	Cetacean
A. Lobsters		
B. Dolphins		
C. Shrimps		
D. Porpoises		

5. According to the professor, what is untrue about the traits of the blue-ringed octopuses?

(A) They use coloration to caution predators.

(B) Their toxicity is very deadly.

(C) People can develop the immunity, if it's the second bite from them.

(D) Other than their venom, they can spill the ink cloud.

▶▶ 新托福聽力解析

1. 這題詢問的是聽力細節的部份，D 選項的敘述中有 only 過於絕對，且聽力訊息開頭即有提到 another victory on land，可以得知章魚不僅能於水中活動，故答案為選項 D。

2. 這題是詢問為什麼教授提到 giant octopus' phenomenal attack to the shark。可以整合幾個部分的聽力訊息後，推測出其實要表明的是 To show that in nature there are no guarantee.，故可以得知答案為選項 B。

3. 這題詢問學生為什麼會講該段話 but it somehow shows that size matters when it comes to an attack…like small snakes get eaten by a larger lizard and a full-grown mantis can take down a very small snake.，最正確的選項其實是要表明 To show that size will somehow determine the ultimate victory，故答案為選項 A。

4. 這題是考兩種海洋生物間的區隔，其實文中有提到好幾種生物，題目也可能改考其他兩種生物的比較，在聽力時要注意或記下每個生物屬於哪個類別就能答對這題，答案分別為 AC 和 BD。

5. 這題詢問的是聽力細節的部份，C 選項的敘述中 People can develop the immunity, if it's the second bite from them.，聽力訊息中並未提到這部分，故要小心，這題答案為選項 C。

......

答案：1. D 2. B 3. A 4. AC/BD 5. C

影子跟讀練習 MP3 025

做完題目後，除了對答案知道錯的部分在哪外，更重要的是要修正自己聽力根本的問題，即聽力理解力和聽力專注力，聽力專注力的修正能逐步強化本身的聽力實力，所以現在請根據聽力內容「逐個段落」、「數個段落」或「整篇」進行跟讀練習，提升在實際考場時專注聽完每個訊息、定位出關鍵考點和搭配筆記回答完所有題目。Go!

| **Professor** |

As you can see from the video, a crab stays pretty vigilant on the shore. All of a sudden, an octopus shows up unannounced dragging the crab, which struggles hard to escape, into the water. This demonstrates octopus' another victory on land. Octopuses have been known for their high intelligence, remarkable camouflage, and ink. They are the master of the marine creatures. Their inborn talent allows them to inhabit different marine habitats.

從視頻中你可以看到，螃蟹在岸上保持高度警戒。然後突然間，章魚無聲地出現，把仍在掙扎的螃蟹拖進水裡。這顯示了章魚在陸地上的另一個勝利。章魚以它們高度的智力、驚人的偽裝和墨水聞名。它們是海洋生物中的主宰者。章魚天生的能力顯示出它們居住於不同的海洋棲地。

字彙輔助

1. vigilant 警惕的
2. unannounced 突然的、未經宣布的
3. struggle 掙扎
4. demonstrate 顯示、示範
5. victory 勝利
6. intelligence 智力
7. camouflage 偽裝
8. inhabit 居住
9. marine 海洋的
10. habitat 棲地

Crustaceans and mollusks are on their food list. Prey will be injected with a paralyzing saliva and disjointed with their beaks. Clams and crabs, although equipped with a hard shell, can't withstand the toxic saliva they secrete. The enzyme of the saliva will dissolve the calcium structure of the shell. Without the protection of the shell, the prey will be consumed in an instant.

　甲殼綱動物和軟體動物都在它們的食物清單上。獵物會被注射具癱瘓能力的唾液並會被章魚的喙肢解。蛤蠣和螃蟹，儘管都裝備著堅硬的外殼，卻無法抵禦章魚分泌的唾液毒素。唾液中的酵素會將鈣結構的殼分解。沒有了外殼的保護，獵物就會即刻被食用。

字彙輔助

1. Crustacean 甲殼綱動物
2. mollusk 軟體動物
3. paralyzing 癱瘓的
4. saliva 唾液
5. disjointed 肢解
6. harden 使…堅硬
7. withstand 抵禦
8. enzyme 酵素
9. dissolve 分解
10. calcium 鈣

Even though they seem powerful compared to some fish, crustaceans, and mollusks, octopuses have their natural enemies, too. They can be preyed on by cetaceans, sharks, pinnipeds, sea otters, or sea birds, but recently, an astounding video revealed a giant octopus taking down a shark, too⋯perhaps they're not that approachable and meek, right? They can be as aggressive as they seem.

即使它們在有些魚、甲殼綱動物和軟體動物中看似強大，章魚也有它們自己的天敵。他們會被鯨類動物、鯊魚、鰭足類動物、海獺或海鳥捕食，但最近一個驚人的視頻揭露大型章魚也拿下鯊魚⋯或許它們沒那麼容易接近或溫和，對吧？它們跟看起來一樣具攻擊性。

字彙輔助

1 cetacean 鯨類動物　　2 pinniped 鰭足類動物

3 approachable 易親近的　　4 meek 溫和的

| Student A |

It's incredible⋯I'm still having a hard time believing that. The video captures the phenomenal attack of the octopus. Poor shark⋯but it somehow shows that size matters when it comes to an attack⋯like small snakes getting eaten by a larger lizard and a full-grown mantis can take down a very small snake⋯

這很難以置信⋯仍需要些時間來消化這個事實。視頻捕捉到非凡的章魚攻擊畫面。可憐的鯊魚。但某種程度上來說，這顯示出當提到攻擊時，這跟體態有關。像是小型蛇被較大的蜥蜴捕食，體態生長成熟的螳螂能夠拿下體態非常小的蛇一樣。

| **Professor** |

That's correct. We can't really tell who's winning until it's near the end⋯All things can change in the blink of an eye. A doomed prey can sometimes find itself a moment to escape⋯All of a sudden it totally saves itself from being the meal of another creature. Or a predator can successfully plot the whole scheme to capture its prey in a moment. All prey have their defense mechanisms, too.

| 教授 |

正確。所有的事情能於片刻間改變。劫數難逃的獵物可能有時候發現了能逃走的時刻。突然間，它救了自己免於成為其他生物的餐點。或者是捕食者能成功的密謀計劃整個騙局於片刻間捕到獵物。所有個獵物也都有它們的防禦機制。

字彙輔助

1. phenomenal 非凡的、傑出的
2. lizard 蜥蜴
3. mantis 螳螂
4. doomed 註定的
5. scheme 計謀

| Student B |

I'm not sure I follow…what are crustaceans? What are cetaceans? What are pinnipeds?

| 學生 B |

我不太確定我有跟上…什麼是甲殼綱動物？什麼是鯨類動物？什麼是鰭足類動物？

| Professor |

Oops!…totally forgot to mention the definition of them. Crustaceans may seem like a big word but they are often the food we order when we're in a restaurant. I think you know what they are. For example, shrimps, crabs, and lobsters belong to the category of the crustaceans. We eat them very often. Like octopuses, we have to break down their harden armor to eat the soft tissue inside. Cetaceans, on the other hand, are much bigger than crustaceans. They are as familiar to us as crustaceans. Let me list three cetaceans for you…or is there anyone else who wants to try that…

| 教授 |

喔～都忘了要提關於它們的定義。甲殼綱動物似乎像個大詞彙，但它們通常就是我們在餐廳時會點的食物。我認為你知道它們為何？蝦子、螃蟹和龍蝦都屬於甲殼綱動物的範疇。我們很常以它們為食。至於章魚，我們必須要拆解它們堅硬的裝甲來吃裡頭柔軟的組織。鯨類動物，另一方面，是比甲殼綱動物更大的生物。它們也同甲殼綱動物為我們所熟悉。讓我列出三個鯨類動物給你。或者是有任何人想要試試看。

| Student A |

Marine creatures?

| 學生 A |

海洋生物嗎？

| Professor |

Yes, marine creatures…marine mammals…to be more specific… they are welcomed mammals like we often see them perform in the zoo or circus…

| 教授 |

是的，是海洋生物…海洋哺乳類動物…但更具體些…它們像是我們通常在動物園或馬戲團看到表演的受歡迎的哺乳類動物。

| Student C |

Whales… dolphins…and porpoises…

| 學生 A |

鯨魚…海豚…和鼠海豚。

字彙輔助

1 mammal 哺乳類動物
2 welcome 歡迎
3 perform 執行、表演

| **Professor** |

Excellent! Let's continue…pinnipeds are another word for seals. They are semi-aquatic marine mammals… pinnipeds, cetaceans, and crustaceans are all familiar marine mammals to us… Let's go back to what we've discussed. The defense mechanism. Octopuses have their own defense mechanisms, too. They secrete ink. They are equipped with an ink sac, so when threatened, they spew out an ink cloud to distract their predator…so that they will have a higher chance to escape. The vision of the predators is blocked by a sudden pouring of the ink. This will give octopuses a few seconds to escape. Sometimes they are lucky enough to escape…at other times…it just won't work.

| 教授 |

優秀…讓我們繼續…鰭足類動物是海豹的換句話說。它們是半水生海洋哺乳類動物。 鰭足類動物、鯨類動物和甲殼綱動物都是我們所熟悉的海洋哺乳類動物。讓我們回到我們已經討論過的部分，防禦機制。章魚也有自我的防禦機制。它們分泌墨水。它們配有墨水囊，所以當受到威脅時，它們會噴出墨水雲來分散捕食者的注意...如此一來就有更多的逃生機會。捕食者的勢力會受到突然湧現的墨水阻

擋。這會給章魚幾秒時間逃生。有時它們能很幸運的逃走，但有時這並不管用。

Aside from the ink cloud, octopuses are venomous. Blue-ringed octopuses are extremely venomous. In nature, having venom gives you an upper hand. It more or less protects you from getting eaten, unless the predator is immune to the potency of the venom or the predator coevolves to be resistant to the venom. Also, the coloration also exhibits as a warning to the predator. It sends out a clear message, "Don't come near me!"

除了墨水雲之外，章魚也有毒性。藍環章魚異常的毒。在自然界中，有毒性讓你佔上風。這或多或少能保護你免於被捕食，除非捕食者能免於毒性的效力或捕食者共同演化出對毒性的抵抗力。而且，顏色也顯示出對捕食者的警告。毒性傳遞出清楚的訊息：『別靠近我！』

---

3 venomous 有毒的

4 immune 免疫於

5 potency 力量、效力

6 resistant 抵抗的

7 coloration 顏色

8 warning 警告

With summer vacation coming up…as a professor, I've got to warn you about jellyfish and blue-ringed octopuses. They sometimes surface to a shallow water. Blue-ringed octopuses are especially deadly to humans. So just be careful when you swim in the shallow water. When threatened, they are not lovely and docile as they seem. The toxicity of the blue-ringed octopuses can kill you in a minute. I guess that's all for today.

隨著暑假的到來，身為教授，我想要提醒你們關於水母和藍環章魚。它們有時候會浮現到淺水水域。藍環章魚對人類有致命的傷害。所以當你游泳在淺水水域時要小心。當受到威脅時，藍環章魚不會像看起來的那樣可愛且溫馴。藍環章魚的毒性能於片刻間殺了你。我想今天就到這邊。

字彙輔助

1 jellyfish 水母

2 surface 浮現

3 shallow 淺水水域的

4 especially 特別地

5 deadly 致命的

6 docile 溫馴的

7 toxicity 毒性

1. According to the professor, what is untrue about the traits of the octopus?

2. Why does the professor mention the giant octopus' phenomenal attack on the shark?

3. Listen again to part of the lecture. Then answer the question.
    Student:···I'm still having a hard time believing that. The video captures the phenomenal attack of the octopus. Poor shark···but it somehow shows that size matters when it comes to an attack···like small snakes get eaten by a larger lizard and a full-grown mantis can take down a very small snake···

    Why does the student say "but it somehow shows that size matters when it comes to an attack···like small snakes getting eaten by a larger lizard and a full-grown mantis can take down a very small snake···"?

4. The following statements list marine creatures and their categories.
    Click the correct box for each category

5. According to the professor, what is untrue about the traits of the blue-ringed octopuses?

▶▶ 記筆記與聽力訊息

| Instruction | MP3 025

新托福聽力與其他聽力測驗不同，可以於聽力的紙上記筆記，除了寫試題外，更重要的一點是訓練自己能夠將聽完一段訊息後，將重要的聽力訊息都記到。也可以將自己聽到跟記到的重點訊息跟試題做比對，因為試題考的就是長對話跟講座中出現的重點，能修正自己篩選聽力訊息重點的能力。

| 聽力重點 |

- 記筆記有很多方式，包含符號跟自己習慣的縮寫字等等，可以找出最適合自己的模式，一定要自己重聽音檔作練習數次。
- 這篇是關於海洋生物學，前面段落其實都是鋪陳和引導入題的敘述，蠻容易理解，但要注意生物特性和細節部分的題目，另外就是章魚的特性和天敵，還有其他物種的分類和最後總結的部分。

Main idea ❶
Their inborn talent allows them to inhabit different marine habitats.

octopus	❶ talent：high intelligence, remarkable camouflage, and ink
	❷ food：**Crustaceans and mollusks** (Clams and crabs), **fish**
	❸ Prey will be injected with a paralyzing saliva and disjointed with their beaks
	❹ saliva：dissolve the calcium structure
	❺ natural enemies：cetaceans, sharks, pinnipeds, sea otters, or sea birds

Main idea ❷
However, another phenomenal attack of the giant octopus takes down a shark, which leads us to think that size matters when it comes to an attack.

application	small snakes get eaten by a larger lizard and a full-grown mantis can take down a very small snake
details	things can change in the blink of an eye.

Main idea ❸
Definition of the crustaceans, cetaceans, pinnipeds

crustaceans	shrimps, crabs, and lobsters

cetaceans	**whales, dolphins, and porpoises**
pinnipeds	**seals**
octopus	❻ an ink sac
	❼ venomous
Blue-ringed octopuses	❶ extremely venomous/deadly to human beings
	❷ coloration
shallow water	jellyfish and blue-ringed octopuses

Note

Instruction | MP3 025

　　現在請再聽一次音檔，並做下列的測驗，檢視自己能否完成此填空測驗和強化自己聽力能力和拼字能力，降低並修正自己漏聽到聽力訊息的機會，大幅提升英考實力。

1. From the video as you can see, a crab stays pretty v____ _____ on the shore…then all of a sudden, an octopus shows up u_____…dragging the crab, which s_____ ___ hard to escape, into the water.

2. This d_____ octopus' another v_____ on land.

3. Octopuses have been known for their high i_____, r_____ c_____, and ink.

4. Their i_____ talent allows them to i_____ different m_____ h_____.

5. C_____ and m_____ are on their food list.

6. Prey will be i_____ with a p_____ s_____ and d_____ with their beaks.

7. Clams and crabs, although equipped with a h_____ s_____, can't withstand the toxin saliva they s_____

___.

8. The e_____ of the saliva will d_____ the c_____
   ____ s_____ of the shell. Without the protection of
   the shell, the prey will be c_____ in an instant.

9. They can be preyed on by c_____, sharks, p_____
   __, s_____, or sea birds.

10. but recently, an a_____ video revealed a giant
    octopus takes down a shark, too…perhaps they're not
    that a_____ and m_____, right?

11. The poor shark…but it somehow shows that size
    matters when it comes to an attack…like small snakes
    get eaten by a larger l_____ and a f_____ m____
    _____ can take down a very small snake…

12. Or a predator can successfully plot the whole s_____
    to c_____ its prey in a moment.

13. For example, shrimps, crabs, and l_____ b_____
    to the category of the c_____.

14. We eat them very often. Like octopuses, we have to
    break down their hard armor to eat the s_____ t____
    _____ inside.

15. They are equipped with an ink s_____, so when threatened, they spew out an ink c_____ to d_____ their predator···so that they will have a higher chance to escape.

16. The v_____ of the predators is b_____ by a s__ _____ pouring of the ink.

17. B_____ o_____ are extremely venomous.

18. In nature, having venom gives you an upper hand. It more or less protects you from getting eaten, unless the predator is i_____ to the p_____ of the venom or the predator c_____ to be r_____ to the venom.

19. Also, the c_____ also e_____ as a w_____ to the predator. It sends out a clear message that···don't come near me···

20. J_____ and b_____ o_____ sometimes surface to a s_____ water, and they are especially deadly to humans.

| 答案 |

1. vigilant, unannounced, struggles
2. demonstrates, victory
3. intelligence, remarkable camouflage
4. inborn, inhabit, marine, habitats
5. Crustaceans, mollusks
6. Injected, paralyzing saliva, disjointed
7. hard shell, secrete
8. enzyme, dissolve, calcium structure, consumed
9. cetaceans, pinnipeds, sea otters
10. astounding, approachable, meek
11. lizard, full-grown mantis
12. scheme, capture
13. lobsters, belong, crustaceans
14. soft, tissue
15. sac, cloud, distract
16. vision, blocked, sudden
17. Blue-ringed octopuses
18. immune, potency, coevolves, resistant
19. coloration, exhibits, warning
20. Jellyfish, blue-ringed, octopuses, shallow

▶▶ 摘要能力

| Instruction | MP3 025

　　除了閱讀測驗外，其實培養能在聽完一大段訊息後，以口述講述剛才聽到的聽力訊息是學習語言和表達很重要的一件事，讓自己養成具備這樣的能力，除了能在聽力測驗中獲取高分外，也能在新托福寫作跟口說的整合題型上大有斬獲喔！所以快來練習，除了書中提供的參考答案外，自己可以試著重新聽過音檔一遍後，摘要出英文訊息並朗讀出來。

Note

▶▶ 參考答案

Three traits of the octopus package them with the ability to inhabit different marine habitats, taking down prey, such as crustaceans and mollusks. Despite these they have their natural enemies, too. They are vulnerable to the attack of cetaceans, sharks, pinnipeds, sea otters, or sea birds. However, another phenomenal attack of the giant octopus takes down a shark, which leads us to think that size matters when it comes to the attack. We cannot really say about the outcome since things can change in the blink of the eye. Shrimps, crabs, and lobsters belong to the category of the crustaceans. Cetaceans, on the other hand, refer to whales, dolphins, and porpoises. The defense mechanisms have allowed animals to have a high successful survival rate. Octopuses, with the ability to spill ink, is one of the examples, although this will not always work. Aside from the ink cloud, the venom and coloration are also the defense mechanism. Blue-ringed octopuses are the representative, and their toxicity can kill you in a minute.

6 ▶▶ Psychology：Underemployment 年輕人都面對的困境學非所用/畢業後低就

▶▶ **聽力試題** `MP3 026`

1. According to the professor, what is untrue about the underemployment phenomenon?

   (A) Even if it's not during the economic downturn, people can't find desired jobs.

   (B) People are not courageous enough to acknowledge this phenomenon.

   (C) The only solution to this is to follow guidelines given by educators and parents.

   (D) Conventional ways are not suitable for today's situations.

2. What are the major differences between the lucky few and the ones who can't find jobs?

   (A) The lucky few are satisfied with the job they get.

   (B) The lucky few eventually have to face the music.

   (C) Those who can't find jobs have to do jobs that do not need a great diploma.

   (D) Those who can't find jobs will instead have a working holiday in Australia.

3. Listen again to part of the lecture. Then answer the question.
    (A) To show interviewers are good at detecting the intention of interviewees.
    (B) To show interviewers should be like golden retrievers to be qualified for their jobs.
    (C) To refute the idea that interviewers are acting like golden retrievers.
    (D) To show interviewers favor candidates who raise golden retrievers.

4. Why does the professor mention parents as the responsible ones for the phenomenon?
    (A) To show the phenomenon hits especially hard in eastern countries in Asia.
    (B) To show it seems ridiculous but it is true.
    (C) To show parents are the ones to be blamed on because they are preventing their kids from growing up.
    (D) To show how wonderful that parents can view kids' fantastic diploma as a golden ticket to the job.

5. According to the professor, what is true about the underemployment phenomenon?
    (A) Redundant universities are not the cause.
    (B) Perhaps today's parents and educators should alter their sayings by educating their kids to be well-prepared.

(C) The fancy diploma is still a guarantee to our success.

(D) We do not have to do something extra if we follow conventional routes.

答案：1. C 2. C 3. A 4. C 5. B

▶▶ 新托福聽力解析

1. 這題詢問的是聽力細節的部份，C 選項的敘述中 The only solution to this is to follow guideline given by educators and parents 與聽力訊息不符，故可以得知答案為選項 C。

2. 這題是詢問幸運錄取者和找不到工作者兩者間的差異，要注意聽力訊息中兩者的差異和相似的敘述，最終可以得出答案為選項 C，找不到工作者最終從事不需要好文憑的工作。

3. 這題詢問學生為什麼會講 Interviewers have a hunch that they won't do that for long. They are like golden retrievers or something…all of a sudden getting pretty good at their senses.，要注意其他混淆的選項，其實主要是要表明 To show interviewers are good at detecting the intention of interviewees，故答案為選項 A。

4. 這題詢問為什麼父母會需要為此事負責呢？，要注意其他選項敘述為聽力中提到過的訊息，但並非這個題目問的原因，最後得出答案為選項 C。

5. 這題詢問的是聽力細節的部份，但是是詢問正確的部分，也要注意其他同義詞轉換，可以得知答案為選項 B，Perhaps today's parents and educators should alter their sayings by educating their kids to be well-prepared.。

影子跟讀練習 MP3 026

　　做完題目後，除了對答案知道錯的部分在哪外，更重要的是要修正自己聽力根本的問題，即聽力理解力和聽力專注力，聽力專注力的修正能逐步強化本身的聽力實力，所以現在請根據聽力內容「逐個段落」、「數個段落」或「整篇」進行跟讀練習，提升在實際考場時專注聽完每個訊息、定位出關鍵考點和搭配筆記回答完所有題目。Go!

| Professor |

　　"Underemployment" has been a big issue in our lives because it's highly related to a person's development right after we graduate. Traditionally, we follow the route set by our parents and educators, hoping that one day　right after we graduate…we will be able to stand on our own feet, and earn a pretty decent salary based on the skills we have learned during four years of undergraduate study. But the fact is that that's never been the case. Traditional ways of going to a great school in high schools and colleges cannot be a panacea in today's job search. Lots of people are undergoing a certain change…A word they are so timid to mention… underemployment. Even if the whole economy seems pretty sound and prosperous, people can't seem to find the job they want, let alone during the economy downturn. I'm just as puzzled as several researchers as to what seems to go wrong for our education.

　　「未充分就業」已經是我們生活中很重大的議題因為這與一位畢業生畢業後的個人發展有高度的相關性。傳統上，我們遵循著我們父母和教育家的路走，希望有一天，在我們畢業後，我們能夠獨立，並根據我們四年大學期間所學的技能賺取相當足夠的薪水。但是事實是這卻不是這麼回事。傳統方式教導我們在高中和大學時唸好學校已經無法成為現今求職的萬靈丹。許多人正經歷著特定的改變，一個他們不敢提及的字彙，「未充分就業」。即使整個經濟看似相當穩健和繁榮，人們似乎無法找到他們想要的工作，更別說是在經濟蕭條時期。我也幾個研究人員一樣為了我們教育到底哪裡出錯了這部分感到困惑。

Underemployment is like a wave, pervading among today's younger generation. It's like no one can be immune from it. People can't find their dream jobs right after they graduate. The specialty and skills learned during four years of undergraduate study seem of little or no use in job searching. A lot of them are pretty depressed. Some evade this phenomenon by having a working holiday in Australia or other countries, but eventually they still have to go back and start from scratch. Some are reluctant to do their jobs even if they are the lucky few who get the job after graduation.

「未充分就業」像是一波浪潮蔓延在現今的年輕世代裡。像是沒人可以免受其害。人們在畢業後找不到他們夢想的工作。在四年大學期間所學的專長和技能似乎對於求職有些微或完全沒有幫助。許多人感到相當沮喪。有些人藉由到澳洲或其他國家打工度假來逃避這個現象，但是他們終究需要回國且一切從頭開始。有些人勉強做著工作即使他們是少數自大學畢業後就幸運找到工作者。

字彙輔助

1. pervade 瀰漫於、遍及於
2. specialty 專業、專長
3. depressed 沮喪的
4. evade 規避
5. phenomenon 現象
6. reluctant 勉強的

Even though they get to utilize their skills, they are resenting the low salary given by some corporations. They prefer to stay at home waiting for a golden opportunity. Some wait longer than predicted or imagined. Others hold a grudge inside doing the job that's totally irrelevant to their major. Heading to the office with a mind that says that's not the job I will be doing for the next few years. A few eventually are willing to face the music…trying to make a living by doing a job that doesn't need a glamourous or fantastic diploma, but they find themselves shut down by interviewers. Perhaps no one expects graduates with a top diploma would do such a job or no one would hire someone who just wants to do the job temporarily. Interviewers have a hunch that they won't do that for long. They are like golden retrievers or something…all of a sudden getting pretty good at their senses.

即使他們能使用他們的技能，他們對於有些公司所給予的低薪感到厭惡。他們情願待在家等待著絕佳的機會降臨。有些畢業生所等待的時間遠長於他們所預測或想像的。另一些畢業生抱持著怨恨在心頭，做著與他們大學專業無關的工作。步向辦公室的途中心裡想著，這不是我接下來幾年想要從事的工作。有些人最終願意面對現實,試著做著能夠維生的工作，這些工作絲毫不需要光鮮或夢幻的學歷，但他們發現自己被面試官拒於門外。或許是因為沒有人期待頂著頂尖文憑光環的畢業生會做這樣子的工作，也或者是沒人願意雇用一個只想要做短期工作的員工。面試官直覺感受到他們不會待很久。面試官就像是黃金獵犬一般，突然間對於自己的感官能力異常敏銳。

字彙輔助

1. utilize 利用
2. resent 憎恨
3. corporation 公司
4. golden 黃金的、絕佳的
5. opportunity 機會
6. grudge 恨
7. irrelevant 無關的
8. glamourous 富有魅力的
9. diploma 文憑

Parents can do nothing about it. They view their kids as

outstanding as what their diploma seems like. Some give an encouraging talk to the kid that a good job takes time to find, but this leads to another phenomenon dragging their kids down the drain. Others are too protective of their kids. All these are hurting their kids from taking a step further, impeding them to achieve something or regain their confidence. The phenomenon hits especially hard in eastern countries in Asia. A Japanese father is not worrying about his kid not having a job⋯but is worrying about whether his savings left after he dies are enough for his son. It seems ridiculous, but it's the fact.

父母也無能為力。他們把孩子想成如同他們文憑般的傑出。有些人給予小孩鼓勵性的談話講述著好工作是需要時間尋找的，但是這也導致另一個現象，將他們自己的孩子拖到谷底。其他父母則是過於保護自己的孩子。這些都會傷害小孩子向前邁出一步，阻礙他們成就一些是或是找回自己的自信。這個現象對於東方的亞洲國家打擊更重。一位日本父親並不擔心自己的小孩沒有工作，而是擔心自己的存款在自己過世後足夠他兒子使用嗎？這看似荒謬和卻是事實。

字彙輔助

1 outstanding 傑出的

2 encouraging 鼓勵的

3 protective 保護的

4 impede 阻礙

5 achieve 達成

6 regain 恢復

7 confidence 自信

Perhaps we should really do some serious thinking about this phenomenon··· After all, a person without a job he or she likes is like having no goals in life, having no purpose or passion in life···Another thing to be blamed on is superfluous universities. There are just too many universities out there. The diploma is not as useful or glamorous as it used to be.

或許我們應該要對關於這個現象做些深度思考⋯畢竟一個沒有自己喜歡工作的人，就如同人生中毫無目標一般，人生中毫無任何目的或熱情⋯另一個是要歸咎於過多的大學。就是有太多的大學了。文憑就不像過往那樣有用和光鮮。

字彙輔助

1. purpose 目的
2. passion 熱情
3. superfluous 多餘的
4. useful 有用的

Perhaps today's parents and educators should modify their sayings by educating their kids to be well-prepared, instead of following the traditional route. After all, a fancy diploma is pretty insignificant in job-searching. It might work for some occasions, but it's not a guarantee. It can only open a door for you···but we shouldn't value the diploma as a guarantee to our success. We should probably view it as a basis, and we should do something extra, like a right mindset to be well-prepared for the underemployment problems. Life is long. We can only pray the underemployment won't be that long. (chuckling)

或許今天的父母和教育家應該要修改他們的說法，教育他們的孩子更充分準備或別遵循傳統的道路走。畢竟，一個華麗的文憑在求職上是相當無用的。它在有些情況下有用，但是它並非保證。它能為你開啟一道門，但我們不應該將文憑視為我們成功的保證。我們應該要將它視為是基礎之外再多做些什麼才是，像是有正確的心態才能更完備的面對「未充分就業」的問題。人生漫長。我們只能夠禱告「未充分就業」的問題不會維持那麼久（笑）。

字彙輔助

1. modify 修改
2. well-prepared 充分準備的
3. insignificant 微不足道的
4. guarantee 保證
5. mindset 心態

▶▶ 試題聽力原文

1. According to the professor, what is untrue about the underemployment phenomenon?

2. What are the major differences between the lucky few and the ones who can't find jobs?

3. Listen again to part of the lecture. Then answer the

question.

Professor: Perhaps no one expects graduates with a top diploma would do such job or no one would hire someone who just wants to do the job for the temporarily. Interviewers have a hunch that they won't do that for long. They are like a golden retriever or something…all of a sudden getting pretty good at their senses.

Why does the professor say "Interviewers have a hunch that they won't do that for long. They are like a golden retriever or something…all of a sudden getting pretty good at their senses."?

4. Why does the professor mention parents as the responsible ones for the phenomenon?

5. According to the professor, what is true about the underemployment phenomenon?

▶▶ 記筆記與聽力訊息

| Instruction | MP3 026

　　新托福聽力與其他聽力測驗不同，可以於聽力的紙上記筆記，除了寫試題外，更重要的一點是訓練自己能夠將聽完一段訊息後，將重要的聽力訊息都記到。也可以將自己聽到跟記到的重點訊息跟試題做比對，因為試題考的就是長對話跟講座中出現的重點，能修正自己篩選聽力訊息重點的能力。

｜聽力重點｜

- 記筆記有很多方式，包含符號跟自己習慣的縮寫字等等，可以找出最適合自己的模式，一定要自己重聽音檔作練習數次。

- 這篇是關於心理學和社會現象的敘述，**這篇很生活化訊息不難理解，也跟考生年紀層重疊，會更好答，可以參考列表的筆記，句子可以再簡化，然後是注意細節性的題型。**

Note

Main idea ❶

- the problem of underemployment and its influence on graduates
- Traditional ways (X)

Main idea ❷ no one can be immune from this phenomenon

---

phenomenon	The specialty and skills = little, no use
	❶ getaway：working holidays in Australia
	❷ lucky few：reluctant to do, resent low salary
	❸ unemployed：wait for a golden opportunity
	❹ others：hold grudge
	❺ a few：irrelevant to their major, underemployment

Main idea ❸

- Parents can do nothing about it. What parents do eventually prevents their kids from advancing. The phenomenon hits especially hard in eastern countries in Asia.

---

example	❶ view their kids as outstanding as what their diploma seems like
	❷ give an encouraging talk

Main idea ❹

- The phenomenon hits especially hard in eastern countries in Asia.

example   Japanese father

Main idea ❺

- The diploma is not as useful and glamorous as it used to since there are so many superfluous universities.

Main idea ❻

- Graduates should not view the diploma as a guarantee to future success, but should prepare their kids to counter underemployment trends.

Note

▶▶ 填空測驗

| Instruction | MP3 026

　　現在請再聽一次音檔，並做下列的測驗，檢視自己能否完成此填空測驗和強化自己聽力能力和拼字能力，降低並修正自己漏聽到聽力訊息的機會，大幅提升英考實力。

1. "U_____" has been a big issue in our lives because it's highly related to a person's d_____ right after we graduate.

2. Traditionally, we follow the r_____ set by our parents and educators, hoping that one day…right after we graduate…we will be able to stand on our own feet, earn a pretty d_____ s_____ based on what skills we have learned during four years of u_____ study.

3. T_____ ways of going to a great school in high schools and colleges cannot be a p_____ in today's job search.

4. Even if the whole e_____ seems pretty sound and p_____, people can't seem to find the job they want, let alone during the economy d_____.

5. I'm just as p_____ as several r_____ as to what seems to go wrong for our e_____.

6. The s_____ and skills learned during four years of undergraduate study seem of little or no use in job s____ _____.

7. Some e_____ this p_____ by having a working holiday in Australia or other countries, but eventually they still have to go back and start from scratch.

8. Some are r_____ to do their jobs even if they are the l_____ few who get the job after g_____.

9. Even though they get to u_____ their skills, they are r_____ the low salary given by some c_____.

10. They prefer to stay at home waiting for a g_____ o__ _____ to s_____. Some wait longer than predicted or imagined.

11. Another hold g_____ inside doing the job that's totally i_____ to their m_____.

12. A few eventually are willing to face the m_____ ⋯ trying to make a living by doing a job that doesn't need a g_____ or fantastic d_____, but they find themselves shut down by i_____.

13. Perhaps no one expects graduates with a top d_____

would do such a job or no one would h_____ someone who just wants to do the job t_____.

14. Interviewers have a h_____ that they won't do that for long. They are like golden r_____ or something… all of a sudden getting pretty good at their s_____.

15. They view their kids as o_____ as what their diploma seems like.

16. Some give an e_____ talk to the kid that a good job takes time to find, but this leads to another phenomenon dragging their kids down the d_____.

17. Others are too p_____ of their kids. All these are hurting their kids from taking a step further, i_____ them to achieve something or regain their c_____.

18. After all, a person without a job he or she likes is like having no goals in life, having no purpose or p_____ in life.

19. Another thing to be blamed is s_____ universities. There are just too many universities out there. The diploma is not as useful or glamorous as it used to be.

20. After all, a fancy diploma is pretty i_____ in job-

searching. It might work for some o_____, but it's not a guarantee. It can only open a door for you⋯but we shouldn't value the diploma as a guarantee to our success.

| 答案 |

1. Underemployment, development
2. route, decent salary, undergraduate
3. Traditional, panacea
4. economy, prosperous, downturn
5. puzzled, researchers, education
6. specialty, searching
7. evade, phenomenon
8. reluctant, lucky, graduation
9. utilize, resenting, corporations
10. golden, opportunity, surface
11. grudge, irrelevant, major
12. music, glamourous, diploma, interviewers
13. diploma, hire, temporarily
14. hunch, retrievers, senses
15. outstanding
16. encouraging, drain
17. protective, impeding, confidence
18. passion
19. superfluous, universities
20. insignificant, occasions

▶▶▶ 摘要能力

| Instruction | MP3 026

　　除了閱讀測驗外，其實培養能在聽完一大段訊息後，以口述講述剛才聽到的聽力訊息是學習語言和表達很重要的一件事，讓自己養成具備這樣的能力，除了能在聽力測驗中獲取高分外，也能在新托福寫作跟口說的整合題型上大有斬獲喔！所以快來練習，除了書中提供的參考答案外，自己可以試著重新聽過音檔一遍後，摘要出英文訊息並朗讀出來。

Note

▶▶ 參考答案

Traditional ways of going to a great school in high schools and colleges cannot be a panacea in today's job search. Lots of people are undergoing a certain change, a change we are too timid to mention, underemployment. Even if the whole economy seems pretty sound and prosperous, people can't seem to find the job they want, let alone during the economic downturn. The specialty and skills learned during four years of the undergraduate study seem of little or no use in job searching. No matter how graduates respond to these changes, it seems inevitable that they are unable to reverse the trend. Parents are with their two hands tied behind their back as well. Coming up with solutions, such as giving an encouraging talk or others, only impedes their kids from moving forward. Also, the diploma is not as useful and glamorous as it used to since there are too many superfluous universities out there. Today's parents and educators should probably educate their kids to have the right attitude by knowing that they should not view the diploma as a guarantee to future success, but prepare their kids to counter underemployment trends.

▶▶ **聽力試題** MP3 027

1. Listen again to part of the lecture. Then answer the question.
   (A) To show how much she likes golden retrievers in the hospital.
   (B) To show she has doubts in herself about working in the hospital.
   (C) To show finding inner voices inside us can make our life painful.
   (D) To show wrestling golden retrievers is the best way to accumulate work experiences.

2. Listen again to part of the lecture. Then answer the question.
   (A) To show the professor hates the ending of the story.
   (B) To show the professor wants the student to be open to the ending part.
   (C) To refute that the students already know how the story ends.
   (D) To show the story ends as unexpected to readers.

3. Listen again to part of the lecture. Then answer the question.
   (A) To show we cannot truly count on family members and friends.
   (B) To show they are always the last to stand up for us.
   (C) To show answers from them are not helpful for a person's growth.
   (D) To show friendship will not always last.

4. According to the professor, what is untrue about the Lea Chadwell?
   (A) She eventually works as a vet tech at an animal hospital.
   (B) Making cookies is what she feels passionate about.
   (C) Everyone starts to tell her she should own her bakery some day.
   (D) She did not go to Portland because her mentor does not want her there.

5. What can be inferred about starting a new startup from the lecture?
   (A) It involves taking risks, stepping out of one's comfort zone.
   (B) It requires a steady income to support the need.
   (C) It involves the support from friends and family members.
   (D) It reduces a person's chance of finding a sense of

purpose.

▶▶ 新托福聽力解析

1. 這題詢問教授為什麼要說 So she asks herself like "am I really going to be wrestling golden retrievers when I'm 65，其實最主要的原因是 To show she has doubts in herself about working in the hospital.，她其實是產生自我懷疑，內心聲音告訴她是否自己到 65 歲都要在動物醫院工作，所以答案為選項 B。

2. 這題詢問教授為什麼要說 It's a little surprising to find that the story ends that way，可以得知答案為選項 D，其實對讀者來說是感到意外的。

3. 這題詢問教授為什麼要說 Family members and friends are the last person you should seek advice from… we are not discussing this today…but stop seeking advice from them…，其實要注意的是避免用自己常識去做判斷且題目中有提到 according to the professor，這題答案為選項 C。

4. 這題詢問細節的部分，所以其實有聽懂女主角要做的每件事跟流程就能答對這題，D 選項是錯誤的因為她有跟 mentor 學習到，故答案為 D。

5. 這題是考推測能力，答案為選項 A，其實創業就包含了要脫離舒適圈，而非穩定且領固定薪資等等。

答案：1. B 2. D 3. C 4. D 5. A

影子跟讀練習 MP3 027

做完題目後，除了對答案知道錯的部分在哪外，更重要的是要修正自己聽力根本的問題，即聽力理解力和聽力專注力，聽力專注力的修正能逐步強化本身的聽力實力，所以現在請根據聽力內容「逐個段落」、「數個段落」或「整篇」進行跟讀練習，提升在實際考場時專注聽完每個訊息、定位出關鍵考點和搭配筆記回答完所有題目。Go!

No matter how old we are or how many achievements we have accomplished, we all have been looking for a purpose for living, a sense of purpose that will make us feel fulfilled. Some have made it, successfully starting a new startup. It's such a joy for them to do things that mean so much to them after working for a certain amount of time, doing things that mean nothing to them.

不論我們幾歲或我們達成了多少的成就，我們都尋找著生活的目的，一個目的感能讓我們感到完整。有些人已經達到了，成功地創立了一個新創公司。這是如此的喜悅，對於他們來說做這些事對他們意義重大，在工作了特定的時間，做了對於他們毫無意義的事後。

字彙輔助

1 achievement 成就

2 accomplish 達成

3 purpose 目的

4 joy 樂趣

It's adventurous and risky for some people simply because they're afraid of stepping out of their comfort zone. They are afraid of losing a fixed income that comes in every month. They need security. They have that kind of burden.

對於一些人來說這是具冒險性和有風險的，因為他們懼怕跳脫他們自己的舒適圈。他們如此懼怕沒有每個月的固定收入。他們需要穩定感。他們有著這樣的負擔。

字彙輔助

1. adventurous 冒險的
2. comfort 舒適
3. fixed 固定的
4. income 收入
5. security 安全

But the thing is we all need to find our inner voice, finding a moment that makes us great or something. That's why I'm recommending you to read "The Power of Moments" written by Chip Heath and Dan Heath. In the book, you will find how a short or unexpected experience can elevate us to a point that we can also have spectacular moments of our own.

但事情是我們都需要尋找我們的內在聲音，找尋某一刻能使我們偉大。這也是我推薦你們閱讀由奇普西斯和丹西斯所寫的「時刻的力量」。在他們的書中你會發現短暫或意想不到的經驗可以提升我們到某種程度，讓我們能有驚人的時刻。

字彙輔助

1. inner 內部的
2. recommend 推薦
3. unexpected 出乎意料外的
4. elevate 提高
5. spectacular 壯觀的

The first thing we should do is to create them. We cannot expect things to happen in a certain way if we just sit there and do nothing. Things just do not go that way. We have to seize every moment and be able to create them for ourselves. In chapter six, Stretch for Insight, it reveals a case for us to rethink for ourselves. It's worth reading. We all have time that we are asking ourselves…like am I heading to the right direction… the right path for our career and we just can't stop us for thinking about that kind of question… no matter how confident we are or how many things we have achieved…we all have these doubts and voices inside each of us…even during every phase of our lives.

第一件事我們必須做的是創造它們。我們不能期待事情會以特定的方式進展，如果我們只是坐著卻毫無動靜。事情不會這樣演變。我們必須抓住每個時刻且能夠替自己創造它們。在第六章「洞察力的延展」中，它揭露著一個讓我們能重新省思自我的案例。這值得閱讀。我們都有些時候我們詢問自己：『像是我們是朝著對的方向前進嗎？我們職涯走在對的路上嗎？』。我們就是無法停下來思考像這樣

影子跟讀

學術場景

校園場景

子的問題，不論我們多麼有自信或是達成了多少事。在我們每個人心中都有著疑惑和聲音，甚至是在我們生活中的每個階段。

字彙輔助

1. expect 期待
2. rethink 重新思考
3. direction 方向
4. reveal 揭露
5. confident 自信的
6. phase 階段

Let's take a look at the case by ourselves. Lea Chadwell is the heroine. She is proactive and she is unlike many graduates who are undergoing an underemployment phase. She gets her dream job as a vet tech, being able to work at an animal hospital. That sounds like a pretty good start simply because if you want something in your life, you have to be bold and willing to do things to get what you want. But the story does not end here. It's back to what I have said. The voice inside each one of us that is asking ourselves, "Am I doing the right things? Am I accumulating the experience ready for our next job?" So, she asks herself, like "Am I really going to be wrestling golden retrievers when I'm 65?"

讓我們自己看下這個案例。李·才特薇爾是女主角。她積極主動且她不像許多畢業生那樣經歷著「學非所用」階段。她得到自己想要的夢想工作成為獸醫技術人員，能夠替動物醫院工作。這像是個相當好了開端，僅因為如果你人生中想要一些事，你必須要大膽且願意做些事去得到自己想要的。但故事並未在這劃下句點。這回到我剛才所説過的。在我們每個人的心中，我們都在詢問著自己關於我們做對的事情嗎？我們累積著對的經驗，讓我們邁向下個工作做好準備嗎？所以她也詢問自己：像是「在我 65 歲時我還會真的想要與黃金獵犬角力嗎？」。

字彙輔助

1 **heroine** 女主角
2 **proactive** 積極的
3 **hospital** 醫院
4 **accumulate** 累積
5 **wrestling** 與…角力/搏鬥
6 **golden retriever** 黃金獵犬

Then she does things that impress most of us. Perhaps it is rare in Asian countries. You can't possibly make such a bold move. People around you are often discouraging you from reaching goals. People value security over everything. Family members and friends are the last person you should seek advice from. We are not discussing this today.…but stop seeking advice from them…kidding.

然後她做了讓我們都感到欽佩的事。或許這在亞洲國家中較不常見。你不可能做這樣大膽的舉動。圍繞著你的人們通常都對於你想要達成的目標進行勸阻。人們把穩定性看得重於任何事。家庭成員和朋友們都該是你最後尋求意見的人，但這並非我們今天要討論的部分…但停止向他們尋求意見…開玩笑的。

After that she started doing things she is passionate about: making cookies and so on. As it turns out everyone starts to tell her she should open her bakery someday. It's another big move for her as well and it's pretty commendable. She then test-drives herself by imitating someone else who is doing what she dreams about…to see what they are doing. Things progressed well when she flew to Portland, getting a mentor to teach her the bakery business.

在那之後她開始做了她有熱情的事：烹飪餅乾等等的。最後事情的發展是每個人開始告訴她，有天她應該要開間自己的烘培店。這對她而言是另一個重大的舉動而且這相當值得讚許。然後她就測試性的開始模仿其他正在從事她夢想工作的人，看他們在做些什麼。事情進展良好且當她飛去波蘭時獲得另一個導師教授她烘培事業。

Pretty awesome, right? She eventually went back home resolving to open the shop one day. She had a step-by-step preparation to get closer to her dream. After those preparations, she intended to open the shop. It's like a dream come true. Normally, people are not as gallant as the heroine. But the story does end here. It's a little surprising to find that the story ends that way. I'm not telling you what happened after that. Why not...It's more fun if you get to finish the reading yourself. Regardless of the result or the story, I want you all to walk out of this classroom being equipped with the ability to do things that matter the most to you and step out of your comfort zone. I guess that's all for today's session.

相當棒，對吧？她最終回到家決心有天開店。她有著循序漸進的準備使她能更接近自己的夢想。在那些準備後，她打算開店。這像是夢想成真。通常人們不會想女主角那樣那麼勇敢。但是故事並非以此做結束。很訝異故事的結尾會是這樣結束。而我不會告訴你們接下來事情的進展。為什麼不要呢？…你們自己完成閱讀的話會更有趣，儘管故事的結尾是這樣。我想要你們都走出這間教室後，都能有著具備從事對自己而言最至關重要的事的能力和踏出舒適圈。我想今天的課程就到此為止。

字彙輔助

1 resolving 決心　　**2** gallant 大膽的

3 ability 能力　　**4** comfort 舒適

▶▶ 試題聽力原文

1. Listen again to part of the lecture. Then answer the question.

   Professor: But the story does not end here⋯it's back to what I have said. The voice inside each one of us that is asking ourselves am I doing the right things? Am I accumulating the experience ready for our next job? So she asks herself like "Am I really going to be wrestling golden retrievers when I'm 65?"

   Why does the professor say "So she asks herself like "am I really going to be wrestling golden retrievers when I'm 65?""?

2. Listen again to part of the lecture. Then answer the question.

   Professor: After those preparations, she tended to open the shop. It's like dream coming true. Normally, people are not as gallant as the heroine. But the story does end here. It's a little surprising to find that the story ends that way.

   Why does the professor say "It's a little surprising to find that the story ends that way"?

3. Listen again to part of the lecture. Then answer the question.

Professor: People around you are often discouraging you from reaching a goal. People value security over everything else. Family members and friends are the last person you should seek advice from⋯but we are not discussing this today⋯but stop seeking advice from them⋯

Why does the professor say "Family members and friends are the last person you should seek advice from⋯but we are not discussing this today⋯but stop seeking advice from them⋯"?

4. According to the professor, what is untrue about the Lea Chadwell?

5. What can be inferred about starting a new startup from the lecture?

▶▶ 記筆記與聽力訊息

| Instruction | MP3 027

　　新托福聽力與其他聽力測驗不同，可以於聽力的紙上記筆記，除了寫試題外，更重要的一點是訓練自己能夠將聽完一段訊息後，將重要的聽力訊息都記到。也可以將自己聽到跟記到的重點訊息跟試題做比對，因為試題考的就是長對話跟講座中出現的重點，能修正自己篩選聽力訊息重點的能力。

| 聽力重點 |

- 記筆記有很多方式，包含符號跟自己習慣的縮寫字等等，可以找出最適合自己的模式，一定要自己重聽音檔作練習數次。

- 這篇是關於商業類話題，**前面段落其實都是鋪陳和引導性句子所以其實理解就可以了，重點可以放在書中女主角的部分還有一系列的創業步驟，這樣就大概掌握出考點了。**

Note

▶▶ 參考筆記

Main idea ❶

● Having a sense of purpose will make us feel fulfilled, and some have made it by starting a new startup.

| step | ❶ involve risks |
| | ❷ step out of the comfort zone/ let go of security |

Main idea ❷

● we all need to find our inner voice and cannot sit there and do nothing

books	The Power of Moments
case	Lea Chadwell
	❶ Get a dream job as a vet tech
	❷ rethink about the job
	❸ make a bold move
	❹ doing things that she is passionate about： bakery
	❺ test-drive herself by imitating a Portland mentor
	❻ open the shop

Main idea ❸

● To walk out of this classroom being equipped with the ability to do things that matter the most to you and step out of your comfort zone

▶▶ 填空測驗

| Instruction | MP3 027

　　現在請再聽一次音檔，並做下列的測驗，檢視自己能否完成此填空測驗和強化自己聽力能力和拼字能力，降低並修正自己漏聽到聽力訊息的機會，大幅提升應考實力。

1. No matter how old we are or how many a_____ we have accomplished, we all have been looking for a purpose for living, a sense of purpose that will make us feel f_____.

2. Some have made it, successfully starting a new s_____.

3. It's a_____ and risky for some simply because they're so afraid of stepping out of their c_____ zone.

4. They are so afraid of losing a f_____ i_____ that comes in every month. They need s_____.

5. But the thing is we all need to find our i_____ v_____, finding a moment that makes us great or something.

6. In their book, you will find how a short or u_____ experience can e_____ us to a point that we can also

have s_____ moments of our own.

7. We have to s_____ every moment and be able to create them for ourselves.

8. No matter how c_____ we are or how many things we have achieved…we all have these doubts and voices inside each of us…even during every p_____ of our lives.

9. She gets her d_____ job as a vet tech, being able to work at an a_____ hospital.

10. Am I a_____ the experience ready for our next job? So she asks herself like "am I really going to be w_____ __ golden retrievers when I'm 65?"

11. Then she does things that i_____ most of us.

12. Perhaps it is rare in Asian countries. You can't possibly make such a b_____ move.

13. People around you are often d_____ you from reaching goals. People value s_____ over everything else.

14. As it turns out everyone starts to tell her she should

open her bakery some day···it's another big move for her as well and it's pretty commendable.

15. Things p_____ well when she flew to Portland, getting a m_____ to teach her the b_____ business.

16. She had a step-by-step p_____ for her to get closer to her dream.

17. Normally, people are not as g_____ as the h_____ __.

18. It's a little s_____ to find that the story ends that way.

19. it's more fun if you get to finish the r_____ yourself.

20. Regardless of the r_____ or the story, I want you all to walk out of this c_____ being equipped with the ability to do things that matter the most to you and step out of your comfort zone.

答案

1. achievements, fulfilled
2. startup
3. adventurous, comfort
4. fixed, income, security
5. inner, voice
6. unexpected, elevate, spectacular
7. seize
8. confident, phase
9. dream, animal
10. accumulating, wrestling
11. impress
12. bold
13. discouraging, security
14. commendable
15. progressed, mentor, bakery
16. preparation
17. gallant, heroine
18. surprising
19. reading
20. result, classroom

▶▶ 摘要能力

| Instruction | 〔MP3 **027**〕

　　除了閱讀測驗外，其實培養能在聽完一大段訊息後，以口述講述剛才聽到的聽力訊息是學習語言和表達很重要的一件事，讓自己養成具備這樣的能力，除了能在聽力測驗中獲取高分外，也能在新托福寫作跟口說的整合題型上大有斬獲喔！所以快來練習，除了書中提供的參考答案外，自己可以試著重新聽過音檔一遍後，摘要出英文訊息並朗讀出來。

Note

▶▶ 參考答案

We all need to find the true voice within us, and we have to admit that this is an era where true success rests on taking risks and having the courage to step out one's comfort zone. The Power of Moments reveals some insights for us to find rare and unexpected experiences so that we can all find a spectacular moment. In chapter six, the heroine gets the dream job as a vet tech, but soon finds herself getting trapped. She begins to wonder is this what she will be doing for a living, wrestling golden retrievers in her 65. She eventually makes a bold move by flying to Portland to mimic what her mentor is doing. She arrives at home, feeling certain that she needs to open the shop. The story does not end as what readers would expect, but what we can learn from her is her courage to do things.

Part 3

校園話題

篇章概述

校園場景收錄了 11 篇貼近生活的校園話題，當中還融入一些較趣味性的用語，像是「你的午餐還躺在那」等等的，讓你備考也不枯燥。此外，還探討了許多現代年輕人息息相關的議題，有空也可以翻翻相關書籍，解解惑，畢竟腦海中一直塞英文，每天能塞的英文也有限，邊唸英文邊思考自己未來也不錯喔。

1 ▶▶ 心理學專題：鳩摩智也是靠「刻意練習」練就絕世武功嗎？

▶▶ **聽力試題** MP3 028

1. Why does the student visit the professor?
   (A) To join the professor for the cheese bagel
   (B) To inquire why the professor feels disappointed about student's report
   (C) To inquire why the professor is into Chinese fictions
   (D) To discuss the book he read

2. What can be inferred about the student?
   (A) He's been eyeing for professor's bagel since he got here.
   (B) He is in the middle of something that cannot be interrupted.
   (C) His research through Chinese fictions comes from professor's influence.
   (D) His epiphany comes from reading other book.

3. Listen again to part of the conversation. Then answer the question.
   (A) Cards are the control of one's destiny.
   (B) No one can be in the advantageous position all the

time

(C) Things will be smoother if one holds all the cards.

(D) Card holders possess extremely powerful ability.

4. According to the conservation, what is untrue about the seventy-two arts of Shaolin?

(A) Da Mo is the only person known to have mastered the seventy-two arts of Shaolin.

(B) Jiumozhi beguiles others by using other kong fu skills.

(C) Jiumozhi might fool others, but his tactic is transparent to Xu Zhu.

(D) The abbot is defeated by Xu Zhu during the flight.

5. What will the professor probably do next?

(A) Start reading students' report on Mozart and athletes

(B) Make sure the student sticks to what he's been working on.

(C) Take a walk because he has been sitting for a long time

(D) Finish the cheese bagel

▶▶ 新托福聽力解析

1. 這題詢問的是學生為何拜訪教授。要注意文章開頭跟文章結尾的對話，還有細節性的干擾選項，其實最主要的原因是跟教授討論他近期看過的其他書籍，所以答案為選項 **D**。

2. 這題是詢問可以推測出學生的什麼，也是要注意聽力中的細節。對話中有出現 **it hit me** 等可以得知學生是從閱讀其他書籍後有了這樣的頓悟，所以答案為選項 **D**。

3. 這題是詢問教授說某句話的意涵比較需要推測能力。但可以從 **no one holds all the cards** 字面上去理解，沒有人可以總是占上風的，對應選項 **B** 的敘述，沒有人總是處於有利的位置。

4. 這題詢問聽力訊息中的敘述何者為非。其實要多注意功夫跟鳩摩智習武等的訊息。可參考學習法中記筆記列出的表格，其實訊息有記到這題其實不難回答，另外要注意的是選項 **D**，此訊息在段落中未提及，要特別注意。

5. 這題是考教授接下來可能做什麼，其實最有可能的是完成未吃完的午餐，故答案為選項 **D**。

$$\text{答案：} 1.\ D\ 2.\ D\ 3.\ B\ 4.\ D\ 5.\ D$$

影子跟讀練習 MP3 028

做完題目後，除了對答案知道錯的部分在哪外，更重要的是要修正自己聽力根本的問題，即聽力理解力和聽力專注力，聽力專注力的修正能逐步強化本身的聽力實力，所以現在請根據聽力內容「逐個段落」、「數個段落」或「整篇」進行跟讀練習，提升在實際考場時專注聽完每個訊息、定位出關鍵考點和搭配筆記回答完所有題目。Go!

| Student |

Sorry to interrupt. It seems that you're right in the middle of something.

| 學生 |

抱歉打斷你...似乎你正有點事要忙。

| Professor |

Don't worry about it. If you mean the cheese bagel I just had a bite of, it can certainly be finished it in a minute or two. So what's up? And please have a seat…

| 教授 |

別擔心。如果你指的是我才剛咬一口的起司貝果的話，我確實在一到兩分鐘能完成的事，所以有什麼事呢？請坐。

字彙輔助

1. interrupt 干擾　　2. in the middle of something 有事
3. bagel 貝果　　　　4. finish 完成

| **Student** |

I was just reading this book about the deliberate practice⋯ then it hit me⋯Are Jiumozhi's (鳩摩智) kong fu skills a result of deliberate practice?

| **學生** |

我閱讀了一本關於刻意練習的書然後突然想到鳩摩智的功夫技能也是刻意練習的結果嗎？

| **Professor** |

I can't believe you are into Chinese fiction, and the answer is YES. I'm feeling a little disappointed about several books, not mentioning something as intriguing as this. They all want to focus on their studies on well-known athletes.

| **教授** |

我不敢相信你也喜歡中國小說呢，而答案是「是的」。我對於幾本書感到有點失望，都沒提到像是像這個題材一樣有趣的。他們都只想要將他們的研究重點放在知名的運動員身上。

字彙輔助

1 deliberate 故意的、刻意的　2 practice 練習

3 result 結果　4 well-known 知名的

| Student |

Jiumozhi claims that he masters seventy-two arts of Shaolin, which is unlikely because Da Mo is the only person who's been known to master seventy-two arts of Shaolin.

| 學生 |

鳩摩智宣稱他精通了少林 72 絕技…這幾乎不可能因為達摩祖師是唯一一個已知精通少林 72 絕技的人。

| Professor |

That's correct. A later account by an abbot reveals that he couldn't have achieved such a feat. People are as perplexed as the abbot about what Jiumozhi uses at Shaolin temple is actually the seventy-two arts of Shaolin. There must be something that they all fail to notice. But you know what, you can't fool everyone. Sometimes no one holds all the cards. It's just not how things go. His fight with Xu Zhu says a lot about that.

| 教授 |

確實如此。後來聽一個方丈的敘述，接露出他不可能達成這樣

255

的成就。人們跟方丈同樣感到困惑的是，鳩摩智在少林寺使用的武功確實是少林 72 絕技。這中間一定有些東西是他們都未能察覺到的部分。但是你知道嗎？…你無法蒙騙所有人。有時候沒人可以總是佔盡優勢，事情的發展不會是這樣的。他與虛竹的戰鬥就説明了一切。

字彙輔助

1. master 精通
2. account 敘述
3. perplexed 困惑的
4. notice 注意到

| Student |

That's right. They both know the Unseen Power. Clearly Jiumozhi memorizes the seventy-two arts of Shaolin. He watches how other people perform the seventy-two arts of Shaolin. He emulates how they perform them. Thus creating a false impression that he is performing the seventy-two arts of Shaolin but in fact he is using the Unseen Power to create the illusions. Only the person who studies the Unseen Power knows the difference…

| 學生 |

確實如此。他們都知道小無相公。顯然鳩摩智背誦少林 72 絕技他觀察其他人如何運行少林 72 絕技。他仿效他們如何運行。因此造成一個假象，就是他使用的武功像是少林 72 絕技但是實際上他是使用小無相公製造幻覺。只有懂得小無相公的人知道之間的差異。

字彙輔助

1 memorize 記住　　　2 watch 觀看
3 false 錯誤的　　　　4 impression 印象
5 illusion 幻覺

| Professor |

It's clearly a deliberate practice. Using Unseen Power to do a deliberate practice of the seventy-two arts of Shaolin and other kong fu skills. It's just a weird way to do a deliberate practice.

| 教授 |

這顯然是刻意練習。使用小無相公去刻意練習少林 72 絕技和其他功夫技能。這是用奇怪的方式去做刻意練習。

| Student |

Perhaps I should write the mid-term paper about the deliberate practice by using fictional characters in those works of fiction. I'll do a thorough research. I promise.

| 學生 |

或許我應該要在期中報告寫份關於刻意練習。但是是使用那些小説中虛構的人物角色...跟你保證...我會做詳盡的研究。

字彙輔助

1 weird 奇怪的　　　　2 perhaps 或許
3 mid-term 期中的　　　4 fictional 虛構的

| Professor |

That sounds intriguing. I'm kind of tired from reading about the same thing. Students write about Mozart and athletes. I'm sure that will do you good too, doing something unusual and different.

| 教授 |

聽起來蠻有趣的。我有點厭倦閱讀同樣的東西了。學生都寫關於莫札特和運動員。我相信這對你蠻好的，做些不尋常且與眾不同的研究。

字彙輔助

1. intriguing 引起興趣的
2. Mozart 莫札特
3. unusual 不尋常的
4. different 不同的

| Student |

What can I say, taking the road less traveled by.

| 學生 |

我還能說什麼呢。走人煙罕至的道路。

| Professor |

Now if you don't mind I have a very important thing to turn to…(staring…)

| 教授 |

如果你不介意的話，我有更重要的是要做了。（注視...）

| Student |

Right, your lunch! Seems it's been sitting there for a long time.

| 學生 |

對吼，你的午餐！似乎已經躺在那很久了。

| Professor |

ha ha

| 教授 |

哈哈。

字彙輔助

1 don't mind 不介意
2 staring 注視
3 lunch 午餐
4 seem 似乎

▶▶ 試題聽力原文

1. Why does the student visit the professor?
2. What can be inferred about the student?
3. Listen again to part of the conversation. Then answer the question.

   Professor: A later account by an abbot reveals that he couldn't have achieved such a feat…but people are as perplexed as the abbot about what Jiumozhi uses at Shaolin temple is actually the seventy-two arts of Shaolin. There must be something that they all fail to notice. But you know what…You can't fool everyone… Sometimes **no one holds all the cards**…it's just not how things go.

   What does the professor imply when he says "**no one holds all the cards**"?
4. According to the conservation, what is untrue about the seventy-two arts of Shaolin?
5. What will the professor probably do next?

▶▶ 記筆記與聽力訊息

| Instruction | MP3 028

　　新托福聽力與其他聽力測驗不同，可以於聽力的紙上記筆記，除了寫試題外，更重要的一點是訓練自己能夠將聽完一段訊息後，將重要的聽力訊息都記到。也可以將自己聽到跟記到的重點訊息跟試題做比對，因為試題考的就是長對話跟講座中出現的重點，能修正自己篩選聽力訊息重點的能力。

| 聽力重點 |

- 記筆記有很多方式，包含符號跟自己習慣的縮寫字等等，可以找出最適合自己的模式，一定要自己重聽音檔作練習數次。

- 這篇是關於校園類話題但有融入武俠人物應用到心理學中的研究和 peak 中提到的刻意練習，**重點可以放在與教授間的討論還有鳩摩智和其他人的關係。**

▶▶ 參考筆記

Main idea ❶ Jiumozhi's kong fu skills, a result of deliberate practice (correct)	
Main idea ❷ seventy-two arts of Shaolin	
master	Da Mo/only person
claim/emulate	Jiumozhi (by using the Unseen Power)
beguiled/ perplexed	abbot and others
See through	Xu Zhu
Main idea ❸ Using Unseen Power to do a deliberate practice of the seventy-two arts of Shaolin and other kong fu skills/unusual	
student	write the mid-term paper about the deliberate practice···but by using fictional characters in those fictions
professor	Intriguing/tired of reading examples from Mozart and athletes

Note

| Instruction | MP3 028

　　現在請再聽一次音檔，並做下列的測驗，檢視自己能否完成此填空測驗和強化自己聽力能力和拼字能力，降低並修正自己漏聽到聽力訊息的機會，大幅提升應考實力。

1. The c_____ b_____ can be finished in a minute or two according to the professor.

2. The professor is surprised to find that the student is intrigued about C_____ f_____.

3. The professor feels disappointed at studies focusing on w_____ a_____.

4. It's h_____ u_____ for someone like Jiumozhi to master seventy-two arts of Shaolin, since Da Mo is the only person who's been known to master seventy-two arts of Shaolin.

5. People are as p_____ as the a_____ about what Jiumozhi uses at Shaolin temple is actually the seventy-two arts of Shaolin.

6. By o_____ how others p_____ the seventy-two arts of Shaolin, he fools others.

7. He m_____ others so that people will have a f_____ ___ i_____ that he actually masters it.

8. Only the person who studies the Unseen Power knows the difference and won't be fooled by the i_____ created by Jiumozhi.

9. He uses the Unseen Power to do a d_____ p_____ of the seventy-two arts of Shaolin and other kong fu skills.

10. The student g_____ that he will do a t_____ r_____ when he is working on the mid-term paper.

11. The professor finds his idea i_____ and he always expects students to do something n_____ and different.

12. Mozart and athletes are quite c_____ in students' writing.

| 答案 |
1. cheese, bagel
2. Chinese, fiction
3. well-known, athletes
4. highly, unlikely
5. perplexed, abbot
6. observing, perform

7. mimics, false, impressions
8. illusions
9. deliberate, practice
10. guarantees, thorough, research
11. intriguing, novel
12. common

▶▶ 摘要能力

| Instruction | MP3 028

　　除了閱讀測驗外，其實培養能在聽完一大段訊息後，以口述講述剛才聽到的聽力訊息是學習語言和表達很重要的一件事，讓自己養成具備這樣的能力，除了能在聽力測驗中獲取高分外，也能在新托福寫作跟口說的整合題型上大有斬獲喔！所以快來練習，除了書中提供的參考答案外，自己可以試著重新聽過音檔一遍後，摘要出英文訊息並朗讀出來。

Note

▶▶ 參考答案

The student has come up with something unusual. A further look into it unmasks the fact the Jiumozhi's kong fu skills are a result of deliberate practice. From what he self-proclaims that he masters seventy-two arts of Shaolin, there must be something that others and the abbot have failed to notice. Doing a little thinking can reveal the fact that he uses the Unseen Power to emulates how others perform them and create the illusions. Deep down he knows nothing about seventy-two arts of Shaolin. This is an unusual example of doing a deliberate practice. The student intends to write a mid-term paper about the deliberate practice by using fictional characters in in those works of fiction, and the professor deems it as intriguing since other students will write expected responses, such as Mozart and athletes.

▶▶ **聽力試題** MP3 029

1. Why does the student visit the professor?
    (A) To show how she loves the professor's history course
    (B) To discuss which dress she should be wearing for the contest
    (C) To get the compliment from the professor
    (D) To discuss that she can't get over the lose

2. What are the speakers mainly discussing?
    (A) How to win the beauty pageant
    (B) How to be as successful as Warren Buffet
    (C) The right mindset after losing
    (D) How to be a famous spokesperson

3. Why does the professor mention Warren Buffet?
    (A) To show that he was not that outstanding
    (B) To show that she can still go to Harvard after losing the pageant
    (C) To show that obsessions to Harvard can hurt her in some ways
    (D) To share a story that the student can relate

4. Listen again to part of the conversation. Then answer the question.
   (A) She wants the student to grab the chance.
   (B) She wants the student to be more confident about herself.
   (C) She wants the student to be well-prepared.
   (D) She is afraid that the student will be disqualified.

5. Listen again to part of the conversation. Then answer the question.
   (A) Things can sometimes be disastrous.
   (B) Things can't work out well all the time.
   (C) Things don't work out can be a blessing in disguise.
   (D) The rest of the things can work well, if something bad happens first.

1. 這題詢問的是學生為何拜訪教授，要注意一些對話干擾訊息，其實最終的目的是選項 D，To discuss that she can't get over the lose，學生其實因為選美比賽落選無法克服這個挫敗而去找教授。

2. 這題是詢問說話者主要討論的是什麼，也要注意干擾選項，主要並非是如何贏選美比賽或是多成功，而是有正確的心態，故答案為選項 C。

3. 這題是詢問為什麼教授提到股神巴菲特，其實主要是教授想要藉由分享一則故事讓學生能夠 relate，進而轉換心情，得知失敗並非什麼大事，成功者其實也都有過許多不為人知的挫折，故答案為選項 D。

4. 這題詢問教授為什麼會講該段話，I wouldn't even qualify to be in such a contest，其實主要是想要藉由貶低自己跟分享自己經驗，讓學生知道自己其實已經表現很好了，教授自己本身都沒資格參加，故答案為選項 B。

5. 這題詢問教授為什麼會講該段話，things that seem disastrous at the time usually do work out for the best，其實主要是要表明選項 C 的意思，故答案為選項 C。

··

答案：1. D 2. C 3. D 4. B 5. C

影子跟讀練習 MP3 029

做完題目後，除了對答案知道錯的部分在哪外，更重要的是要修正自己聽力根本的問題，即聽力理解力和聽力專注力，聽力專注力的修正能逐步強化本身的聽力實力，所以現在請根據聽力內容「逐個段落」、「數個段落」或「整篇」進行跟讀練習，提升在實際考場時專注聽完每個訊息、定位出關鍵考點和搭配筆記回答完所有題目。Go!

| Professor |

Long time no see. A year after you took my history course. You look lovely today.

| 教授 |

嗨！在修我歷史課的一年後，好久不見了。你今天看起來很美。

| Student |

I came to see you about something.

| 學生 |

我來找你是因為有些事。

| Professor |

Wow! You're still wearing those skirts? It's just too

attractive, you know. Even though I'm a female, I just think you're born with this. I can't take my eyes off you.

| 教授 |

哇！你仍穿著那些裙子？真的太吸引人了！你知道即使我是女性，我總覺得這是你與生俱來的，我無法將目光從你身上移開。

| **Student** |

Thanks! I'll take that as a compliment.

| 學生 |

謝謝！我會把這個當成是稱讚。

字彙輔助

1 history 歷史　　　　　2 attractive 有吸引力的
3 female 女性　　　　　4 compliment 稱讚

| **Professor** |

What's wrong? You look like you're are upset.

| 教授 |

發生什麼事了嗎？你看起來相當心煩意亂。

| **Student** |

Thanks…that kind of cheers me up a bit…I just have this feeling that my life is over…These lingering feelings just won't go away…for a while…

｜學生｜

謝謝…這玩笑真的讓我開心了些…我只是有種感覺就是我的人生完了…這種感覺一直縈繞在心頭…有好一會兒都揮之不去…。

｜Professor｜

What happened?

｜教授｜

發生什麼事了？

｜Student｜

Ever since I lost the beauty pageant, I feel like my life is over.

｜學生｜

自從我參加選美比賽落選後，我就覺得我的人生完了。

字彙輔助

1. upset 心煩意亂的
2. lingering 縈繞的
3. feelings 感覺
4. beauty pageant 選美比賽

｜Professor｜

Oh, that! I'm sure you've learned a lot through the whole preparation process.

| 教授 |

噢，那個啊！我相信在這整個準備過程中你有學到了很多東西。

Student

Yes. But I'm disappointed with myself. I did not even make it into top twenty.

| 學生 |

是沒錯！但是我對自己感到很失望。我甚至沒有進到前 **20** 強。

Professor

Just don't feel that way. You're beautiful. You possess the rare quality of beauty. You should feel grateful for that. Plus it's just a competition. Back in the day, I wouldn't even qualify to be in such a contest.

| 教授 |

別這樣想！妳很漂亮！你擁有著很罕見的特質和美貌。你應該要對此感到感恩。再說這只是場比賽。回想到過去，我根本沒有資格參加這樣的比賽。

Student

Seriously?

| 學生 |

真的嗎？

字彙輔助

1. process 過程
2. possessing 持有
3. quality 品質
4. competition 競爭

| Professor |

We all have a moment of dread. It's ok. Let me share a story with you. It's not a story about me. It's about Warren Buffett. He once had this fixation on going to Harvard. It's like every high school kids' dream of going to the Ivy League, and a ten-hour train ride to Chicago turns out to be nothing.

| 教授 |

我們都有感到懼怕的時刻。這是正常的。讓我跟你分享一個故事。但故事不是關於我就是了。這是關於股神巴菲特的故事。他曾經有著要進哈佛就讀的執著，就像是每個高中生的夢想，想著要進常春藤盟校就讀。但是 10 小時前往芝加哥的火車路途卻演變成什麼都沒有。

| Student |

He failed?

| 學生 |

他失敗了嗎？

| Professor |

He was rejected right on the spot.

| 教授 |

他當場被拒絕了。

| **Student** |

No way! How come?

| 學生 |

不可能！怎麼會呢？

字彙輔助

1 moment 時刻

2 dread 懼怕

3 fixation 固定、異常迷戀

4 Ivy League 常春藤盟校

| **Professor** |

It's true. It's not that he is not that great. He was disappointed just like you're now. I'm sure you're feeling a bit about letting other people down. His father had such high hopes for him, but that did not stop him from keeping on moving forward. Look at him now! What he said was **"Things that seem disastrous at the time usually do work out for the best."** I'm sure things are going to turn out to be fine for you. We all have a fixation on something, but that doesn't mean it works the best for us. A lot of successful people don't win a damn contest, but they are the most well-known spokespersons representing the famous cosmetics lines.

| 教授 |

這是真的。這並不是說他不優秀，但是他也是像你現在一樣感到失望。我相信你也覺得讓其他人失望了。他的父親也對他有著很高的期望，但是這不能停止他向前邁進。看他現在就知道了。而他說的是「事情在當下看起來似乎糟透了，但是通常最後結果都適得其所」所以我相信事情最後發展對你來說也都會是好的。我們都會執著某些事。但是這不代表著那件事對我們來說會是最好的。而且很多成功的人都沒贏那該死的比賽，但是他們都成了知名的代言人，代表知名的化妝品系列。

| **Student** |

Right! I'm feeling a bit better now. Thank you for your time.

| 學生 |

確實如此。我現在覺得好多了。謝謝你的時間。

| **Professor** |

Just don't ever let people who care about you feel worried…ok?

| 教授 |

別讓在乎你的人感到擔心好嗎？

| **Student** |

I promise.

| 學生 |

我保證。

---

1 disappoint 失望　　　2 disastrous 災難性的

3 successful 成功的　　　4 spokesperson 代言人

▶▶▶ 試題聽力原文

1. Why does the student visit the professor?

2. What are the speakers mainly discussing?

3. Why does the professor mention Warren Buffet?

4. Listen again to part of the conversation. Then answer the question.
   Professor: just don't feel that way··· you're beautiful··· you possess the rare quality of beauty··· you should feel grateful for that··· plus it's just a competition··· and back in the day··· I wouldn't even qualify to be in such a···

   What does the professor mean when she says this? I wouldn't even qualify to be in such a···

5. Listen again to part of the conversation. Then answer the question.
   Professor: I'm sure you're feeling a bit about letting other people down, too···his father had such high hopes for him···but that does not stop him from keeping on moving forward··· and look at him now···what he said was "things that seem disastrous at the time usually do work out for the best"···so I'm sure things are going to

turn out to be fine at you, too. We all have a fixation on something…but that doesn't mean it works best to us…

What does the professor mean when she says this? "things that seem disastrous at the time usually do work out for the best"…

▶▶ 記筆記與聽力訊息

| Instruction | MP3 029

　　新托福聽力與其他聽力測驗不同，可以於聽力的紙上記筆記，除了寫試題外，更重要的一點是訓練自己能夠將聽完一段訊息後，將重要的聽力訊息都記到。也可以將自己聽到跟記到的重點訊息跟試題做比對，因為試題考的就是長對話跟講座中出現的重點，能修正自己篩選聽力訊息重點的能力。

| 聽力重點 |

- 記筆記有很多方式，包含符號跟自己習慣的縮寫字等等，可以找出最適合自己的模式，一定要自己重聽音檔作練習數次。
- 這篇是關於校園類話題但有提到選美比賽和巴菲特的小故事，**要注意推測類的考題和應用。**

Note

Main idea ❶ Lingering feelings of not being able to make to the top 20 of the beauty pageant contest make the student depressed.

professor ❶ saying something assuring and encouraging
❷ share the story of Warren Buffett for the student to relate
● rejected by Harvard
● **"things that seem disastrous at the time usually do work out for the best"**

Main idea ❷ Winning a contest has nothing to do with future success

Note

▶▶▶ 填空測驗

| Instruction | MP3 029

現在請再聽一次音檔，並做下列的測驗，檢視自己能否完成此填空測驗和強化自己聽力能力和拼字能力，降低並修正自己漏聽到聽力訊息的機會，大幅提升英考實力。

1. The professor thinks the student is too a_____ to wear s_____.

2. The student takes the professor's praise as a c_____.

3. L_____ feelings of failing at something is the reason the student is upset.

4. The professor believes that she must have learned something through the whole p_____ process.

5. The student possesses the r_____ quality of b_____.

6. The professor would not even q_____ for attending in a c_____ like the beauty pageant.

7. Warren Buffett once had this f_____ of going to Harvard, but was r_____ right on the scene.

8. His father had a high h_____ for him.

9. What he said was "things that seem d_____ at the time usually do work out for the best".

10. Many people don't win the contest, but they are s_____.

11. S_____ of the cosmetic lines don't win a damn contest.

| 答案 |
1. attractive, skirts
2. compliment
3. Lingering
4. Preparation
5. rare, beauty
6. qualify, contest
7. fixation, rejected
8. hope
9. disastrous
10. successful
11. Spokespersons

▶▶ 摘要能力

| Instruction | MP3 029

　　除了閱讀測驗外，其實培養能在聽完一大段訊息後，以口述講述剛才聽到的聽力訊息是學習語言和表達很重要的一件事，讓自己養成具備這樣的能力，除了能在聽力測驗中獲取高分外，也能在新托福寫作跟口說的整合題型上大有斬獲喔！所以快來練習，除了書中提供的參考答案外，自己可以試著重新聽過音檔一遍後，摘要出英文訊息並朗讀出來。

▶▶ 參考答案

　　Lingering feelings of not being able to make to the top 20 of the beauty pageant contest make the student depressed. The professor encourages her by guiding her and complimenting her, and making her realize people all have a moment of dread sometimes. She then shares the story of the Warren Buffett with the student. Buffet's failure of going to the Harvard turns out to be a blessing in disguise. He is now a successful businessman and no one would ever care that he was once rejected on the spot. They share the same feelings of letting others down. What Buffet said was "things that seem disastrous at the time usually do work out for the best." After hearing the inspiring story, the student feels a lot better.

3 ▶▶ 求職與學歷：難道這就是耶魯大學學歷的價值！？

▶▶ **聽力試題** (MP3 030)

1. Why does the student visit the professor?
   (A) To let the professor know how bad the economy is out there.
   (B) To inquire how to get a journalist position.
   (C) To inquire how to maintain good appearance.
   (D) To vent that he can't find a job.

2. What can be inferred about the student?
   (A) He wants to be as good-looking as Cooper
   (B) He wants to be a serious journalist
   (C) He wants to apply for the entry-level position job at ABC as well
   (D) He laments the value of a Yale education

3. Listen to part of the lecture and answer the question
   (A) Because the professor wants him to be daring and different.
   (B) Because the professor thinks he picks the wrong part to read.
   (C) Because other parts are what he will be benefited

from.

(D) Because the student is the one who needs constant guidance and unfocused.

4. Listen to part of the lecture and answer the question

(A) To show only perfect candidates can get the full-time job.

(B) To demonstrate sometimes it's one of the ways to get the desired full-time position.

(C) To elucidate working part-time can be so beneficial for one's career.

(D) To further explain people working at home are more trustworthy than employees working in the office.

5. What will the student probably do next?

(A) Schedule the interview for Studio 598

(B) Take the summer internship job at Studio 555

(C) Prepare for the scheduled interview

(D) Take the part-time job first

▶▶ 新托福聽力解析

1. 這題詢問的是學生為何拜訪教授，要注意文章開頭跟文章結尾的對話，還有細節性的干擾選項，其實最主要的原因是跟教授聊近況表示自己尚未找到工作，要注意 vent 這個字，在教科書或單字書不常見，但在生活口語中很常用，表示宣洩一個狀況，這題答案為選項 D。

2. 這題是詢問可以推測出學生的什麼，也是要注意聽力中的細節，對話中其實清楚表明 he laments the value of a Yale education，所以答案為選項 D。

3. 這題是詢問教授說某句話的意涵，比較需要推測能力，教授其實想要學生不要只看到 Cooper 寫的抱怨的話，而是抱怨後 cooper 又下了多少努力才拿到全職工作，所以才說了這句話，故答案為選項 C。

4. 這題是詢問教授說某句話的意涵，比較需要推測能力，教授其實也是想向學生指出另一件事，答案為選項 B，這也是大家常忽略的部分，因為有時候全職工作是這樣來的，一次性就要找到夢幻工作其實蠻難。

5. 這題是考學生接下來可能做什麼，根據文意其實是準備教授替他安排的面試機會，故答案為選項 C。

....

答案：1. D 2. D 3. C 4. B 5. C

影子跟讀練習  MP3 030

做完題目後，除了對答案知道錯的部分在哪外，更重要的是要修正自己聽力根本的問題，即聽力理解力和聽力專注力，聽力專注力的修正能逐步強化本身的聽力實力，所以現在請根據聽力內容「逐個段落」、「數個段落」或「整篇」進行跟讀練習，提升在實際考場時專注聽完每個訊息、定位出關鍵考點和搭配筆記回答完所有題目。Go!

| Professor |

A year after graduation, how's everything going?

| 教授 |

畢業一年後，一切都還好嗎？

| Student |

I just can't seem to find the job I want. I just can't help but lament something like "**such is the value of a Yale education**"

| 學生 |

我就是似乎沒辦法找到我想要的工作。我就是不得不感嘆一些像是「就是耶魯大學學歷的價值」的話。

| **Professor** |

What?

| **教授** |

什麼？

| **Student** |

I'm like the journalist Anderson Cooper. Only he is better looking than I am.

| **學生** |

我就像是新聞記者安德生‧庫柏只是他比我好看很多。

字彙輔助

1. graduation 畢業
2. lament 感嘆
3. Yale 耶魯
4. journalist 新聞記者

| **Student** |

I read somewhere that he once applied for an entry-level job at ABC. It's like kind of the job that does not require a fancy degree as Ivy Leagues, but he couldn't get the interview. I'm feeling like I'm stuck.

| **學生** |

我從有個地方讀到的，他曾應徵 ABC 廣播公司的基層工作。像這樣的工作根本不用像是需要到常春藤盟校這樣的夢幻學歷但是他根

本無法獲得面試機會...我覺得我被困住了。

| Professor |

Did you finish the whole reading?

| 教授 |

你有讀完全部嗎？

| Student |

He sent the application to several other similar companies, but he couldn't get a reply there, either.

| 學生 |

他寄了其他應徵函到同性質的幾間公司。但是他也沒有獲得任何回覆。

字彙輔助

1 apply 申請
3 fancy 夢幻的

2 entry-level 基層的
4 interview 面試

......

| Professor |

What you should be focusing on is other things he wrote about like he is a big believer of creating your opportunity. It's true that we create our own luck. We should always do that. Acting passively the whole time still won't change things. Be proactive.

教授

你應該要將重點放在他所寫的其他事上面，像是他是深信人是要自己為自己創造機會的。這是真的。我們自身的運氣是要我們自己創造的。我們應該要總是這樣做。總是表現得很被動並不能改變事情，要積極主動。

Student

That's correct! I should be more proactive and should focus a little bit more on how to get my foot in the door.…doing anything…just to get to that…

學生

確實如此...我應該要更積極主動而且應該要把重點放在如何拿到門票...做任何事...就是做到就是了...

字彙輔助

1 focus 專注在   **2** create 創造

3 passively 被動地   **4** change 改變

Professor

He has to sacrifice a lot of things to get hired as a full-time correspondent. For some reasons, I just don't think employers are going to hire someone to work full time since there's a risk involved. Sometimes people working part-time at home eventually earn the trust to work full-time if there is a new position opening up. Sometimes there is no way that you can get the job if no one leaves, and when the opportunity presents itself, you have to be ready. Otherwise, it will just slip away. For example, if a friend of mine is looking for a person to work at Studio 598. Are you ready for the job?

| 教授 |

他必須要犧牲很多事情才能獲得雇用為全職的特派員工作...某些原因，我想雇主不太可能會去雇用全職員工...因為當中涉及到了風險...有時候人們在家做兼職而最終卻贏得了信任而獲取了全職工作...如果有新的職缺出現...有時候你不可能得到工作因為沒人離職...而且當機會出現時...你必須要準備好...否則...機會就會溜走了...例如，如果我的一位朋友正要找一位在 598 工作室的工作者...你覺覺得自己準備好了嗎？

| **Student** |

What are the requirements for that job? I think I'm ready. I mean I guess I'm ready.

| 學生 |

那份工作的條件是什麼呢？我認為我準備好了。我指的是我想我準備好了。

| **Professor** |

You guess? You should feel certain about that.

你想？你應該要很確定才是。

| **Student** |

I once had a summer job. Although it was part-time, it was at Studio 555.

| 學生 |

我曾有份暑期的工作…儘管是兼職的…但是是在工作室 555。

| **Professor** |

And?

| 教授 |

然後呢？

字彙輔助

| 1 | sacrifice 犧牲 | 2 | employer 雇主 |
| 3 | position 職位 | 4 | requirement 條件 |

| **Student** |

Perhaps that could be the thing to impress them if I had an interview with them. I totally forgot to write that on my resume.

| 學生 |

或許這可以是能打動他們的事，如果我有與他們面試的機會。我全然忘記要把這個寫在我的履歷上面了。

| **Professor** |

I'm going to make a call to them and schedule an interview. You will have a week to prepare your resume andwhat you're gonna say.

| 教授 |

我去打個電話給他們，然後安排面試。你會有一週的時間可以準備你的履歷及你要說些什麼。可以嗎？

| **Student** |

Thank you! I can't believe it. It's like a dream come true. At least I have a chance to meet with them. I won't let you down. Thanks.

| 學生 |

謝謝你。我不敢相信這就對我來說就像是夢想成真一樣。至少我有機會能見到他們。我不會讓你失望的。謝謝。

字彙輔助

1. resume 履歷
2. schedule 安排
3. prepare 準備
4. chance 機會

1. Why does the student visit the professor?
2. What can be inferred about the student?
3. Listen to part of the lecture and answer the question
   Professor: What you should be focusing on is other things he wrote, like he is a big believer of creating your opportunity. It's true that we create our own luck. We should always do that. Acting passively the whole time still won't change things. Be proactive!

   Why does the professor say "What you should be focusing on is other things he wrote"?
4. Listen to part of the lecture and answer the question
   Professor: He has to sacrifice a lot of things to get hired as a full-time correspondent. For some reasons, I just don't think employers are going to hire someone to work full time since there's a risk involved. Sometimes people working part-time at home eventually earn the trust to work full-time. If there is a new position opening up, sometimes there is no way that you can get the job if no one leaves.

   Why does the professor say "I just don't think employers are going to hire someone to work full time since there's a risk involved. Sometimes people working part-time at home eventually earn the trust to work full-time."

5. What will the student probably do next?

Note

▶▶▶ 記筆記與聽力訊息

　　新托福聽力與其他聽力測驗不同，可以於聽力的紙上記筆記，除了寫試題外，更重要的一點是訓練自己能夠將聽完一段訊息後，將重要的聽力訊息都記到。也可以將自己聽到跟記到的重點訊息跟試題做比對，因為試題考的就是長對話跟講座中出現的重點，能修正自己篩選聽力訊息重點的能力。

| 聽力重點 |

- 記筆記有很多方式，包含符號跟自己習慣的縮寫字等等，可以找出最適合自己的模式，一定要自己重聽音檔作練習數次。
- 這篇是關於校園類話題有提到價值觀和學歷的部分，**教授給的建議是主要的考點。**

▶▶ **參考筆記**

Main idea ❶ uncertain for the future	
statement	**such is the value of a Yale education**/ Anderson Cooper+student
student	cooper couldn't get the reply
professor	should be focusing on things that will help him ● a big believer of creating your opportunity/ create our own luck ● proactive ● sacrifices that Cooper made to get the full-time position
Other ways	by working part-time at home
professor	● want him to be well-prepared ● set up the interview for him
student	forgot the list of the part-time work experience on a resume

▶▶ 填空測驗

| **Instruction** | MP3 030

現在請再聽一次音檔，並做下列的測驗，檢視自己能否完成此填空測驗和強化自己聽力能力和拼字能力，降低並修正自己漏聽到聽力訊息的機會，大幅提升英考實力。

1. A year after graduation, the student is still j_____ and thinks Y_____ education is of no use when it comes to finding a job.

2. The student mentions about Anderson Cooper, a j_____ ____, who is more g_____ than himself.

3. He once applied for an e_____ job at ABC, but he couldn't get the i_____.

4. He didn't get the r_____ even though he sent _____ ____ to other similar companies.

5. The professor suggests him to shift his focus into something useful. The journalist is a big b_____ who believes that people should create the opportunity for themselves.

6. The student should be more p_____.

7. Before getting h_____ as a full-time c_____, the journalist sacrifices lots of things to make that happen.

8. It's possible to eventually work f_____, if you earn the t_____ by working part-time.

9. For the unready one, the opportunity will s_____ away.

10. The student had a previous working experience at Studio 555, but it's p_____.

11. The student is idiotic by not writing the important thing on his r_____.

12. The student will have a week to prepare for the s_____ interview.

| 答案 |

1. jobless, Yale
2. journalist, good-looking
3. entry-level, interview
4. reply, applications
5. believer
6. proactive
7. hired, correspondent
8. full-time, trust

影子跟讀

學術場景

校園場景

9. slip
10. part-time
11. resume
12. scheduled

▶▶ 摘要能力

| Instruction | MP3 030

　　除了閱讀測驗外，其實培養能在聽完一大段訊息後，以口述講述剛才聽到的聽力訊息是學習語言和表達很重要的一件事，讓自己養成具備這樣的能力，除了能在聽力測驗中獲取高分外，也能在新托福寫作跟口說的整合題型上大有斬獲喔！所以快來練習，除了書中提供的參考答案外，自己可以試著重新聽過音檔一遍後，摘要出英文訊息並朗讀出來。

Note

▶▶▶ 參考答案

A year after graduation, the student is still jobless, pretty uncertain about his future. He laments what Anderson Cooper one said "such is the value of a Yale education". Cooper didn't get the reply from ABC and similar companies. But the professor reminds the student of focusing on things that will help him to figure out the problem. Cooper has made lots of sacrifice to get the full-time job as a journalist. Staying proactive and creating one's own luck are what the student should do. It's quite possible that until someone leaves, there is no new recruitment, and sometimes you can eventually get the full-time job by working part-time at first. The professor lets him know that he should be well-prepared and she sets up the interview for the student.

▶▶ **聽力試題** MP3 031

1. Why does the student visit the professor?
    (A) Because he wants to ask something about the mid-term paper
    (B) Because he wants the professor to be hard on him
    (C) Because he is worried about his future
    (D) Because he wants to be an Ivy League student

2. Listen again to part of the conversation. Then answer the question.
    (A) Having a fancy degree matters to make things smooth.
    (B) One should be free from roughness, if one possesses a prestigious degree.
    (C) Having a fancy degree increases the probability of the smooth sailing.
    (D) Learning how to sail can make things smoothness.

3. Listen again to part of the conversation. Then answer the question.
    (A) One really needs a fancy degree.

(B) Traveling a more gilded path is very important.

(C) People with prestigious degrees can end up in having the same result as someone who does not.

(D) She wants to travel a more gilded path, too.

4. Listen again to part of the conversation. Then answer the question.

(A) How you are perceived in the school is not the same as how you are viewed in the workplace.

(B) The wind will help you through when you are outside the school.

(C) The wind matters especially in the very beginning.

(D) With fancy degrees, you can walk like everyone beneath you.

5. What will the student probably do next?

(A) Find a paid summer internship job

(B) Head to the next class

(C) Answer the vibrated phone

(D) Learn something theory-based

▶▶ 新托福聽力解析

1. 這題詢問的是學生為何拜訪教授，要注意一些對話干擾訊息，其實最終的目的是選項 C，學生其實擔憂自己的未來，所以才去找教授聊聊。

2. 這題是詢問為什麼學生要說 like with this degree…it should be like smooth sailing，其實是 B 選項的同義轉換，故答案為選項 B，擁有好學歷不代表會一帆風順。

3. 這題是詢問為什麼教授提到 Traveling a more gilded path, she'd arrived at the very same destination，其實主要是選項 C，People with prestigious degrees can end up in having the same result as someone who does not 的同義表達，故答案為選項 C。

4. 這題詢問教授為什麼會講該段話，but it's only in the school…like a wind blowing on your forehead…you feel so great…but in reality you still have to start somewhere from the very beginning，其實主要是想表明 how you are perceived in the school is not the same as how you are viewed in the workplace，在學校的表現和職場是不可相提並論的，故答案為選項 A。

5. 這題詢問學生接下來會做什麼，故答案為選項 B。

答案：1. C 2. B 3. C 4. A 5. B

影子跟讀練習 MP3 031

做完題目後，除了對答案知道錯的部分在哪外，更重要的是要修正自己聽力根本的問題，即聽力理解力和聽力專注力，聽力專注力的修正能逐步強化本身的聽力實力，所以現在請根據聽力內容「逐個段落」、「數個段落」或「整篇」進行跟讀練習，提升在實際考場時專注聽完每個訊息、定位出關鍵考點和搭配筆記回答完所有題目。**Go!**

| Professor |

Please come in. By the look on your face,⋯I'm pretty sure it's not about the mid-term paper⋯perhaps I should be a little hard on you⋯so that you won't have time to think about something else⋯

| 教授 |

請進來吧⋯看你臉上的表情⋯我相當肯定這不是關於期中報告⋯或許我應該要對你更嚴格才是⋯這樣你就沒時間去想其他東西了⋯。

| Student |

ha ha⋯thanks though⋯but I was thinking about other things⋯things like my future⋯I'm now an Ivy League student⋯

學生

哈哈…謝謝了…我只是在想關於其他的事…像是我的未來…我現在是常春藤盟校的學生…

Professor

yes…you're…and?

教授

是的…你是…然後呢？

Student

I just start to envision my future…that's all… and I just don't want anything to go wrong…like with this degree…it should be like smooth sailing, right…but I recently found out from a friend who is two years older than me…and it turns out it's just not the case…

學生

我只是開始展望自己的未來…就這樣而已…還有我不想要任何差錯…像是擁有這個學歷…應該就要像是一帆風順那樣，對吧！…但是我近期發現到一位比我年長兩年的朋友…最後事情發展是…完全不是那麼回事…。

Professor

What can I say? It's life and the most important thing is"Where You Go Is Not Who You Will Be"

| 教授 |

我還能説甚麼呢？這就是人生而且重要的是「唸哪所學校不代表你未來的成就」。

| Student |

How come?

| 學生 |

怎麼説？

字彙輔助

1　envision 展望　　　2　degree 學歷
3　smooth sailing　一帆風順　　4　important 重要的

| Professor |

What do you mean how? It's a book my daughter recently read. Not like that I will ever have time to read.⋯ you know⋯but it's true⋯and it's good for her to learn this at her age⋯even though she is only 15⋯but "Where You Go Is Not Who You Will Be"⋯in the introduction of the book it says "Traveling a more gilded path, she'd arrived at the very same destination"⋯and it's true⋯having an Ivy League education as a start doesn't not mean you will win at the end⋯there are other factors involved⋯

| 教授 |

「怎麼說」你指的是什麼...這是我女兒剛讀完的一本書...像我就不像是那種會有時間去閱讀的人...你知道的...但這是實話...而且以她的年紀來說學習這個對她來講是好的...即使她才只有 15 歲而已...但是「唸哪所學校不代表你未來的成就」... 在書中介紹寫到「學習旅程走過鍍金的道路,她抵達了相同的目的地」確實是這樣。有著常春藤盟校的教育為開端不意謂著你會贏在終點。還有其他因素牽涉在其中。

| Student |

perhaps I should read that book too…

| 學生 |

或許我也該閱讀那本書...。

字彙輔助

1 introduction 介紹　　2 gilded 鍍金的
3 destination 目的地　　4 education 教育

| Professor |

yep…perhaps…right after you graduate…you might learn that a lot of job applicants who don't have a degree fancier than you…but they are getting the job…or are working in the same division as you…and you have all the puzzled look like why…But don't. That's not the attitude I want you to possess. You should be open about that.

| 教授 |

是的…或許…在你畢業後…你可能會學習到很多工作的應徵者沒有比你更美好的學歷…但是他們卻獲得工作了，或與你在同個部門工作。而你有著困惑的神情像是為什麼呢？但是不要有這種想法！這不是我所希望你抱有的態度。你應該要更開放才是。

| Student |

I guess…perhaps

| 學生 |

我想…或許是吧。

| Professor |

our society is so wrapped up on the fancy degrees… the fixation and obsessions with the Ivies it's only in the school…like a wind blowing on your forehead…you feel so great…but in reality you still have to start somewhere from the very beginning…work at the entry-level job…no one starts working at a higher level position right after they graduate…trust me…unless your family owns the company…

| 教授 |

我們的社會太注重夢幻學歷。…執著和迷戀常春藤盟校。…這僅限於在學校裡，…像是有陣風往你前額吹去。…你覺得棒透了。…但是現實生活中你仍要從最開始的地方開頭。…在最基層的地方開始工作。...相信我，...沒有人是在畢業後就從事較高階的工作，...除非你的家庭擁有公司...。

| Student |

I'm thinking about taking a summer internship even if it's not paid. At least I can learning something that's not theory-based.

| 學生 |

我正想到要參加暑期工讀的工作即使這份工作不支薪。至少我能學習到一些不是以理論為基礎的東西。

| Professor |

You go ahead. My phone just vibrated. It's my daughter. Sorry I have to take this.

| 教授 |

你儘管去做吧。我的手機剛響了。是我女兒。抱歉我必須要接這通電話。

| Student |

Thank you for your time. I've a class at four so I'll see you later.

| 學生 |

謝謝你抽空。我四點還有課，所以等會兒見。

字彙輔助

1 applicant 申請者　　　**2** division 部門

3 attitude 態度　　　　　**4** obsession 迷戀

▶▶ 試題聽力原文

1. Why does the student visit the professor?

2. Listen again to part of the conversation. Then answer the question.
   Student: I just start to envision my future…that's all… and I just don't want anything to go wrong…like with this degree…it should be like smooth sailing, right…but I recently found out from a friend who is two years older than me…and it turns out it's just not the case…

   What does the student mean when he says "like with this degree…it should be like smooth sailing"?

3. Listen again to part of the conversation. Then answer the question.
   Professor: not like that I will ever have time to read…you know…but it's true…and it's good for her to learn this at her age…even though she is only 15…but "Where You

Go Is Not Who You Will Be"··· in the introduction of the book it says "Traveling a more gilded path, she'd arrived at the very same destination"···and it's true having an Ivy League education as a start doesn't not mean you will win at the end···there are other factors involved···

What does the professor mean when she says "Traveling a more gilded path, she'd arrived at the very same destination"?

4. Listen again to part of the conversation. Then answer the question.
   Professor: our society is so wrapped up on the fancy degrees··· the fixation and obsessions with the Ivies··· but it's only in the school···like a wind blowing on your forehead···you feel so great···but in reality you still have to start somewhere from the very beginning···work at the entry-level job···

What does the professor mean when she says "but it's only in the school···like a wind blowing on your forehead···you feel so great···but in reality you still have to start somewhere from the very beginning"?

5. What will the student probably do next?

▶▶ 記筆記與聽力訊息

| Instruction | `MP3 031`

新托福聽力與其他聽力測驗不同，可以於聽力的紙上記筆記，除了寫試題外，更重要的一點是訓練自己能夠將聽完一段訊息後，將重要的聽力訊息都記到。也可以將自己聽到跟記到的重點訊息跟試題做比對，因為試題考的就是長對話跟講座中出現的重點，能修正自己篩選聽力訊息重點的能力。

| 聽力重點 |

- 記筆記有很多方式，包含符號跟自己習慣的縮寫字等等，可以找出最適合自己的模式，一定要自己重聽音檔作練習數次。

- 這篇是校園類話題但有提到書籍和未來，**可以參考下述列表中的 main idea，掌握主旨就差不多了**，不一定要每句都記起來。

Note

Main idea ❶	fancy degrees don't equal smooth sailing in life
Professor	"Where You Go Is Not Who You Will Be"
Main idea ❷	Having an Ivy League education as a start doesn't not mean you will win at the end and there are other factors involved in the greater success in life
Professor	want him to possess the right attitude
Main idea ❸	society's fixation and obsessions with the Ivies, but in real life, we all have to start at the very beginning
student	plan to take the summer internship jobs to learn something practical

Note

▶▶ 填空測驗

| Instruction | MP3 031

現在請再聽一次音檔，並做下列的測驗，檢視自己能否完成此填空測驗和強化自己聽力能力和拼字能力，降低並修正自己漏聽到聽力訊息的機會，大幅提升英考實力。

1. By the look on the student's face, the professor understands that he is not here for the m_____ paper.

2. As an I_____ L_____ student, the student doesn't want anything to go wrong.

3. He thinks that with this kind of degree, life should be like s_____ s_____.

4. The professor thinks it's good for her d_____ to read books, such as Where You Go Is Not Who You Will Be, even though she is young.

5. In the introduction of the book it says "Traveling a more g_____ path, she'd arrived at the very same d_____".

6. There are other f_____ that will influence a person's future.

7. Sometimes a_____ having f_____ degrees are getting the same job as candidates who do not possess them.

8. A_____ is what the professor deems important to the work.

9. The f_____ and o_____ with Ivies are an unavoidable phenomenon.

10. In real life, right after we graduate, we all start not by working at a h_____ level position, but by working at an e_____ job.

11. The student will not get p_____ by taking the summer i_____.

12. The student wants to learn something p_____, contrary to something t_____.

答案

1. mid-term
2. Ivy League
3. smooth sailing
4. daughter
5. gilded, destination
6. factors

7. applicants, fancier
8. Attitude
9. fixation, obsessions
10. higher, entry-level
11. paid, internship
12. practical, theory-based

▶▶ 摘要能力

| Instruction | MP3 031

除了閱讀測驗外,其實培養能在聽完一大段訊息後,以口述講述剛才聽到的聽力訊息是學習語言和表達很重要的一件事,讓自己養成具備這樣的能力,除了能在聽力測驗中獲取高分外,也能在新托福寫作跟口說的整合題型上大有斬獲喔!所以快來練習,除了書中提供的參考答案外,自己可以試著重新聽過音檔一遍後,摘要出英文訊息並朗讀出來。

Note

▶▶參考答案

The student expects his life should be like smooth sailing because he will have a gilded degree right after he graduates. The prospect of the student's friend proves that the future will not be what he thinks it is. The professor has a chat with him about the book "Where You Go Is Not Who You Will Be", the book that her daughter just read. It's true that there are other factors that will influence a person's future success. The professor wants him to have the right mindset in the workplace. Our society is so wrapped up on the fancy degrees. (the fixation and obsessions with the Ivies) In the workplace, we all start from the very beginning, a position of the entry-level job. Eventually, the student plans to find a summer internship so that he will learn something practical.

▶▶ **聽力試題** MP3 032

1. Why does the student visit the professor?
   (A) Because he has love troubles
   (B) Because he wants to change the professor's impression on him
   (C) Because he does not want others view professor as a lazy person
   (D) Because he wants the professor to do the prediction for him.

2. Why does the student respond to the professor by saying "am I that transparent"?
   (A) Because he wonders why the professor detects his motive before he asks
   (B) Because he has secrets he does not want others to know
   (C) Because he is surprised to find that others would ask the same question as he does
   (D) Because he does not want to be seen through

3. Why does the professor mention the book "The

Achievement Habit"?

(A) To make the student intrigued about a research project

(B) To help the student make predictions about life

(C) To clear up doubts about life

(D) To tell the student that "go with the flow" is not wise

4. Listen again to part of the conversation. Then answer the question.

(A) The journey of life can be in a straight line

(B) We can't predict it correctly all the time

(C) The journey of life can be in a zigzag line

(D) Making accurate predictions will lead our life to a nonlinear route

5. What will the professor probably do next?

(A) Memorize those sentences

(B) make sure the student inform other students

(C) resume the unfinished research

(D) keep the paper

▶▶ 新托福聽力解析

1. 這題詢問的是學生為何拜訪教授，要注意一些對話干擾訊息，學生並非有感情困擾等等，其實最主要的目的是選項 D，學生其實擔憂自己的未來，希望教授可以做些預測，所以才去找教授聊聊。

2. 這題是詢問為什麼學生要說 am I that transparent?，學生其實想表明自己有這麼明顯嗎，這是 A 選項的同義轉換，故答案為選項 A，。

3. 這題是詢問為什麼教授提到 The Achievement Habit 這本書呢，其實主要因為選項 C 的原因，對生命釋疑，故答案為選項 C。

4. 這題詢問教授為什麼會講該段話，Life is not something you can predict. The journey is sometimes nonlinear…，要注意選項的一些同義詞改寫，其實主要是想表明 the journey of life can be in a zigzag line，故答案為選項 C。

5. 這題詢問教授接下來會做什麼，訊息中有提到教授會繼續做研究，所以答案為選項 C。

答案：1. D 2. A 3. C 4. C 5. C

做完題目後，除了對答案知道錯的部分在哪外，更重要的是要修正自己聽力根本的問題，即聽力理解力和聽力專注力，聽力專注力的修正能逐步強化本身的聽力實力，所以現在請根據聽力內容「逐個段落」、「數個段落」或「整篇」進行跟讀練習，提升在實際考場時專注聽完每個訊息、定位出關鍵考點和搭配筆記回答完所有題目。Go!

| Professor |

Not again!

| 教授 |

怎麼又是這個。

| Student |

What do you mean by "not again"?

| 學生 |

「怎麼又是這個」你指的是什麼呢？...

| Professor |

it seems that you're also the one who tries to ask me something about predicting a career path or something…

| 教授 |

似乎你也是要問我一些關於預測職業軌跡或什麼的...。

| Student |

Am I that transparent? I do want to ask you something other than this…like love troubles or something…but I just don't have those kinds of problems…Plus, right after graduation, the career is so important.

| 學生 |

我有這麼明顯嗎？我也想要問你與這個話題不同的事...像是關於感情困擾或什麼的事...但是我就沒有這些問題...再說，畢業後...職業很重要...。

| Professor |

I'm giving you answers, but just don't think of me as a lazy professor.

| 教授 |

我會給你答案但是別把我當成懶惰的教授就是了。

| Student |

Of course I won't. Especially when I'm the one asking you the favor.

| 學生 |

我當然不會...尤其是我是尋求幫助的人...。

| Professor |

Read the paper. I've prepared this since day one. I've been asked this for so many times.

| 教授 |

讀這份文件...從第一天開始，我已經準備好這個了...我已經被問太多次了...。

| Student |

ok…I'm reading now…

| 學生 |

好的...我準備好了...。

字彙輔助

1 predicting 預測　　　　**2** transparent 透明的

3 trouble 麻煩　　　　　**4** professor 教授

| Professor |

Go ahead.

| 教授 |

唸吧。

| Student |

"Life is an adventure, so loosen up, stop trying to figure

it out, and just go with the flow." "My life is punctuated by milestones that would have never happened except for the combination of unplanned and improbable chance events." Who wrote this?

| 學生 |

「人生像是一場冒險，所以敞開胸懷，不要試著想要盡窺全貌，只要順著走就好了。」。「我的一生有許多里程碑，但若不是意外與看來不可能出現的因緣巧合，這些里程碑也不可能出現」。

| Professor |

Bernard Roth, the author of The Achievement Habit.

| 教授 |

博納德·羅斯，把成功變成習慣的作者。

| Student |

Wow…

| 學生 |

哇…。

字彙輔助

1. adventure 冒險
2. loosen 鬆開
3. combination 結合
4. unplanned 未規劃的
5. improbable 不可能的

| **Professor** |

It's true. If you're intrigued, you can go read the whole book by yourself. The thing I want to point out is you don't have to plan the whole thing, like having a long-term plan or something. Sometimes it happens suddenly. Like in the book life-changing opportunities have come to him from unexpected phone calls. You don't need a fortune teller telling you what you will have become in the next ten years. Or like an anxious ant on the hot pot trying to figure out what you're going to be. Stop making predications and do the right thing. Life is not something you can predict. The journey is sometimes nonlinear.

| 教授 |

確實如此。如果你感到有興趣的話，你可以自己去讀完整本書。我想要指出的是你不用想要計劃整個事情，像是有長期的計劃或什麼的。有時候事情就這樣突然發生了。像是這書中改變人生的機會就是經由突如其來的電話。你不需要算命師去告訴你在接下來的十年會成為什麼樣的人？或像是熱鍋上焦慮的螞蟻般試圖想要了解你將成為什麼？停止做預測和做正確的事。人生不是你可以預測的。人生的旅程有時候是非線性的。

字彙輔助

1. unexpected 出乎意料之外的
2. fortune 幸運、財富
3. predication 預測
4. nonlinear 非線性的

| Student |

Perhaps we shouldn't be doing the predicting things after all. Why hasn't anyone told me this before?

| 學生 |

或許我們最終都不應該要預測事情。為什麼之前沒有人告訴我這些呢？

| Professor |

But you know now, right? I think you will be just fine. Don't be too fixated on doing something. Sometimes it will just come your way at the right time. Embrace what life has given you, ok?

| 教授 |

但你現在知道了，對吧？我想你會沒問題的。別太執著要做某些事。有時候在對的時候事情自己會照你想要的發展走。擁抱人生所賦予你的，好嗎？

| Student |

OK…can I keep the paper…even if it's just several sentences…it means a lot to me…

| 學生 |

好的…我能保留這文件嗎…即使只有幾句話…這對我來說意義重大…。

| Professor |

You can keep it if you want.I have it memorized right in my head. I can write another one in case there is another student like you begging me to tell him or her life trajectory.

| 教授 |

如果你想要的話，你可以保留。我早就背起來了。就在我腦袋裡。我能寫另一份以防又有另一位學生像你一樣要我告訴他或她人生軌跡的事。

| Student |

Ha ha…

| 學生 |

哈哈…。

| Professor |

And if you don't mind I have to get back to my research…ok…

| 教授 |

還有如果你不介意的話我要繼續回到我的研究了…好嗎…

| Student |

See you in tomorrow's class. Bye.

明天的課堂上見。再見了。

字彙輔助

1 embrace 擁抱　　　　　2 beg 乞求
3 trajectory 軌跡　　　　4 research 研究

▶▶ 試題聽力原文

1. Why does the student visit the professor?

2. Why does the student respond to the professor by saying "am I that transparent"?

3. Why does the professor mention the book "The Achievement Habit"?

4. Listen again to part of the conversation. Then answer the question.
   Professor: Sometimes it happens all of a sudden, like in the book life-changing opportunities have come to him from unexpected phone calls. You don't need a fortune teller telling you what you will have become in the next ten years? Or like an anxious ant on the hot pot trying to figure out what you're going to be? Stop making

predications and do the right thing. Life is not something you can predict. The journey is sometimes nonlinear⋯

What does the professor mean when he says "Life is not something you can predict. The journey is sometimes nonlinear⋯"

5. What will the professor probably do next?

▶▶ 記筆記與聽力訊息

| Instruction | MP3 032

　　新托福聽力與其他聽力測驗不同，可以於聽力的紙上記筆記，除了寫試題外，更重要的一點是訓練自己能夠將聽完一段訊息後，將重要的聽力訊息都記到。也可以將自己聽到跟記到的重點訊息跟試題做比對，因為試題考的就是長對話跟講座中出現的重點，能修正自己篩選聽力訊息重點的能力。

| 聽力重點 |

- 記筆記有很多方式，包含符號跟自己習慣的縮寫字等等，可以找出最適合自己的模式，一定要自己重聽音檔作練習數次。

- 這篇是校園類話題但有提到書籍和未來，**可以參考下述列表中的 main idea，掌握主旨就差不多了，另外要注意教授提到這本書的部分，和推測類考題的應答，這篇需要更多的推測能力。**

▶▶ **參考筆記**

Main idea ❶ getting asked about predicting a career path

professor wants him to read the paper

- "Life is an adventure, so loosen up, stop trying to figure it out, and just go with the flow."
- "My life is punctuated by milestones that would have never happened except for the combination of unplanned and improbable chance events."

Books

- Bernard Roth, the author of The Achievement Habit
  - life-changing opportunities have come to him from unexpected phone calls.

Main Idea ❷

- Life is not something you can predict. The journey is sometimes nonlinear.
- Sometimes it will just come your way at the right time⋯ embrace what life has given you.

Instruction | MP3 032

現在請再聽一次音檔，並做下列的測驗，檢視自己能否完成此填空測驗和強化自己聽力能力和拼字能力，降低並修正自己漏聽到聽力訊息的機會，大幅提升英考實力。

1. The professor is tired of being asked about the s_____ __ questions about p_____ a career path or something.

2. The student doesn't have the problem like l_____ t__ _____.

3. The professor doesn't want to be viewed as a l_____ professor.

4. The professor wants the student to read the paper that he has p_____ since day one.

5. "Life is an a_____, so loosen up, stop trying to figure it out, and just go with the f_____."

6. "My life is punctuated by m_____ that would have never happened except for the combination of u_____ __ and i_____ chance events."

7. L_____ opportunities have come to the author from u_____ phone calls.

8. The j_____ of our life is n_____ so making p____ _____ is of no use.

9. Sometimes you just have to e_____ what life has given you.

10. There might be some students out there wanting to ask the professor about l_____ t_____.

| 答案 |

1. same, predicting
2. love troubles
3. lazy
4. prepared
5. adventure, flow
6. milestones, unplanned, improbable
7. life-changing, unexpected
8. journey, nonlinear, predications
9. embrace
10. life, trajectory

▶▶ 摘要能力

　　除了閱讀測驗外，其實培養能在聽完一大段訊息後，以口述講述剛才聽到的聽力訊息是學習語言和表達很重要的一件事，讓自己養成具備這樣的能力，除了能在聽力測驗中獲取高分外，也能在新托福寫作跟口說的整合題型上大有斬獲喔！所以快來練習，除了書中提供的參考答案外，自己可以試著重新聽過音檔一遍後，摘要出英文訊息並朗讀出來。

Note

▶▶ 參考答案

Once again, the professor is asked about the predication of a career path for the future. He wants the student to read the prepared paper, with answers on it. Those sentences are from the book The Achievement Habit, written by Bernard Roth. The author tells readers that life-changing opportunities have come to him from unexpected phone calls. We should understand that life is not something we can predict, and the journey is sometimes nonlinear. The professor wants the student to know things will come your way and just embrace what life has given us.

6 ▶▶ 商業話題探討：Give and Take，所以哈利波特是 giver 嗎?

▶▶ **聽力試題** MP3 033

1. What are the speakers mainly discussing?
   (A) How to write Harry Potter
   (B) How to avoid digression from the main topic
   (C) How to outperform classmates
   (D) Work on a report through fictional characters

2. Why does the professor say "what do you have in mind"?
   (A) He wants the student to do something as he asked.
   (B) He wants to know how the student thinks.
   (C) He does not want someone who changes his mind very often
   (D) He wants the student to make up his mind

3. Listen again to part of the conversation. Then answer the question.
   (A) Matchers always expect something in return
   (B) Matchers will lose if they give something first
   (C) Matchers won't forget to return things
   (D) Matchers will return similar or equitable favors to others

4. Listen again to part of the conversation. Then answer the question.
   (A) Takers think all people can be defeated.
   (B) In order to win, you don't have to act like takers because there are other ways.
   (C) Success favors takers in some ways
   (D) Defeating people gives takers a leg up in the game

5. What will the student probably do next?
   (A) Help audiences relate to the idea
   (B) Remind his friends that don't be a taker
   (C) Spend less time with classmates
   (D) Reread details so he can work on the writing

1. 這題詢問的是說話者主要是討論什麼，主要原因是選項 D，其他都是干擾選項。

2. 這題是詢問為什麼教授要說 what do you have in mind，其實是想詢問學生有什麼想法嗎，為 B 選項的同義轉換，故答案為選項 B，他想知道學生在想什麼。

3. 這題是詢問為什麼教授提到 Matchers value a fair return，要注意每個選項的敘述，有的過於絕對或不符合，最符合的是選項 D，Matchers will return similar or equitable favors to others 為教授講到的句子的同義表達，故答案為選項 D。

4. 這題詢問教授為什麼會講該段話，success doesn't mean you have to defeat people like what most takers do，其實是只選項 C 的敘述，其他敘述有些在文中未提到要注意，故答案為選項 B。

5. 這題詢問學生接下來會做什麼，文中有提到仍需要回顧一些小說中的細節，故答案為選項 D。

....

答案： 1.D 2. B 3. D 4. B 5. D

影子跟讀練習 MP3 033

做完題目後，除了對答案知道錯的部分在哪外，更重要的是要修正自己聽力根本的問題，即聽力理解力和聽力專注力，聽力專注力的修正能逐步強化本身的聽力實力，所以現在請根據聽力內容「逐個段落」、「數個段落」或「整篇」進行跟讀練習，提升在實際考場時專注聽完每個訊息、定位出關鍵考點和搭配筆記回答完所有題目。Go!

| Professor |

Hi.

| 教授 |

嗨。

| Student |

I just want to discuss with you about the report on Give and Take.

| 學生 |

我只是想要跟你討論關於「給予和奪取」這本書的報告。

| Professor |

What do you have in mind?

你心裡有什麼想法嗎？

| Student |

I was thinking about writing about Harry Potter.

| 學生 |

我在想要寫關於哈利波特。

| Professor |

Why Harry Potter?

| 教授 |

為什麼是哈利波特？

| Student |

I know how it sounds like a digression from the topic for a bit, but after rereading it, I think it's quite relevant to what we have discussed so far about previous lectures. I actually wrote it down. Let me read those sentences for you.

| 學生 |

我知道這聽起來有點離題了。但是在讀過之後，我認為這與我們之前幾次講課中所討論到的部分相當有關連性。實際上我把它寫下來了。讓我讀那些句子給你聽。

"Cedric still didn't know about the dragons. The only champion who didn't. If Harry was right in thinking that Maxime and Karkaroff would have told Fleur and Krum."

「西追仍不知曉關於龍的事。唯一一位不知道的鬥士，如果哈利思考的是正確的話，美心夫人和卡卡夫可能已經告訴芙兒和克朗。」

字彙輔助

1. digress 離題
2. relevant 相關的
3. dragon 龍
4. champion 鬥士

"Cedric, said Harry, "the first task is dragons. We're on an even footing now, aren't we?"

"He said I owe you one for telling me about the dragons. Now just mull things over in the hot water. It will help you think."

「哈利說道：西追，第一個任務是龍！我們現在在相同的起跑點了，對吧？」

「西追回說：你告訴我關於龍的事讓我欠你一個人情。只要在熱水中好好深思下。它能幫助你思考。」

So Harry is a giver, and in return Cedric tells him about the secret of the second task which is to take a bath and he will eventually crack the puzzle. Harry couldn't have worked out those, if he hadn't have helped Cedric in the first place. So to me Cedric is perhaps a matcher, somewhere between a taker and a giver. Matchers value a fair return.

所以哈利波特是給予者，而西追為了回報哈利告訴他關於第二項任務的秘密，也就是洗個澡，然後他最終就會解開謎題。哈利波特不可能解開謎題，如果他當初沒有幫助西追，對吧？對我而言，西追或許是位相配者，大概在奪取者和給予者中間，配對者重視對等的回報。

| **Professor** |

That sounds intriguing.

| **教授** |

聽起來挺有趣的。

| **Student** |

I kind of understand what it means that you have to give something in order to receive something, and success doesn't mean you have to defeat people like what most takers do. Givers are not losers. Harry Potter is doing the right thing informing Cedric that the first task is dragons. Being a giver gives you a lot of advantages over others. It's for the long-term. Even though it will have a certain cost at first, whereas takers enjoy the fruit early on but they can only win something for the very short-term.

| 學生 |

我有點了解了為什麼你必須要給予進而獲取東西的意思了。成功不意謂著你必須要擊敗人，像是所有奪取者那樣。而給予者不是輸家。哈利波特告訴西追第一個任務是龍就是做了件對的事。身為給予者賦予你比其他人來説有更多優勢。這是長期的。即使這在開頭會有確切的成本在。而奪取者享有初期的果實但他們卻只能非常短暫地贏一些東西。

字彙輔助

1　footing 起跑點
2　crack 解開
3　defeat 擊敗
4　advantage 優勢

| Professor |

Yep! That's why we know "It's easier to win if everybody wants you to win". Perhaps you should write about defining the role of being a taker, a matcher, and a giver through fictional characters in Harry Potter Series. I really look forward to reading what you are going to write.

| 教授 |

對啊...這也是為什麼我們知道「如果每個人都希望你贏的話，將會贏得更容易。」。或許你應該要寫透過哈利波特虛構的人物去定義成為奪取者、配對者和給予者的角色。很期待讀你要寫得部分。

| Student |

Thanks. I still need some time to go over some details of

347

the fiction.

| 學生 |

謝謝！我仍需要一些時間去重溫小説細節。

| **Professor** |

I'm sure you will just be fine. Using those characters can make readers and audiences more resonate to the concept.

| 教授 |

我想你會沒問題的。使用那些角色讓讀者和觀眾都更能對這些概念有更多的共鳴。

字彙輔助

1. fictional 虛構的
2. character 角色
3. audience 觀眾
4. resonate 共鳴

▶▶ **試題聽力原文**

1. What are the speakers mainly discussing?

2. Why does the professor say "what do you have in mind"?

3. Listen again to part of the conversation. Then answer the question.
   Student: so Harry is a giver…and in return Cedric tells

him about the secret of the second task…which is to take a bath and he will eventually crack the puzzle… Harry couldn't have worked out those, if he hadn't have helped Cedric in the first place, right…and to me Cedric is perhaps a matcher…somewhere between a taker and a giver…Matchers value a fair return…

What does the student mean when she says "Matchers value a fair return"?

4. Listen again to part of the conversation. Then answer the question.

Student: I kind of understand what it means that you have to give something in order to receive something… and success doesn't mean you have to defeat people like what most takers do…and givers are not losers…and Harry Potter is doing the right thing informing Cedric that the first task is dragons…being a giver gives you a lot of advantages over others.

What does the student mean when she says "success doesn't mean you have to defeat people like what most takers do"?

5. What will the student probably do next?

▶▶ 記筆記與聽力訊息

| Instruction | MP3 033

　　新托福聽力與其他聽力測驗不同，可以於聽力的紙上記筆記，除了寫試題外，更重要的一點是訓練自己能夠將聽完一段訊息後，將重要的聽力訊息都記到。也可以將自己聽到跟記到的重點訊息跟試題做比對，因為試題考的就是長對話跟講座中出現的重點，能修正自己篩選聽力訊息重點的能力。

| 聽力重點 |

- 記筆記有很多方式，包含符號跟自己習慣的縮寫字等等，可以找出最適合自己的模式，一定要自己重聽音檔作練習數次。

- 這篇是關於校園類話題有提到書籍和哈利波特，**要掌握推測題型和了解 taker, matcher, giver 間的關係和教授給的建議**。

Note

▶▶ 參考筆記

Main idea ❶ report on Give and Take + Harry Potter	
sentences	Harry informs Cedric about the first task Cedric returns that favor by telling Harry the second task
role	Giver, taker, matcher giver：Harry matcher：Cedric, value a fair return

Main idea ❷

- success doesn't mean you have to defeat people like what most takers do.
- Takers can only win something for a very short-term. "It's easier to win if everybody wants you to win".

suggestion	❶ write about defining the role of being a taker, a matcher, and a giver through fictional characters in Harry Potter Series. ❷ using those characters can make readers and audiences more resonate to the concept

| Instruction | MP3 033

現在請再聽一次音檔，並做下列的測驗，檢視自己能否完成此填空測驗和強化自己聽力能力和拼字能力，降低並修正自己漏聽到聽力訊息的機會，大幅提升英考實力。

1. The professor w_____ why the student wants to writing the topic relating to Harry Potter.

2. However, the student explains that it might sound like d_____ from the main theme, but it's actually quite r_____.

3. Those sentences include things like Cedric is the only c__ _____ who didn't know anything about the first task.

4. Harry is kind enough to tell Cedric that the first task is d_____.

5. Cedric in return r_____ the f_____.

6. According to the student, Harry is a g_____, whereas Cedric is a m_____.

7. Matchers value a fair return, so they are somewhere between a t_____ and a giver

8. In real life, you don't have to be like a taker because winning does not mean you have to d_____ someone.

9. Takers enjoy the f_____ from the very beginning, but will not win the race in the l_____ term.

10. As a saying goes, "It's e_____ to win if everybody wants you to win".

11. The student will write about the topic but by using f____ _____ c_____.

12. Writing the report through this will make readers and audiences more r_____ to the concept.

| 答案 |

1. wonders
2. digress, relevant
3. champion
4. dragons
5. returns, favor
6. giver, matcher
7. taker
8. defeat
9. fruits, long

10. easier
11. fictional, characters
12. resonate

▶▶ 摘要能力

| **Instruction** | MP3 033

　　除了閱讀測驗外，其實培養能在聽完一大段訊息後，以口述講述剛才聽到的聽力訊息是學習語言和表達很重要的一件事，讓自己養成具備這樣的能力，除了能在聽力測驗中獲取高分外，也能在新托福寫作跟口說的整合題型上大有斬獲喔！所以快來練習，除了書中提供的參考答案外，自己可以試著重新聽過音檔一遍後，摘要出英文訊息並朗讀出來。

Note

▶▶ **參考答案**

　　The student has come up with something novel to do. He will do what they have discussed so far from previous lectures about characters of Harry Potter. Harry is kind enough to inform Cedric, his competitor, the first task. In return, he gets the information about the second task from Cedric. Harry is obviously a giver, and Cedric more like a matcher. Matchers value a fair return. It's important to know that we do not have to be like takers to win. What takers get is very short-term. The professor advises him to write the definition of the role of being a taker, a matcher, and a giver but through fictional characters in Harry Potter Series. Using those characters can make readers and audiences more resonate to the concept.

▶▶ **聽力試題** `MP3 034`

1. What are speakers mainly discussing?

   (A) How to get off the lingered feelings.

   (B) How to make classmates intrigued into what you say

   (C) A person's ability to learn through other books

   (D) Science is the key to one's learning

2. Listen again to part of the conversation. Then answer the question.

   (A) Because others already view it as a golden rule

   (B) Because there are no golden rules.

   (C) Because golden rules require far more hours

   (D) Because there are some defects in this theory.

3. What can be inferred about the student?

   (A) He needs a travel companion.

   (B) He needs an epiphany for the final report.

   (C) He hardly knows anyone in the class.

   (D) He needs friends of similar interests.

4. Listen again to part of the conversation. Then answer the question.

(A) The professor wants him to be glamorous.

(B) The author of Outliers has other considerations.

(C) The professor favors Peak over Outliers.

(D) The defect in Outliers makes it less appealing.

5. What will the student probably do next?

(A) Visit the professor's office

(B) Schedule the professor's doctor appointment.

(C) Finish reading Outliers

(D) Ask the professor how to succeed on Thursday

▶▶ 新托福聽力解析

1. 這題詢問的是說話者主要是在討論什麼，要注意一些對話干擾訊息，其實最終的目的是選項 C，主要是在討論學習以及透過其他書籍討論一個人的學習能力，故答案為選項 C。

2. 這題是詢問為什麼學生要說 it's a part that we haven't covered that…it's a great rule of course…but we shouldn't view it as a golden rule，要注意其他干擾選項，其實是書中有提到其他書的缺陷部分，所以才會說也別將這當成 golden rule，故答案為選項 D，因為理論中有缺失。

3. 這題是詢問可以推測出學生什麼，根據教授的察覺，學生其實需要的是有興趣相同的朋友，故答案為選項 D。

4. 這題詢問教授為什麼會講該段話，…especially you can

analyze what Outliers fails to take into account…it's not as glamorous to you…when there are other things that need to be taken into consideration…，其實主要是想表明 The defect in Outliers makes it less appealing.，故答案為選項 D。

5. 這題詢問學生接下來會做什麼，根據聽力後段的敘述，可以得知學生還有可能於週四去找教授，故答案為選項 A。

答案：1. C 2. D 3. D 4. D 5. A

 ## 影子跟讀練習 MP3 034

做完題目後，除了對答案知道錯的部分在哪外，更重要的是要修正自己聽力根本的問題，即聽力理解力和聽力專注力，聽力專注力的修正能逐步強化本身的聽力實力，所以現在請根據聽力內容「逐個段落」、「數個段落」或「整篇」進行跟讀練習，提升在實際考場時專注聽完每個訊息、定位出關鍵考點和搭配筆記回答完所有題目。Go!

| Professor |

I was just heading out. What's up?

| 教授 |

我正要外出。有什麼事嗎？

| Student |

I have a question I just can't get off my mind.

| 學生 |

我有個問題我一直縈繞在心裡。

| Professor |

What question?

| 教授 |

什麼問題呢？

| Student |

it's about something you said the other day. About learning?

| 學生 |

是關於你前幾天說有關學習的部分？

| Professor |

Right! We covered so many things about whether a person's ability to learn is innate or acquired.

| 教授 |

是的。我們談到許多事情，關於一個人的學習能力是與生俱來的還是後天學習的。

| Student |

I was reading a book, "Peak - Secrets from the NEW Science of Expertise." It reveals the ten-thousand-hour rule is not true.

| 學生 |

我讀了一本書，「刻意練習-來自新科學專業的秘密」。它揭露了關於一萬小時規則是錯誤的。

字彙輔助

1 innate 先天的

2 acquired 後天養成的

3 Expertise 專業

4 rule 規則

| Professor |

It's a part that we haven't covered yet. It's a great rule of course, but we shouldn't view it as a golden rule. It's quite possible that people can achieve their goal with far fewer than those hours. You don't have to think that you do need to practice that amount of time to achieve your goal. It can impede you from thinking the goal can't be done. I'm sure you can find several examples in the book, right?

| 教授 |

這是我們尚未談到的部分。這當然是很棒的規則。但我們不該把它視為是黃金準則。而且人們非常可能在少於那些時數就達成了他們的目標。所以你不用認為你需要練習到那樣的時間才能達到你的目標。它能阻礙你思考著某些目標而相對的無法達成。我相信你能夠在書中找到幾個例子，對吧？

| Student |

Right. I just had this epiphany while reading the book. I guess I just want to discuss what I have read with someone.

| 學生 |

對的。我只是在讀這本書的時候有些頓悟。我想我只是想要與人討論我所讀過的部分。

字彙輔助

1. cover 涵蓋
2. achieve 達成
3. impede 阻礙
4. example 例子

| Professor |

Especially when you can't find someone who works as hard as you do. I get that. I was once a student. I've been there. I know how it feels when you want to discuss something and your classmates are just not the right audience. All they talk about is traveling and many other things.

| 教授 |

是的。特別是當你無法找到一位像你這樣努力的人。我懂！我也曾是學生。我是過來人。我了解這種感覺。當你想要討論某些事，但你的同班同學卻不是正確的對象。他們都只想要談論旅行和其他事情。

| Student |

Thank you for your understanding. thanks…for a moment I'm feeling like you know me or something…

| 學生 |

謝謝你的理解。謝謝…有一會兒，好像感覺你懂我或什麼的…

| Professor |

If you have anything you'd like to discuss, you can come to my office. That's the purpose of office hours.

| 教授 |

如果你有任何你想要討論的，你可以來我的辦公室。這也是設立諮詢時間的目的。

| Student |

Thank you.

| 學生 |

謝謝。

| Professor |

I'm sure finishing reading Peak will give you a leg up if

you are working on the final report, especially you can analyze what Outliers fails to take into account. It's not as glamorous when there are other things that need to be taken into consideration, but we just can't ignore evidence that one needs to make a lot of effort even if it means doing fewer than 10,000 hours to succeed. Now I have other things I really have to go see to. I've got a doctor's appointment, so perhaps you should come at 9AM on thursday morning. My office hours are from 9AM to 12PM if you still have something you'd like to ask me.

| 教授 |

　　我想讀完刻意練習一書能對於你在寫期末報告有所幫助。特別是你能去分析為什麼異數一書未能考量到的部分。異數沒有你想的那麼棒了吧？當還有其他考量是你需要列入考慮。但是我們不可能忽略事實，就是若要成功，需要付出很多的努力即使這意謂著花費少於一萬小時的時數。現在我有其它是我必須要去忙.。我也個醫生的約診。或許你應該在週四早上九點過來。我的諮詢時間是從九點到十二點，如果你仍有些東西是你想要問我的話。

| **Student** |

Thank you. I guess I will finish reading the book by then. I am really looking forward to that. Take care.

| 學生 |

　　謝謝。那時候我想我應該就完成閱讀這本書了。很期待。保重。

1 analyze 分析　　　　　**2** consideration 考量

3 ignore 忽略　　　　　**4** appointment 約定

▶▶ 試題聽力原文

1. What are the speakers mainly discussing?

2. Listen again to part of the conversation. Then answer the question.

   Professor: it's a part that we haven't covered that⋯it's a great rule of course⋯but we shouldn't view it as a golden rule⋯and it's quite possible that people can achieve their goal with far fewer than those hours⋯so you don't have to think that you do need to practice that amount of time to achieve your goal⋯it can impede you from thinking that the goal can't be done⋯

   Why does the professor say "it's a part that we haven't covered that⋯it's a great rule of course⋯but we shouldn't view it as a golden rule"?

3. What can be inferred about the student?

4. Listen again to part of the conversation. Then answer the question.

Professor: I'm sure finishing reading Peak⋯will give you a leg up if you are working on the final report⋯especially you can analyze what Outliers fails to take into account⋯it's not as glamorous to you⋯when there are other things that need to be taken into consideration⋯but we just can't ignore evidence that to succeed, one needs to make a lot of effort even if it means doing less than 10,000 hours⋯

What does the professor mean when he says "⋯especially you can analyze what Outliers has failed to take into account⋯it's not as glamorous to you when there are other things that need to be taken into consideration⋯"

5. What will the student probably do next?

▶▶ 記筆記與聽力訊息

Instruction MP3 034

　　新托福聽力與其他聽力測驗不同，可以於聽力的紙上記筆記，除了寫試題外，更重要的一點是訓練自己能夠將聽完一段訊息後，將重要的聽力訊息都記到。也可以將自己聽到跟記到的重點訊息跟試題做比對，因為試題考的就是長對話跟講座中出現的重點，能修正自己篩選聽力訊息重點的能力。

| 聽力重點 |

- 記筆記有很多方式，包含符號跟自己習慣的縮寫字等等，可以找出最適合自己的模式，一定要自己重聽音檔作練習數次。
- 這篇是關於校園類話題，**有提到刻意練習和異數這兩本書，要注意異數缺陷的部分還有教授給的建議。**

Note

▶▶ 參考筆記

Main idea ❶ whether a person's ability to learn is innate or acquired

student	defects about the ten-thousand-hour rule

professor	<ul><li>people can achieve their goal with far fewer than those hours</li><li>mislead people into thinking goals can't be done</li><li>finishing reading PEAK will give him a leg up for his final report. He can analyze what Outliers fail to take into account.</li></ul>

Note

| Instruction | MP3 034

　　現在請再聽一次音檔，並做下列的測驗，檢視自己能否完成此填空測驗和強化自己聽力能力和拼字能力，降低並修正自己漏聽到聽力訊息的機會，大幅提升英考實力。

| Professor |

1. There is something that I_____ in the mind of the student so he came to the professor.

2. During the course, they have talked about whether a person's ability to learn is i_____ or a_____.

3. According to the professor, the ten-thousand-hour rule is a great one, but not a g_____ one.

4. Thinking in accordance with the ten-thousand-hour rule can i_____ a person's ability to achieve a goal.

5. The student was having an e_____ while reading PEAK.

6. The professor gets the feeling of not having someone to talk to, especially one's c_____ are so different from the student.

7. The professor deems that having finished reading PEAK will be a b_____ for the student to work on the final report.

8. It will help the student a_____ what other book fails to take into account.

9. After reading PEAK, Outliers is not g_____ any more.

10. The professor is having a doctor's a_____ so he wants the student to come to the office at another time.

11. The office hour is on T_____ morning.

12. By then, the student will have f_____ reading the book.

| 答案 |

1. lingers
2. iinnate, acquired
3. golden
4. impede
5. epiphany
6. classmates
7. boost
8. analyze
9. glamorous

10. appointment
11. Thursday
12. finished

▶▶ 摘要能力

| **Instruction** | MP3 034

　　除了閱讀測驗外，其實培養能在聽完一大段訊息後，以口述講述剛才聽到的聽力訊息是學習語言和表達很重要的一件事，讓自己養成具備這樣的能力，除了能在聽力測驗中獲取高分外，也能在新托福寫作跟口說的整合題型上大有斬獲喔！所以快來練習，除了書中提供的參考答案外，自己可以試著重新聽過音檔一遍後，摘要出英文訊息並朗讀出來。

Note

▶▶ **參考答案**

Whether a person's ability to learn is innate or acquired has long been debated, and it's quite worth discussing. The student reads relevant readings from other book, Peak, and is surprised to find that the ten-thousand-hour rule has some defects. The professor guides the student through letting him know that people can achieve their goal with far fewer than those hours, and the theory from Outliers can delude people into thinking that goals can't be done. Eventually, the professor wants the student to feel welcomed if he wants to discuss with him during office hours, and thinks that finishing reading PEAK will give him a leg up for his final report. He can analyze what Outliers to take into account.

▶▶ **聽力試題** `MP3 035`

1. Why does the student visit the professor?

   (A) To borrow books

   (B) To invite the professor to the national contest

   (C) To show off her skillful performance of playing violin

   (D) To ask for a leave of absence

2. What can be inferred from the student?

   (A) She finds most men boring.

   (B) She can't persuade librarians to let her borrow books.

   (C) She has difficulties understanding how men's mind operates.

   (D) Her roommate has difficulties grasping signals sent by men.

3. Why does the professor mention the story of "Four men who went fishing"?

   (A) Because it's important for women to understand her partner's hobby.

   (B) Because she wants to show men can be cleverer

than women.

(C) Because it's the only part in the book that is humorous.

(D) Because it's the attractive part and she will like that.

4. Listen again to part of the conversation. Then answer the question.

(A) Men with the wrong answer can always be exempted from the blame.

(B) She thinks it's totally harmless to girls.

(C) She thinks men should be educated to how girls think, too.

(D) She knows to girls, whoever listens to this response will find that annoying.

5. Listen again to part of the conversation. Then answer the question.

(A) She knows the student will like her even more if she reveals the whole story.

(B) She knows the student doesn't want someone to ruin her fun of reading.

(C) She knows the student will feel intrigued and beg for more

(D) She thinks it's better for the student to read unfinished parts on her own.

▶▶ 新托福聽力解析

1. 這題詢問的是學生為何拜訪教授。要注意一些對話干擾訊息，其實最終的目的是選項 D，學生是想要請假，請假的理由是參賽，其他選項均為張冠李戴。

2. 這題是詢問可以推測出學生什麼，從談話中可以了解到，學生覺得自己不太了解男人在想什麼，故答案為選項 C，She has difficulties understanding how men's mind operates.。

3. 這題是詢問為什麼教授提到 Four men went fishing 的故事呢，其實主要是選項 D，因為這部分很吸引人且有趣，感覺學生也會喜歡這部分，故答案為選項 D。

4. 這題詢問學生為什麼會講該段話，I just don't think men who have ever said that can be alive，其實主要是想表明選項 D 的意思，對女生來説這樣回答很討厭且煩感，故答案為選項 D。

5. 這題詢問教授為什麼會講該段話，其實是教授不想要劇透，想要學生自己完成剩下的部分，故答案為選項 D。

....

答案：1. D 2. C 3. D 4. D 5. D

影子跟讀練習 MP3 035

> 做完題目後，除了對答案知道錯的部分在哪外，更重要的是要修正自己聽力根本的問題，即聽力理解力和聽力專注力，聽力專注力的修正能逐步強化本身的聽力實力，所以現在請根據聽力內容「逐個段落」、「數個段落」或「整篇」進行跟讀練習，提升在實際考場時專注聽完每個訊息、定位出關鍵考點和搭配筆記回答完所有題目。Go!

| Student |

I just want to inform you that I can't make it to Wednesday's class.

| 學生 |

我想告訴你，週三的課我沒辦法到課。

| Professor |

Why?

| 教授 |

為什麼呢？

| Student |

I'm representing the school to attend the national contest.

| 學生 |

我代表學校參加國家比賽。

| **Professor** |

That's an honor. What instrument do you play?

| 教授 |

哇…這是很榮譽的事…所以你表演什麼樂器呢？

| **Student** |

Violin. I've been playing it since I was a little kid.

| 學生 |

小提琴. 我從小就開始學了。

| **Professor** |

Since I won't do the roll call, don't worry about it.

| 教授 |

既然我也不會點名…所以別擔心…

字彙輔助

1. inform 告知
2. represent 代表
3. honor 榮譽
4. instrument 樂器

| Student |

What's this?

| 學生 |

這是什麼？

| Professor |

You mean the book?

| 教授 |

你是指書籍嗎？

| Student |

I remember I once read about why men and women do think so differently⋯

| 學生 |

我記得我曾讀過關於為什麼男性和女性在思考上會這麼不同。

| Professor |

I guess that's something we have to agree on. Vast differences. My colleague just returned this book to me. This book is different from what you have read.

| 教授 |

我想這也是我們能有共識的部分了。極大的差異。我的同事剛還我這本書。這本書跟你所讀過的很不一樣喔。

| **Student** |

Can I borrow it?

| **學生** |

我能借這本書嗎？

| **Professor** |

Sure! It's quite amazing. It's the kind of the book you will finish in a short time. It has some stories about female and male differences. Very humorous. I bet you are going to like it.

| **教授** |

當然可以。這相當棒。這是本你會在短時間就會看完的一本書。它有些故事是關於女性和男性間的差異，非常幽默。我想你會喜歡的。

| **Student** |

Yes. Actually, I'm having a hard time understanding men.

| **學生** |

是啊...實際上我對於了解男性有困難。

| **Professor** |

You are going to grasp how men think after reading it.

| 教授 |

閱讀後你會很快就能掌握男人在想什麼了。

字彙輔助

1. return 歸還
2. borrow 借閱
3. amazing 驚人的
4. grasp 掌握

| Professor |

I hate to admit it. It's just too hilarious and real. It has this story about four men who went fishing. They are discussing what they have to do to get permission from their wives, and one of them is smart enough to think of something to get away with it. Such a smart move, I think. There're other stories as well. I'm sure you will find it fascinating…

| 教授 |

　　我不想承認，但這真的太好笑而且很逼真。它有個故事是關於四個男人去釣魚的事。他們正討論他們必須做什麼事才能讓妻子准許他們去釣魚。而其中一位聰明到想到能不費吹灰之力就能做到。如此聰明的一招，在我看來，它還有其他故事，我想你也會覺得很有趣。

| Student |

That's kind of making me want to know more.

| 學生 |

這樣真的讓我更想進一步去了解了。

字彙輔助

1. admit 承認
2. hilarious 好笑的
3. permission 准許
4. fascinating 具吸引力的

| Professor |

There are other things you might find interesting, such as the top five questions that frighten most men. They just can't answer those questions well, and we just can't help but ask those kind of questions. Questions like "what are you thinking about? Do you love me? Do I look fat? Do you think she is prettier than me? What would you do if I died?" And of course each with the correct response and inappropriate responses. Reading the incorrect responses made me laugh. Questions like "do you think she is prettier than me." One of the incorrect responses is "Yes, but you have a better personality."

| 教授 |

還有其他你可能會感到有趣的部份。像是五大男人最懼怕被問到的問題。他們就是無法答好那些問題。而我們卻無法不問那些類型的問題，像是「你在想甚麼呢？你愛我嗎？我看起來胖嗎？你認為她比我漂亮嗎？如果我死了你會做什麼呢？」當然每個問題都有著正解和錯誤回答。看錯誤的回答讓我笑番了。像是「你認為她比我漂亮嗎？」這個問題有個錯誤回答就是：「沒錯，但是你個性更好」。

| Student |

ha ha… I just don't think men who have ever said that can be alive.

| 學生 |

哈哈，我只是不覺得男人這樣回答的話還能活著。

| Professor |

Or responses like "not prettier but definitely thinner." I think I will leave other parts for you to read. I don't want to ruin your fun reading the book. Perhaps I'm revealing a little bit too much.

| 教授 |

或是回答像是「沒有妳漂亮但是確實比妳瘦...」，我想我會把其他部分留給妳自己去讀...只是不想要毀掉妳自己閱讀書籍的樂趣了...或許我透露的有點太多了...。

| Student |

That's ok. I'm still curious about how the man gets away with doing something like this. Perhaps buying something nice for his wife?

| 學生 |

還可以。我還是很好其那個男的怎麼擺脫要做些事。或許是買些好東西給自己妻子吧。

| Professor |

You will know the answer when you read it.

| 教授 |

妳自己讀了就會知道囉。

| Student |

OK.

| 學生 |

好吧。

▶▶ 試題聽力原文

1. Why does the student visit the professor?

2. What can be inferred from the student?

3. Why does the professor mention the story of "Four men who went fishing"?

4. Listen again to part of the conversation. Then answer the question.

   Student: ha ha⋯ I just don't think men who have ever said that can be alive⋯

   What does the student mean when she says "I just don't think men who have ever said that can be alive"?

5. Listen again to part of the conversation. Then answer the question.

   Professor: Responses like not prettier but definitely thinner. I think I will leave other parts for you to read. I just don't want to ruin your fun for reading a book. Perhaps I'm revealing a little bit too much.

   What does the professor mean when she says "I think I will leave other parts for you to read. I just don't want to ruin your fun reading the book. Perhaps I'm revealing a little bit too much."

▶▶ 記筆記與聽力訊息

| Instruction | MP3 035

　　新托福聽力與其他聽力測驗不同，可以於聽力的紙上記筆記，除了寫試題外，更重要的一點是訓練自己能夠將聽完一段訊息後，將重要的聽力訊息都記到。也可以將自己聽到跟記到的重點訊息跟試題做比對，因為試題考的就是長對話跟講座中出現的重點，能修正自己篩選聽力訊息重點的能力。

| 聽力重點 |

- 記筆記有很多方式，包含符號跟自己習慣的縮寫字等等，可以找出最適合自己的模式，一定要自己重聽音檔作練習數次。
- 這篇是關於校園類話題，**這篇蠻活潑的要注意語氣和學生與教授間的互動，還有掌握更多較整合性的出題。**

Note

▶▶ 參考筆記

Main idea ❶ asking for a leave of absence for the national contest
Main idea ❷ men and women differences

student	● borrow a book
	● have difficulty understanding men
professor	❶ A story from the book：four men who went fishing
	● one of the men gets the permission from doing nothing
	❷ top five questions that frighten most men
	● with correct and incorrect responses
Incorrect answers	● Yes, but you have a better personality
	● not prettier but definitely thinner
professor	leaves the rest for the student to read

影子跟讀　學術場景　校園場景

　　現在請再聽一次音檔，並做下列的測驗，檢視自己能否完成此填空測驗和強化自己聽力能力和拼字能力，降低並修正自己漏聽到聽力訊息的機會，大幅提升應考實力。

1. The student came to the professor's office asking for a l_____ of a_____ on W_____.

2. The Student is a r_____ of the school for the national c_____.

3. She plays an i_____: v_____ when she was little.

4. The student wants to b_____ the book the professor's c_____ just returned.

5. It includes some stories that the professor finds it very h_____.

6. The students will probably have a better u_____ about men after reading it.

7. The story of four men who went fishing involves the part that they are talking about getting the p_____ from their wives.

8. One of them is i_____ enough to get the grant from his wife without doing anything.

9. Another fascinating part of the book is the top five questions that f_____ most men.

10. I_____ responses make the professor laugh.

11. One of the correct responses is…Yes, but you have a better p_____.

12. The professor fears that she is r_____ too much, so she will l_____ other parts to the student.

| 答案 |

1. leave, absence, Wednesday
2. representative, contest
3. instrument, violin
4. borrow, colleague
5. humorous
6. understanding
7. permission
8. intelligent
9. frighten
10. inappropriate/incorrect
11. personality
12. revealing, leave

▶▶ 摘要能力

| **Instruction** | MP3 035

　　除了閱讀測驗外，其實培養能在聽完一大段訊息後，以口述講述剛才聽到的聽力訊息是學習語言和表達很重要的一件事，讓自己養成具備這樣的能力，除了能在聽力測驗中獲取高分外，也能在新托福寫作跟口說的整合題型上大有斬獲喔！所以快來練習，除了書中提供的參考答案外，自己可以試著重新聽過音檔一遍後，摘要出英文訊息並朗讀出來。

Note

▶▶ 參考答案

The student comes to ask for a leave of absence and happens to find the book on the professor's table. She is so intrigued that she wants to borrow it. The professor assures her that this book is a humorous one since it contains hilarious stories. Four men who went fishing is one of them, but the professor does not tell the student how one of the men gets the permission from his wife. Also, the book includes top five questions that frighten most men and others. Each with correct responses and inappropriate responses. The description makes the students even more interested in reading it. The professor leaves room for the student to explore, hoping that she does not reveal too much.

9 ▶▶ 轉職：Lean In 挺身而進：「如果你坐上一艘 火箭船，別問什麼座位號。趕緊上車。」

▶▶ **聽力試題** MP3 036

1. Why does the student visit the professor?
   (A) Because he needs someone to write the recommendation letter.
   (B) Because he wants to see the professor.
   (C) Because familiar surroundings will help him contemplate.
   (D) Because he wants the professor to cut to the chase.

2. What can be inferred about the student?
   (A) He was not driven and ambitious.
   (B) He has got some offers from other companies.
   (C) He has never heard the book "Lean In".
   (D) It's pretty unstable in his current position.

3. Listen again to part of the conversation. Then answer the question.
   (A) Being on a rocket ship is risky and dangerous.
   (B) If that company is in such fast growth, you grab that in no time.
   (C) Asking seats is not a good way to land a job.

(D) If it's such a great opportunity, being hesitant is wise.

4. Listen again to part of the conversation. Then answer the question.
   (A) You will never know when you are the one who is on the chopping block.
   (B) HR will decide who is made redundant to the company at the end of the year.
   (C) Unessential employees do not know when they can be back.
   (D) Being an essential workforce is important.

5. Listen again to part of the conversation. Then answer the question.
   (A) Because sacrificing some family time is the only solution.
   (B) Because taking a new job often requires payment getting cut.
   (C) Because being on the rocket ship fulfills his dream of being an astronaut.
   (D) Because his inner compass tells him he should step out of the comfort zone.

▶▶ 新托福聽力解析

1. 這題詢問的是學生為何拜訪教授。要注意一些對話干擾訊息。其實最終的目的是選項 C，學生去找教授不是因為要找人寫推薦函等等，是回到校園能夠沉思且順便見教授。

2. 這題是詢問可以推測出學生什麼。要注意一些細節。B 選項的學生其實有幾個 offer 為聽力訊息中提到的，故答案為選項 B。

3. 這題是詢問為什麼教授提到 If you're offered a seat on a rocket ship, you don't ask what seat. You just get on.，這是選項 B，If that company is in such fast growth, you grab that in no time.的同義表達，故答案為選項 B。

4. 這題詢問教授為什麼會講該段話，You just don't know when you're the one that's redundant to the company.，其實是 You will never know when you are the one who is on the chopping block.的同義表達，這題比較難，但可以從 chopping block 推測出是下個被開刀的對象，故答案為選項 A。

5. 這題詢問教授為什麼會講該段話，I guess deep down I'd like to be on a rocket ship, even though it means I have to sacrifice some family time or take a pay cut.，其實是選項 D 的同義表達，這題也需要比較多的推測能力，inner compass 其實就是原因，驅使學生說出跳脫舒適圈這段話。

答案：1. C 2. B 3. B 4. A 5. D

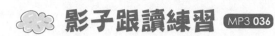 **影子跟讀練習** MP3 036

> 做完題目後，除了對答案知道錯的部分在哪外，更重要的是要修正自己聽力根本的問題，即聽力理解力和聽力專注力，聽力專注力的修正能逐步強化本身的聽力實力，所以現在請根據聽力內容「逐個段落」、「數個段落」或「整篇」進行跟讀練習，提升在實際考場時專注聽完每個訊息、定位出關鍵考點和搭配筆記回答完所有題目。Go!

| Professor |

It's been a long time.

| 教授 |

有好一陣子了…。

| Student |

For sure. It's good to be back actually.

| 學生 |

是啊。確實能回來真好。

| Professor |

How's everything going? Needing someone to write a recommendation letter for you?

| 教授 |

一切還好嗎？需要有人替你寫推薦信嗎？

| **Student** |

That's not the reason I'm back. I came to visit you.

| 學生 |

那不是我回來的原因。我是來看你。

| **Professor** |

Ha ha! Cut to the chase!

| 教授 |

哈哈。切入重點吧。

字彙輔助

1 recommendation 推薦
2 that's not the reason 這不是理由
3 I came to see you 我是來找你的
4 cut to the chase 切入重點

| **Student** |

It's really good to see you. I'm having difficulty deciding which offer I should take from different companies. So I thought maybe returning to a place I was once familiar with can help me contemplate and eventually come up with something.

| 學生 |

真的很高興見到你。我正對於其他公司給的工作機會，不知道該如何決定是好。所以我想或許回到一個我曾熟悉的地方，我能沉思，最終能想出些什麼。

| **Professor** |

I guess that's not a bad start. What's the dilemma?

| 教授 |

我想這個開始不算差。所以困境是什麼呢？

| **Student** |

I'm pretty stable in my current position. Everything seems just fine. Then other opportunities present themselves.

| 學生 |

我在現在的職位相當穩定。每件事都似乎蠻好的，然而其他機會自己出現了...。

字彙輔助

1　difficulty 困難處　　2　campus 校園

3　contemplate 沉思　　4　dilemma 困境

| Professor |

You were so driven and ambitious. If it's a huge opportunity, perhaps you should take it. Have you heard this saying "if you're offered a seat on a rocket ship, you don't ask what seat. You just get on."?

| 教授 |

你過去精力旺盛且具野心。如果一個盛大的機會出現，或許你應該要接受。你聽過這個説法嗎？「如果有人請你上一艘火箭船，別問什麼座位號。趕緊上車。」

| Student |

That's awfully familiar. It's from Lean In?

| 學生 |

這好熟悉喔。是從挺身而進這本書來的嗎？

| Professor |

100 percent correct. That's probably the best piece of career advice. You should value your personal growth more than salary and many other things.

| 教授 |

百分百正確。這或許是最好的職業建議了。你應該更看重你的個人成長，更甚於薪資和許多其他事。

字彙輔助

1 ambitious 野心的　　　　2 rocket 火箭

3 awfully 糟糕的　　　　4 growth 成長

| Student |

Lots of times, familiarity with one's job and surroundings make one's personal growth stagnated. It hampers one's ability to progress.

| 學生 |

許多時候，對一份工作和環境的熟悉度使一個人的個人成長停滯。這阻礙一個人進步的能力。

| Professor |

That's not good for the long-term, especially since the job market is so fickle and things can change in the blink of an eye. You just don't know when you're the one that's redundant to the company. That's why you need to be able to make a job hop every now and then, like after working in a company for three to five years.

| 教授 |

這對於長期來說不是件好事。特別是工作市場如此變幻莫測和事情總是在轉眼間就發生變化，你不知道何時你成了公司多餘的部分。這也是為什麼你會需要偶爾跳槽，像是在公司工作三到五年後。

Student

Perhaps I should rethink the whole thing. I have been in this company for five years now, and working here is like doing the same thing everyday. Everything becomes a routine. Everyone stops learning. People always talk about the trip they're planning to take. I guess deep down I'd like to be on a rocket ship, even though it means I have to sacrifice some family time or take a pay cut.

學生

或許我應該要重新思考整件事。我已經待在這間公司五年了。在這間公司工作就像是一成不變一樣，每件事都變成了例行事務，每個人都停止學習，總是在談論他們要規劃去哪旅行。我想我內心思考著我想要搭上火箭船，即使這意謂著我必須要犧牲家庭時間或減薪接受新工作。

Professor

Sometimes you just don't have the luck to have a second chance, and lots of people are out there looking for that kind of opportunity.

教授

有時候你沒辦法幸運到有第二次機會。而且許多人在等著，尋找著那樣的機會。

字彙輔助

1. familiarity 熟悉
2. stagnate 停滯
3. in a blink of an eye 轉眼間
4. lucky 幸運的

| Student |

Yes, I do think I'm a little bit luckier than my colleagues. I should cherish that. How is everything at school?

| 學生 |

是啊。我想比起我的同事我算有點幸運。...我該珍惜這部分。所以在學校一切都還好嗎？

| Professor |

Petty much the same. Some students are doing some amazing projects. Perhaps I should give a tour at school exhibitions. It's showcasing for two weeks.

| 教授 |

其實都差不多。有些學生正在做很棒的專題。或許我應該要帶你在學校展覽中心導覽一下，展期為兩週。

| Student |

Great.

| 學生 |

很棒！

字彙輔助

1 colleague 同事
2 cherish 珍惜
3 exhibition 展覽中心
4 showcase 展示中心

▶▶ 試題聽力原文

1. Why does the student visit the professor?

2. What can be inferred about the student?

3. Listen again to part of the conversation. Then answer the question.
   Professor: If it's a huge opportunity, perhaps you should take it. Have you heard this saying - "If you're offered a seat on a rocket ship, you don't ask what seat. You just get on."

   What does the professor mean when she says "if you're offered a seat on a rocket ship, you don't ask what seat. You just get on."?

4. Listen again to part of the conversation. Then answer the

question.

Professor: Especially since the job market is so fickle and things can change in the blink of an eye. You just don't know when you're the one that's redundant to the company. That's why you need to be able to make a job hop every now and then, like after working in a company for three to five years.

What does the professor mean when she says " you just don't know when you're the one that's redundant to the company " ?

5. Listen again to part of the conversation. Then answer the question.

Student: Perhaps I should rethink the whole thing. I have been in this company for five years now, and working here is like doing the same thing everyday. Everything becomes a routine. Everyone stops learning. People always talk about the trip they're planning to take. I guess deep down I'd like to be on a rocket ship, even though it means I have to sacrifice some family time or take a pay cut.

Why does the student say " I guess deep down I'd like to be on a rocket ship, even though it means I have to sacrifice some family time or take a pay cut. " ?

| Instruction | [MP3 036]

　　新托福聽力與其他聽力測驗不同，可以於聽力的紙上記筆記，除了寫試題外，更重要的一點是訓練自己能夠將聽完一段訊息後，將重要的聽力訊息都記到。也可以將自己聽到跟記到的重點訊息跟試題做比對，因為試題考的就是長對話跟講座中出現的重點，能修正自己篩選聽力訊息重點的能力。

| 聽力重點 |

- 記筆記有很多方式，包含符號跟自己習慣的縮寫字等等，可以找出最適合自己的模式，一定要自己重聽音檔作練習數次。
- 這篇是關於校園類話題，**要注意學生回學校的目的和教授給的建議，還有推測性題型的考點和引述句同意轉換的表達。**

▶▶ **參考筆記**

Main idea ❶ having difficulty deciding for offers given by other companies	
back	Contemplate/come up with something
About the student	❶ stable in my current position ❷ was so driven and ambitious
suggestions	❶ if you're offered a seat on a rocket ship, you don't ask what seat. You just get on." /Lean In ❷ value more of your personal growth over salary and many other things

Main idea ❷
- familiarity with one's job and surroundings makes one's personal growth stagnated. It hampers one's ability to progress.
- can be made redundant to companies

student	rethink：eventually willing to jump on a rocket ship

| Instruction | MP3 036

　　現在請再聽一次音檔，並做下列的測驗，檢視自己能否完成此填空測驗和強化自己聽力能力和拼字能力，降低並修正自己漏聽到聽力訊息的機會，大幅提升應考實力。

1. It's been a while for the student to be back to the school, but he is not here for the r_____ letter.

2. The student encounters a d_____ on whether he should take the job offer.

3. The campus is a place that was once f_____ to him so that it could be a great place for him to c_____.

4. His current job is pretty s_____, and there are other opportunities.

5. The student seems very tentative to make a move, but the professor mentions that he was d_____ and a__ _____.

6. The professor mentions a saying: "if you're offered a seat on a r_____ ship, you don't ask what seat. You just get on."

7. The saying is probably the best piece of career advice and is a_____ f_____ to the student.

8. The professor mentions something that he should value more about his p_____ g_____.

9. Familiarity with one's job and surroundings can s __ one's ability to grow and h_____ one's ability to progress.

10. Things can change in the blink of an eye, so employees can suddenly be r_____ to the company.

11. The student hates everything has become a daily r_____ ____ and people stop learning.

12. Sometimes you don't get a second c_____ , so when you get one you should probably c_____ it.

| 答案 |

1. recommendation
2. dilemma
3. familiar, contemplate
4. stable
5. driven, ambitious
6. rocket
7. awfully, familiar

8. personal, growth
9. stagnate, hamper
10. redundant
11. routine
12. chance, cherish

▶▶ 摘要能力

| Instruction | MP3 036

　　除了閱讀測驗外，其實培養能在聽完一大段訊息後，以口述講述剛才聽到的聽力訊息是學習語言和表達很重要的一件事，讓自己養成具備這樣的能力，除了能在聽力測驗中獲取高分外，也能在新托福寫作跟口說的整合題型上大有斬獲喔！所以快來練習，除了書中提供的參考答案外，自己可以試著重新聽過音檔一遍後，摘要出英文訊息並朗讀出來。

▶▶ 參考答案

The student is back to the campus because he is having difficulty deciding whether he should accept the offer given by other companies. Returning to the campus might help him contemplate or come up with something. He was once driven and ambitious, according to the professor, and seems now to hold back a bit by not being able to step out of his comfort zone. The professor gives him the advice that he should value his personal growth more than salary and many other things and the best piece of career advice people are all familiar with. "if you're offered a seat on a rocket ship, you don't ask what seat. You just get on." It's from Lean In. Familiarity with one's job and surroundings hampers one's ability to progress. Things can change so fast, so we are uncertain about when we are deemed redundant for the company. The student eventually realizes how rare the opportunity is and thinks he should be on that rocket ship.

▶▶ 聽力試題 MP3 037

1. Why does the student visit the professor?
   (A) To talk about his worried future after the graduation
   (B) To discuss how to play his part as a student
   (C) To discuss the professor's grading policy
   (D) To discuss his scholarship

2. What can be inferred about the student?
   (A) He has ecomonics as the major and philosophy as the minor.
   (B) He does not know what his future employer wants.
   (C) He is worried about grades and scholarship
   (D) He can express himself clearly

3. Listen again to part of the conversation. Then answer the question.
   (A) Because the decision can't reflect what others truly want to do, and she wants him to avoid that trap.
   (B) Because she wants the student to care how others perceive him.
   (C) Because she wants to remind the student it's not

good, if he does such things to others.

(D) Because the student is not beguiled by how others view him.

4. Listen again to part of the conversation. Then answer the question.

(A) She knows not everyone can find the sweet spot.

(B) She believes one needs to be sweet to someone to get that.

(C) She understands it usually takes time to find that.

(D) She wants the student to know that finding these areas that collide is important.

5. What will the student probably do next?

(A) Borrow the book from the library.

(B) Lend the book from the professor

(C) Return the book to the library

(D) Borrow the book from the professor's son

▶▶ 新托福聽力解析

1. 這題詢問的是學生為何拜訪教授。要注意一些對話干擾訊息，其實最終的目的是選項 A，學生其實是畢業後擔憂自己的未來，所以才去找教授聊聊。

2. 這題是詢問從與教授對中可以推測出學生什麼。選項 D 為對話中談到的部分，故答案為選項 D。

3. 這題是詢問為什麼教授提到 sometimes they choose majors or make huge decisions based on how others view themselves, but that's probably the things you shouldn't do，其實教授是想提醒學生，且是 Because the decision can't reflect what others truly want to do, and she wants him to avoid that trap.的同義表達，故答案為選項 A。

4. 這題詢問教授為什麼會講該段話，You need to find them. I mean that's a sweet spot for you.，其實要理解 sweet spot 的意思並推斷出其實是指選項 D，要找到三者重疊的部分就是最適合的區塊，故答案為選項 D。

5. 這題詢問學生接下來會做什麼。要注意干擾選項，學生最可能跟圖書館借書，故答案為選項 A。

....

答案：1. A 2. D 3. A 4. D 5. A

☁ 影子跟讀練習 ▸MP3 037

做完題目後，除了對答案知道錯的部分在哪外，更重要的是要修正自己聽力根本的問題，即聽力理解力和聽力專注力，聽力專注力的修正能逐步強化本身的聽力實力，所以現在請根據聽力內容「逐個段落」、「數個段落」或「整篇」進行跟讀練習，提升在實際考場時專注聽完每個訊息、定位出關鍵考點和搭配筆記回答完所有題目。Go!

| **Student** |

Hi, professor. I just stopped by to see if you have time for a little chat.

| 學生 |

嗨，教授。我只是來看一下你是否有時間聊聊天。

| **Professor** |

You look worried. What's going on?

| 教授 |

你看起來相當憂慮。發生什麼事了嗎？

| **Student** |

I'm starting to worry about my future. That's all.

| 學生 |

我開始對於我的未來感到擔憂。大概是這樣。

| **Professor** |

You just won a scholarship, right?

| 教授 |

你才剛贏得獎學金，對吧？

| Student |

It's not about the scholarship or the grades. I just don't think my future will have anything to do with my grades or scholarship. I'm sure that my future employers are not going to take those into account. They're totally irrelevant.

| 學生 |

這跟獎學金或分數無關。我覺得我的未來與成績或獎學金不相干。我也知道我未來的雇主不會對這個加分。這兩件事沒有關係。

| Professor |

Of course! It's just when you are in school, you still have to play your role. Focus solely on your study!

| 教授 |

當然！只是當你還在學校，你就要扮演好你的角色。全心放在課業上面。

| Student |

I regret majoring in philosophy. And to be honest, I don't like doing research.

| 學生 |

我很後悔選了哲學當主修...而且說實話...我不想要做研究...。

| Professor |

But you seem to know what you are saying in the class.

You know how to articulate yourself and explain things to people. That's a skill required for a certain job…

| 教授 |

但你似乎知道你在課堂要說些什麼，而且你知道要如何表達自己，向其他人解釋事情。這是特定工作很需要的一項技能。

字彙輔助

1. scholarship 獎學金
2. employer 雇主
3. philosophy 哲學
4. articulate 表達

| **Student** |

I'm worried. Even though I'm doing a minor in economics, I'm still trying to figure out a lot of things. I would hate to see myself graduating from a prestigious university, but can't seem to find a job.

| 學生 |

但是我感到擔憂。即使我有著經濟學當副修，我仍試著了解許多事。我不想要看到自己畢業於一間有名氣的大學，卻似乎找不到工作。

| **Professor** |

Having a minor in economics is a great start, but I do think there are lots of things you should know other than professional skills.

| 教授 |

有著經濟學當副主修是很棒的開端。但我認為除了專業能力外，還有許多事情是你應該要知道的。

| Student |

Like what? I'm begging you to tell me more.

| 學生 |

像是什麼呢...我拜託你告訴我更多細節...。

| Professor |

It's not like you just write a great resume, send in your application, have an interview, and eventually get the job…

| 教授 |

這不只是像是寫份很棒的履歷，寄出申請，參加面試，最終獲得工作。

| Student |

That sounds like what it is, right?

| 學生 |

但這聽起來就像是這樣，對吧？

- -

字彙輔助

1 minor 副主修　　　　2 professional 專業的

3 application 申請　　　　**4** interview 面試

Professor

It's not what you think it is. It's important that you get to know yourself. A lot of people don't know who they are, and what they really want. Sometimes they choose majors or make huge decisions based on how others view themselves. But that's probably the things you shouldn't do. You should know your interests, personality, and skills and abilities. There're areas that overlap the three of them. You need to find them. I mean that's a sweet spot for you. It's really unlikely for a shy person to do a sales rep's job. Personalities are like am I outgoing, social, or creative? **"It's the way you like to work and relate to others."** You should know other areas, too. What are skills and abilities that I possess? Am I a team player? Am I good at analyzing problems? "Skills and abilities are **acquired and natural talents; what you can do easily.** Interests are **what excites you.**" You should know all these during your undergraduate years.

教授

但這不像你所想像的那樣。了解自己是件重要的事。許多人不知道自己是誰，想要什麼。有時候他們選擇了一個主修或做了一個重大的決定卻是基於其他人怎麼看待他們。但更重要的是這些是你都不該去做。你該知道自己的興趣、個性和技能與能力。這三樣都重疊到的區塊是你需要探索的。我指的是這會是最適合你的區塊。一個害羞

415

的人不太可能去做業務工作。個性是分析我是個外向的人嗎？社交的嗎？賦有創意的嗎？「這代表著你喜歡工作的方式和如何與人互動的模式。」你也該知道其他區塊才是。我所具備的技能和能力是什麼呢？我是個團隊合作的人嗎？我擅長分析問題嗎？「技能和能力像是後天學習的和先天具備的能力，你能輕易就完成的事。興趣像是什麼能激勵你呢？」在大學這幾年，你應該要知道這些。

| Student |

Wow! Thanks.

| 學生 |

哇！謝謝。

| Professor |

If you'd like to know more about these, perhaps you can borrow a book from the school library. It's called Business Model You. My son just returned the book to the library.

| 教授 |

如果你想要知道更多，或許你可以在圖書館借這本書.。它叫做商業模式。我的兒子剛到圖書館歸還這本書。

| Student |

Thanks again.

| 學生 |

再次謝謝你。

字彙輔助

1. personality 個性
2. outgoing 外向的
3. possess 持有
4. library 圖書館

▶▶ 試題聽力原文

1. Why does the student visit the professor?

2. What can be inferred about the student?

3. Listen again to part of the conversation. Then answer the question.

   Professor: It's not what you think it is. It's important that you get to know yourself. A lot of people don't know who they are, or what they really want. Sometimes they choose majors or make huge decisions based on how others view themselves. But that's probably the things you shouldn't do

   Why does the professor say "sometimes they choose a major or making a huge decision based on how others view themselves…but that's probably the things you shouldn't do"

4. Listen again to part of the conversation. Then answer the

question.
Professor: you should know your interests, personality, and skills and abilities. There're areas that overlap the three of them. You need to find them. I mean that's a sweet spot for you.

Why does the professor say "You need to find them. I mean that's a sweet spot for you"?

5. What will the student probably do next?

▶▶ 記筆記與聽力訊息

| Instruction | MP3 037

　　新托福聽力與其他聽力測驗不同，可以於聽力的紙上記筆記，除了寫試題外，更重要的一點是訓練自己能夠將聽完一段訊息後，將重要的聽力訊息都記到。也可以將自己聽到跟記到的重點訊息跟試題做比對，因為試題考的就是長對話跟講座中出現的重點，能修正自己篩選聽力訊息重點的能力。

| 聽力重點 |

■ 記筆記有很多方式，包含符號跟自己習慣的縮寫字等等，可以找出最適合自己的模式，一定要自己重聽音檔作練習數次。

■ 這篇是關於校園類話題，有提到另一本書，要注意下表中第二個主旨和整合推測的題型。

▶▶ **參考筆記**

Main idea ❶ worried about future ● my future employers are not going to take those into account…it's totally irrelevant	
professor	still you have to play your part
Situation about the student	❶ major in philoshopy with a minor in economics
Main idea ❷	other than professional skills, you should know your interests, personality, and skills and abilities and the overlapped part is your sweet spot. ❶ interests：what excites you ❷ personality：it's the way you like to work and relate to others ❸ skills and abilities：acquired and natural talents; what you can do easily

Note

Instruction | MP3 037

　　現在請再聽一次音檔，並做下列的測驗，檢視自己能否完成此填空測驗和強化自己聽力能力和拼字能力，降低並修正自己漏聽到聽力訊息的機會，大幅提升應考實力。

1. The student who just won the s_____ is pretty worried about his future, so he came to see the professor.

2. Grades and scholarships will not be a key criteria for one's future e_____.

3. Even though those are totally i_____, the professor advises him to play his part as a student.

4. The student majors in p_____, with a minor in e_____.

5. The student expects himself to be a person graduating from a p_____ university and has no worries about his future.

6. Traditional ways of finding a job involve writing a great r_____ …send your a_____ …have the i_____ …and so on.

7. Getting to know y_____ is also very important.

8. Most important of all, you should know your i_____ , p_____, and s_____ and a_____.

9. The o_____ areas are actually a s_____ spot for that person.

10. Personalities are like how you r_____ to others.

11. You also need to know your interests required for the job whether it's a_____ or i_____ skills.

12. Interests are also very important since it's about what e_____ you.

13. The student is able to find Business Model You in the school l_____ since the professor just returned the book.

| 答案 |
1. scholarship
2. employer
3. irrelevant
4. philosophy, economics
5. prestigious
6. resume, application, interview

7. yourself
8. interests, personality, skills, abilities.
9. overlapped, sweet
10. relate
11. acquired, innate
12. excites
13. library

▶▶ 摘要能力

| Instruction | MP3 037

　　除了閱讀測驗外，其實培養能在聽完一大段訊息後，以口述講述剛才聽到的聽力訊息是學習語言和表達很重要的一件事，讓自己養成具備這樣的能力，除了能在聽力測驗中獲取高分外，也能在新托福寫作跟口說的整合題型上大有斬獲喔！所以快來練習，除了書中提供的參考答案外，自己可以試著重新聽過音檔一遍後，摘要出英文訊息並朗讀出來。

▶▶ 參考答案

The student comes to the office hour, not for his scholarship and grades but for his future. The professor advises him that he should still play his part as a student. The student has a major in philosophy with a minor in economics, but he is still worried. He does not want to be the kind of the student graduating from a prestigious university but can't seem to find a job. The professor points out that other than professional skills there're still lots of things he should know. He should know three major things: interests, personality, and skills and abilities. He needs to find the sweet spot the areas that overlap the three of them. He should know all these during his undergraduate years.

11 ▶▶ 運動傷害：由 Lewis Howes, The School of Greatness，從運動傷害中拾回自信

▶▶ **聽力試題** MP3 038

1. Why does the student visit the professor?
   (A) To avoid dreadful coffee
   (B) To borrow a brand-new coffee machine from the professor
   (C) To lighten the professor's mood
   (D) To return the book that the professor left in the classroom

2. What can be inferred from the student?
   (A) He hates his coach.
   (B) He does not want to be the captain.
   (C) He needs time to recover.
   (D) His doctor is responsible for his injury.

3. Listen again to part of the conversation. Then answer the question.
   (A) She does not want the student to injure himself.
   (B) She thinks beating someone won't solve the problem.
   (C) She does not want the student to blame himself.

(D) She thinks not being a captain can prevent him from getting beaten.

4. Listen again to part of the conversation. Then answer the question.

(A) Because he feels bad that the doctor thinks he is a bad person.

(B) Because the doctor is giving him an untrue idea that he will soon get over.

(C) Because the doctor has a wrong impression about him.

(D) Because the report is accidentally switched so the doctor gives him the false impression.

5. Listen again to part of the conversation. Then answer the question.

(A) Because it's hard to retain the glory you have earned.

(B) Because fame and glory won't last.

(C) Because if you don't change the state of mind, fame and glory are transient.

(D) Because the right mindset is the key to turn things around.

1. 這題詢問的是學生為何拜訪教授，要注意一些對話干擾訊息，其實最終的目的是選項 D，學生其實是要歸還教授遺留在教室的書籍，所以才去找教授。

2. 這題是詢問可以推測出學生什麼，其實從對話中可以推測出是他需要時間康復，故答案為選項 C。

3. 這題是詢問為什麼教授提到 you have done such a great job leading the team. Everyone knows it. Stop beating yourself up.，其實主要是選項 C，She does not want the student to blame himself. 的同義表達，故答案為選項 C。

4. 這題詢問教授為什麼會講該段話，The doctor perhaps is giving me the false impression that I will recover sooner than I thought，其實主要是想表明 Because the doctor is giving him an untrue idea that he will soon get over.，醫生給了錯誤印象讓他以為會提早康復，故答案為選項 B。

5. 這題詢問教授為什麼會講該段話 Those dreams of glory and fame came crashing down to earth, but eventually things start to change…and I believe all you have to change is your state of mind and the injury is just temporary，其實是指心態和心境 Because the right mindset is the key to turn things around.，故答案為選項 D。

....

答案： 1. D 2. C 3. C 4. B 5. D

影子跟讀練習 MP3 038

做完題目後，除了對答案知道錯的部分在哪外，更重要的是要修正自己聽力根本的問題，即聽力理解力和聽力專注力，聽力專注力的修正能逐步強化本身的聽力實力，所以現在請根據聽力內容「逐個段落」、「數個段落」或「整篇」進行跟讀練習，提升在實際考場時專注聽完每個訊息、定位出關鍵考點和搭配筆記回答完所有題目。Go!

| Professor |

What is it? Oh! I was such a dummy. I left the book in the classroom. Thanks. Do you want to join me for a cup of coffee?

| 教授 |

這是什麼？喔！我真是個蠢蛋。我把書留在教室了。謝謝！你要加入我也來杯咖啡嗎？

| Student |

I don't think I can say no. It's so exquisite.

| 學生 |

我想我也無法拒絕。好精緻喔。

| Professor |

A brand new coffee machine. It's a gift from a relative. Somewhat fancy, right? Do you want some sugar?

| 教授 |

全新的咖啡機...這是我一個親戚送的禮物...有點豪華，對吧？你要來些糖嗎？

| Student |

Yep. I guess adding some sugar wouldn't hurt. Life is hard as it is.

| 學生 |

要的。我想加些糖無傷大雅。人生夠困難了。

| Professor |

Is everything ok?

| 教授 |

一切都還好吧？

| Student |

Everything is fine. Except that I'm feeling depressed. I just cannot deliver the same performance as I'm used to.

| 學生 |

事情是還好。只是我感到沮喪。我沒辦法展現像以前一樣的演出。

| **Professor** |

Did you talk with your coach about it? No wonder you're feeling a bit low. By the way, how's the coffee?

| 教授 |

你有跟你們教練說嗎？難怪你覺得有點沮喪。附帶一提的是咖啡好喝嗎？

| **Student** |

Wow! It's great, and pretty intense.

| 學生 |

哇...很棒...相當濃...。

| **Professor** |

Yep. It's triple latte.

| 教授 |

是啊...三倍濃縮...拿鐵。

| **Student** |

I talked to the coach about it, but it's still the same.

| 學生 |

我跟教練談過了.但情況還是一樣。

1 dummy 蠢蛋
2 exquisite 精緻的
3 depressed 沮喪的
4 tense 緊張的

| Professor |

What did he say?

| 教授 |

他怎麼說呢？

| Student |

He said to just wait for a bit longer. I do need time to recover.

| 學生 |

他說就在等些時間。我確實需要時間復原。

| Professor |

Why don't you just give yourself a little bit more time. I know you were a captain. You have done such a great job leading the team. Everyone knows it. Stop beating yourself up.

| 教授 |

為什麼你不給自己更多時間呢？我知道你曾是隊長。你已經展

現出能良好的團隊領導能力，大家都知道這點。別再為難你自己了。

| Student |

I know. I just don't like the feeling of sitting on the bench seeing everyone making great progress, but I still need like 6 months to recovery. The doctor is perhaps giving me the false impression that I will recover sooner than I thought. I know there is no way that I can recover that quickly, unless there's a miracle.

| 學生 |

我知道。但是我只是不喜歡這種感覺。坐在板凳上看大家都有很大的進步，而我卻需要六個月的康復時間。醫生或許給我錯覺，讓我覺得我會比想像中更快康復。我知道我不可能復原的這麼快，除非有奇蹟出現。

| Professor |

Just don't think about it that way. You need some meditation time. Perhaps read some books. Do you know Lewis Howes? He once had a career-ending injury. His book is so inspiring. Perhaps you should read it.

| 教授 |

別這樣想吧。你需要一些沉思的時間。或許閱讀些書籍。你知道路易斯‧郝維嗎？它曾經有終結職業的運動傷害。他的書很具啟發性。或許你應該要讀它。

| Student |

what's the name of the book?

| 學生 |

書籍的名字是什麼呢？

| Professor |

The School of Greatness. Sometimes we think there is nothing we can do, but there are plenty of things we can do. He was resting on his sister's couch lamenting and thinking **"those dreams of glory and fame came crashing down to earth"**. But eventually things start to change. I believe what you all have to change is your state of mind. Injury is just temporary. Compared with the lifespan of yours, it's insignificant. You still have a great career ahead of you. The team needs you.

| 教授 |

偉大的學校。有時候我們認為我們無力可為了，但是卻有許多事是我們能做的。他曾在自己妹妹的椅子上感嘆著，想著「那些榮耀的夢想和名聲於一夕間消失殆盡」。但是最終事情開始出現改變，而我相信你必須要改變的是心態。傷害只是暫時的，比起你生命的長度，是很微不足道的。而且在你前方仍有著很好的前程等著你。團隊也還需要你。

| Student |

Thanks for the pep talk. Perhaps I really do need to change what I think of myself. After I recover, I'm going to do something great.

| 學生 |

謝謝你的這些安慰的話。或許我真的需要改變我對於自己的看法。在復原後，我可以做些更棒的事。

字彙輔助

1 pep talk 安慰的話　　**2** lament 感嘆

3 temporary 暫時的　　**4** insignificant 微不足道的

▶▶ 試題聽力原文

1. Why does the student visit the professor?

2. What can be inferred about the student?

3. Listen again to part of the conversation. Then answer the question.
Professor: Why don't you just give yourself a little bit

more time. I know you were a captain. You have done such a great job leading the team. Everyone knows it. Stop beating yourself up.

Why does professor say "You have done such a great job leading the team. Everyone knows it. Stop beating yourself up"?

4. Listen again to part of the conversation. Then answer the question.
Student: I know. I just don't like the feeling of sitting on the bench seeing everyone making great progress, and I still need like 6 months to recover. The doctor is perhaps giving me the false impression that I will recover sooner than I thought. I know there is no way that I can recover that quickly, unless there's a miracle.

Why does the student say "the doctor is perhaps giving me the false impression that I will recover sooner than I thought"?

5. Listen again to part of the conversation. Then answer the question.
Professor: sometimes we think there is nothing we can do. But there are plenty of things we can do. He was resting on his sister's couch lamenting and thinking "those dreams of glory and fame came crashing down to

earth". But eventually things start to change. I believe all you have to change is your state of mind. The injury is just temporary…compared with the lifespan of yours… it's insignificant…

Why does the professor say "those dreams of glory and fame came crashing down to earth. But eventually things start to change, and I believe all you have to change is your state of mind. The injury is just temporary"?

▶▶ 記筆記與聽力訊息

| Instruction | MP3 038

　　新托福聽力與其他聽力測驗不同，可以於聽力的紙上記筆記，除了寫試題外，更重要的一點是訓練自己能夠將聽完一段訊息後，將重要的聽力訊息都記到。也可以將自己聽到跟記到的重點訊息跟試題做比對，因為試題考的就是長對話跟講座中出現的重點，能修正自己選取聽力訊息重點的能力。

| 聽力重點 |

- 記筆記有很多方式，包含符號跟自己習慣的縮寫字等等，可以找出最適合自己的模式，一定要自己重聽音檔作練習數次。
- 這篇是關於校園類話題，**要注意整合和推測題型的出題，還有引述句考點。**

Note

▶▶ 參考筆記

Main idea ❶ injuries and worries make the student depressed	
student	cannot deliver the performance the same as he is used to
professor	❶ suggests him to talk to the coach ❷ compliments him for being a captain
student	❶ the doctor gives him a false impression about recovery time

Main idea ❷

- reading Lewis Howes The School of Greatness can help him get back from track
- don't need to feel like "those dreams of glory and fame came crashing down to earth"

Note

Instruction MP3 038

　　現在請再聽一次音檔，並做下列的測驗，檢視自己能否完成此填空測驗和強化自己聽力能力和拼字能力，降低並修正自己漏聽到聽力訊息的機會，大幅提升英考實力。

1. The professor was such a d＿＿＿＿＿ for leaving the book in the classroom.

2. He then invited the student for a coffee since he got an e ＿＿＿＿＿ coffee machine from a relative.

3. The professor figured that there was something wrong with the student because he felt a little bit d＿＿＿＿＿.

4. He suggested the student talk to his c＿＿＿＿＿ about it, but that didn't help much.

5. The student replied that the r＿＿＿＿＿ time would take a little bit longer.

6. The student was once a c＿＿＿＿＿ of the team.

7. Watching everyone on the field making a great p＿＿＿＿＿ was hard for him.

8. His doctor was giving him a f_____ i_____ that he would recover soon, but the wound would take longer time to heal.

9. The professor suggests him to read Lewis Howes' book, for the author once had a career-ending i_____.

10. The author once lamented that "those dreams of g_____ and f_____ came crashing down to earth"

11. Perhaps the student should focus on changing his state of m_____ since it's just t_____.

12. After all, compared with the lifespan, the wound is relatively i_____.

| 答案 |

1. dummy
2. expensive
3. depressed
4. coach
5. recovery
6. captain
7. progress
8. false impression
9. injury
10. glory, fame

11. mind, temporary

12. insignificant

▶▶ 摘要能力

| Instruction | MP3 038

　　除了閱讀測驗外，其實培養能在聽完一大段訊息後，以口述講述剛才聽到的聽力訊息是學習語言和表達很重要的一件事，讓自己養成具備這樣的能力，除了能在聽力測驗中獲取高分外，也能在新托福寫作跟口説的整合題型上大有斬獲喔！所以快來練習，除了書中提供的參考答案外，自己可以試著重新聽過音檔一遍後，摘要出英文訊息並朗讀出來。

▶▶ 參考答案

The student feels depressed about his performance, fearing that he cannot deliver the performance the same as he used to. Talking to the coach seems of little use. The professor points out his previous performance to ease him mind. Seeing others all making progress makes him feel worse. Doctor is the culprit, too, by giving him the false impression. In fact, the recovery takes like 6 months. The professor suggests him to read The School of Greatness written by Lewis Howes. He was once in his situation so that the student can relate to. We don't have to feel like "those dreams of glory and fame came crashing down to earth", and the recovery time is very insignificant to our lifespan.

頁數	參考書籍	引述的句子
p. 345	*Harry Potter and the Globet of Fire*	He said I owe you one for telling me about the dragons. Just mull things over in the hot water. It'll help you think. (J.K., 2000, p.431)
p. 347	*50 Success Classics*	It's easier to win if everybody wants you to win. (Tom Butler, 2000, p.154)
p. 380	*Why Men Want Sex and Women need Love*	• What are you thinking about? • Do you love me? • Do I look fat? • Do you think she is prettier than me? • What would you do if I died? (Allan and Barbara, 2009, p.197)
p. 380	*Why Men Want Sex and Women need Love*	Yes, but you have a better personality. (Allan and Barbara, 2009, p.198)
p. 381	*Why Men Want Sex and Women need Love*	Not prettier but definitely thinner. (Allan and Barbara, 2009, p.198)
p. 396	*Lean In: For Graduates*	If you're offered a seat on a rocket ship, you don't ask what seat. You just get on. (Sheryl, 2013/2014, p.74)
p. 415	*Business Model You*	• Personality: the way you like to work and relate to others • Interests: what excites you • Skills and Abilities: acquired and natural talents; what you can do easily (Tim, Alexander, and Yves, 2012, p.114)
p. 432	*The School of Greatness*	Those dreams of glory and fame came crashing down to earth. (Preface) (Lewis Howes, 2015, xi)

附錄——引用和出處

頁數	參考書籍	引述的句子
p.151	*The Power of Habit*	Bowman had once made Phelps swim in a Michigan pool in the dark believing that he needed to be ready for any surprise. (Charles, 2012 , p.115)
p.234	*The Power of Moments*	Am I really going to be wrestling golden retrievers when I'm 65? (Chip and Dan, 2017, p. 113)
p.276	*Getting There*	Things that seem disastrous at the time usually do work out for the best. (Gillian, 2015, p.20)
p. 289	*Getting There*	Such is the value of a Yale education. (Gillian, 2015, p.40)
p. 309	*Where You Go Is Not Who You Will Be*	Travelling a more gilded path, she'd arrived at the very same destination. (Frank, 2015, p.2)
p.327 -328	*The Achievement Habit*	Life is an adventure, so loosen up, top trying to figure it out, just go with the flow. (Bernard, 2015, p.220)
p. 328	*The Achievement Habit*	My life is punctuated by milestones that would have never happened except for the combination of unplanned and improbable chance events. (Bernard, 2015, p.223)
p. 345	*Harry Potter and the Globet of Fire*	Cedric still didn't know about the dragons. The only champion who didn't. if Harry was right in thinking that Maxime and Karkaroff would have told Fleur and Krum. (J.K., 2000, p.340)
p.345	*Harry Potter and the Globet of Fire*	Cedric, said Harry, the first task is dragons. (J.K., 2000, p.340)
p.345	*Harry Potter and the Globet of Fire*	We're on an even footing, aren't we? (J.K., 2000, p.341)

國家圖書館出版品預行編目(CIP)資料

新托福100+ iBT聽力/ 韋爾著.
-- 初版. -- 臺北市：倍斯特, 2018.9　面；
公分. --（考用英語系列；12）
ISBN 978-986-96309-4-8（平裝附光碟）
1.托福考試

805.1894　　　　　　　　　　107013279

考用英語　012

新托福100+　iBT聽力（附MP3）

初　　版　　2018年9月
定　　價　　新台幣480元

作　　者　　韋爾
出　　版　　倍斯特出版事業有限公司
發 行 人　　周瑞德
電　　話　　886-2-2351-2007
傳　　真　　886-2-2351-0887
地　　址　　100 台北市中正區福州街1號10樓之2
E - m a i l　　best.books.service@gmail.com
官　　網　　www.bestbookstw.com
執行總監　　齊心瑀
企劃編輯　　陳韋佑
執行編輯　　曾品綺
內頁構成　　菩薩蠻數位文化有限公司
印　　製　　大亞彩色印刷製版股份有限公司

港澳地區總經銷　　泛華發行代理有限公司
地　　址　　香港新界將軍澳工業邨駿昌街7號2樓
電　　話　　852-2798-2323
傳　　真　　852-2796-5471

Simply Learning, Simply Best!

Simply Learning, Simply Best!